Resource Economies

Traverse Davies

November 30, 2017

Resource Economies: Reclaiming the Zombie Apocalypse

World of the Dead, Volume 2

Traverse Davies

Published by Bright Crow Publishing, 2019.

This is a work of fiction. Similarities to real people, places, or events are entirely coincidental.

RESOURCE ECONOMIES: RECLAIMING THE ZOMBIE APOCALYPSE

First edition. April 17, 2019.

ISBN: 978-0995002838

Written by Traverse Davies.

Also by Traverse Davies

World of the Dead
A Long Walk
Resource Economies: Reclaiming the Zombie Apocalypse

Watch for more at https://dreamtime.logic11.com.

Table of Contents

Acknowledgements

First: For my son Alex.

There are a few other people I should thank.

Irina. You supported me while I wrote this, and I am grateful until the end of time. You are my amazing girl, love you always

Marketa. Any errors in this manuscript are mine.

Any errors that are not here are due to the eforts of Marketa Sowers, a great editor (if I'd followed all of her advice this would be a better book I'm sure).

There are a million others, if I thanked everyone I owe thanks to this section would be longer than the rest of the book.

Intro

Tyson decided that he was a miner. It was a better name than scavenger, or vulture. Yes, he was picking through the bones of a dead civilization, pulling whatever nutrients he could from its decaying corpse, but he was doing it with a pick axe - so a miner.

It was hot, sweltering in fact. Who would have thought that they would run into a heat wave in Cape Breton? It didn't help that they had to wear dust masks the whole time, something to keep the mold and powdered gyprock out of their lungs, out of their noses. They worked six abreast, swinging picks into the dead structures that used to make up Sydney, Nova Scotia.

Tyson was young, and strong. When the world died, he'd been a child, too young to understand what was happening. His entire life was lived in this brave new world, a world of salvage, of carrion. His home, the city of New Hope, was the only place he'd ever seen that had living humans in it. Sydney was not that. The zombies roamed, emaciated and decayed, but somehow still moving, as they had been for twenty years. Still, Sydney was a small place, and there was a fence. A large chain link barrier keeping the zombies away from him and his men.

Tyson yelled to the foreman "Hey, time for a break yet?"

"You work until I say convict" the foreman gave him the finger. Tyson figured that meant it was time for a break. The foremen, Jack, was his best friend. A dick, but fun at a party, hard working, a decent guy over all. Tyson and the others sat down and broke out their canteens.

One thing about the reclamation project, you couldn't trust the local water. They had to filter and boil all of it, so it was hard to get enough. A day like this, the mercury hovering around thirty, was hard to deal with. They were all soaked with sweat, dirty and tired. Jack sat down with them.

"Good progress today boys. Keep going at this rate and we might have a full load by... 20 years from now?"

"Shut up ya prick. You want things to go faster, grab a pick and get to work."

"Yeah, I'll do that. We don't need anybody to watch the fence, keep an eye out for z's inside, none of that. I figure we all get eaten it'll keep you from having to do any real work, should make you happy."

Break over they got back to it.

The hours passed, they were deep in the building now. They had managed to pull a couple of hundred pieces of rebar for smelting and recasting (and even a couple dozen that might be usable as is). The sun was heading down, so it was time to get back on ship. Working outside was alright, sleeping outside was way too big a risk. They headed down to the shore, to what was left of the dock.

Tyson noticed something moving from the edge of his vision. Zombies, inside the fence. Not a big deal, they were all armed and capable or they wouldn't have been there. A lot of zombies though. He nudged Brandon, a big guy about his age, and pointed. Brandon tapped Jack. The zombies didn't seem to be heading toward them yet, so they wanted to be silent if they could.

The zombies were shambling, aimless and grotesque. How the hell had a group that size breached the fence? There were a few hundred of them, far too many to fight. Just then one of them seemed to look their way, and he started to move as fast as he could. Jack yelled "Run."

They started to move, fast, toward the dock and the waiting boat. The small boat was their way out, their way home. They had left two guys in the boat to watch it. Emile and Rich. Emile stood up in the bow, looked at them, looked at the horde, and did the unthinkable. He cast off.

It would have been close, but Tyson and his crew would have been there before the zombies reached them, Tyson was sure of it. "You fucking cowards, wait. Fucking wait for fucks sake."

The motorboat was heading out to deep water, to the waiting cargo ship they were using as their home base while they worked. The zombies were coming in from the east, so Jack started running west, fast as he could. Tyson followed, hoping the rest would keep up. They could see the west fence in minutes. It was a no go, there were zombies lined up along it. They turned inland, heading for the south fence. As they ran, the numbers were increasing. Somehow they had gotten surrounded. There shouldn't have been that many zombies here. Initial recon said Sydney was down to a few hundred at most, they were looking at thousands.

Brandon went down, leg caught in one of the many holes in the street. Tyson stopped and started pulling him "Come on man, pull, come on."

"Fuck, fuck, fuck. Don't leave me. Don't let them take me."

His leg was caught, wedged in tight. Tyson pulled, Brandon screamed in pain. His leg didn't come free. Finally, the zombies were too close. Tyson said "Sorry, sorry. Fuck. Sorry." and started running again. He heard Brandon scream as the horde closed on him.

The rest of the group was out of sight. Tyson had no idea where they had gone. He could see the south fence ow. It was as full as the west had been.

He was cornered. This should have been impossible. The boat was there, the fence was there, they should have been fine.

He spotted a hole that looked like it might lead to something, so he jumped into it. No time to look before he leaped. He fell into the darkness, hitting hard ground that knocked the wind out of him. No time to pause, no time to take stock. He stood up, his head wasn't touching the top of his hole, and he started feeling his way along. He could see a little bit from the fading light filtering through the hole.

The smell down here was overwhelming. Mold and rot were the worst of it, but there were undercurrents, chemical and acrid with a hint of something even worse. Tyson was under a collapsed building, but there was nothing to tell him what kind of building it had been to start. He moved deeper, hoping to find a safe spot before the light failed completely.

Of course he had a basic kit, a few minimal supplies in case everything went wrong, but it wasn't much. He was already feeling thirsty after just a few minutes of running.

He spotted a door that was still in a frame, it wasn't locked, so he went inside, cautiously. There was a zombie inside. Impossible to tell what it had been in life, although from the height, Tyson thought it was probably male. He pulled out his blade and casually smashed through its skull.

Tyson closed the door behind him and then pulled out his light. He hadn't wanted to spark it before, the bright bulb would have attracted any zombies in the area. In here, a small closed space, he was probably safe to use it.

RESOURCE ECONOMIES: RECLAIMING THE ZOMBIE APOCALYPSE

In the harsh artificial glow he could see that he was in a furnace room. It was large, but much of the ceiling had fallen in. It was also cold, despite the heat outside. At that moment the cool felt amazing. Tyson found a small corner and set up a mini camp to wait out the night.

The reclaimers are formed

B ennett Matheson was bored. Naomi was giving her usual speech to rally the troops. She was a great speaker, and had a way of connecting with everyone she talked to, but this was the tenth time Bennett had heard this one and no matter how good she still looked, how her flawless dark brown skin still looked like she was the woman he had met eighteen years ago, it was the same material. He knew he should be more invested, that his wife's career was tied to his, but he just wanted to get out there and do stuff. They had been stuck in paperwork for two years, and it was time to make a move.

"It's time to take back the world, to make it ours again. For far too long we have hidden away on our tiny island, let the dead rule and made do with less than we need. We need to bring the fight to them, to carve out pieces of the world for ourselves. It's not enough to eke out a living in tiny pieces. This was our world, it will be again!"

Everyone cheered, everyone clapped. Bennett grabbed her as she walked down.

"Great work, really inspired the troops."

"Yep, everyone loved it... well, almost everyone. I noticed one guy in the back looking like he was starting to nod off." she punched him playfully in the shoulder.

"Sorry babe, it's just that I've heard it once or twice already. Trust me, I was riveted the first six or seven times." He gave her a wink.

They headed to the council meeting. They had allies, people who were sick of living on a tiny little island in the North Atlantic, people who wanted to stop rationing everything all the time, but they also had enemies. Their plans were pretty ambitious, and it would shake things up if they went ahead.

The rest of the council was there, with one major exception, glaring in his absence. Jasper Pellerine, head of civil defense. He would have been the best possible asset, but he was still in his hospital bed, not expected to recover. Anyone else would have been put down already, and if Jasper knew the efforts being used to keep him alive, the effort put into him, he would have been furious. Still, he was probably the only person in New Hope that would warrant that kind of effort. The stroke had been sudden, unexpected. He was in his late fifties, young for that kind of death, but old for these times. Most people in this new world died much more violently, and much younger.

Taylor Pellerine was sitting in his place. Nobody begrudged it to her, in the years since the founding of New Hope she had been one of the greatest assets, a tireless worker and fearless. She led salvage operations for a decade before losing her leg, forcing her to work a desk job.

The biggest opposition was Col. Barbara Miller. A living legend, she had made it on foot from Pittsburgh to New Hope almost nineteen years ago, just months after the city was founded. Her tactics had been a large part of the salvation of the city, but now she was conservative, wanting to keep all the resources they could on hand. This woman, who had walked through a million zombies to reach them, and now she didn't want to open a window for fear of catching cold.

Rounding out the council were John Miller, Barbara's husband, and Tom Elliott. Tom could go either way, while John was clearly in Barbara's corner.

Naomi called the meeting to order.

"Welcome friends, let's get started." Formality had taken a backseat in the new world.

"Our first order of business is the reclamation force project. We have the gear, we have the first group trained. It's time to get on with it, time to start."

Barbara gave Naomi a hostile look "We agreed to let you pilot this idiocy because Jason backed you. Even then, it was planned as a limited scope trial. Without his expertise I don't see how you expect this to succeed. We don't have the manpower to risk so many lives. Maybe in a generation or two, but it's too soon."

Bennett said "No. Look, we are low on resources, in a generation or two we won't have the will, the people, the resources, to do this. We need to start expanding now. We have a generation who have grown up with this as normal, who don't even remember a world without the living dead. By the time our generation dies off there will be nobody around who remembers the old world. Already we have children who don't believe in airplanes, they think they are just a story old people tell about the world before, an exaggeration. If humanity is going to take back the world it has to be directed by people who remember."

"No offense to anyone, but our problems are a bit more immediate than that. We are at half a million people here. Rationing is killing us. We need to expand, there is no other option. If you think we have enough you haven't spent enough time on the east shore. People are out of options. This island is great at growing potatoes, but it's just not that big. We need to expand." Taylor slammed her hands down on the table, clearly frustrated.

There was a knock on the council chamber door, sharp and insistent. "Come, but whatever it is, it better be important." Barbara was clearly irritated, but that was her usual state.

A soldier came in, looking nervous. "It's the Sydney expedition. We just got word from the ship. All the people on shore were lost."

"What? How?" Bennett said.

"A breach in the fence. Details are light."

"Did they see it?"

"No, the team was cut off, the boat pilot took off."

"So, the team could still be alive, hiding in the middle of Sydney with no way to get back home?"

Everyone went silent for a moment. It was the worst-case scenario for a salvage operation.

Bennett was the one to break the silence "We have the first reclamation team ready. Barbara, you wanted a limited scope trial. This is a perfect opportunity. We can send them, see if they can figure out what happened, and clear a section. A proof of concept as it were."

"That's crass even for you. Using a tragedy like this for political gain."

"I'm not. I'm trying to save our people. This is just the best way to achieve that end."

They devolved into argument until finally, Taylor demanded a vote. "Look, we aren't going to settle this. I would love to have consensus, but that ain't going to happen with this group. Let's just vote on it now and be done with it."

In the end, Tom sided with Bennett, Naomi, and Taylor. They needed a simple majority for an operation this size, so it was a go.

Introducing the Reclaimers

The barracks were buzzing with activity. There was a clear division between the long established civil defense team and the newly minted reclamation force. The civil defense team was made up of a random smattering of young people, service was mandatory for two years after turning 18. By contrast the reclamation force was all volunteer, hardened survivors for the most part. They were a small team, only a dozen people so far, but they looked dangerous and competent.

Wayde Conrad, the sergeant for the group, was a 10-year veteran of the civil defense force. When his two years were up he just stayed. He was almost as wide at the shoulders as he was tall. He had a short, wide Mohawk running down the center of his head, and a face that was full of scars. Wayde had dozens of expeditions to the mainland under his belt.

Chad was terrified but trying not to show it. He had just finished his stint in the civil defense force when the chance at the reclamation force came up. He volunteered one night after a major bender - Terry had just left him, and now he was regretting his choice. The civil defense force rarely left the island, and when they did it was short jaunts. The reclamation force was supposed to go out there for months, even years at a time. Sure, the pay was good, but it was hard to spend ration credits if you got eaten while on mission. He was pretty sure he'd just volunteered in a vain attempt to win Terry back.

They were suiting up, getting ready to head out. Chad put on his armour. Most of it was what he was used to, but there was a lightweight chain shirt on top of it all. Chad didn't know what the chain was made of, but it was reportedly lighter and stronger than anything else they had and would stand up to almost anything a zombie could throw at it. The problem was the shirts apparently cost a damned fortune to make. Still, for this force they were throwing out all the stops. On his lower body he had hardened boots that went above his knees and chain pants over padding tucked down into them.

All in all, he had almost no flesh showing. The helmets even had a full-face shield. The whole thing was dark grey, mottled so it didn't stand out too immediately. They had machetes strapped to their waist, handguns on the other side, and rifles slung over their shoulders - but the main weapon was a high-end compound bow. Noise was the enemy out there. Each of them carried 48 arrows.

The rest of their pack was stuff that had been developed just for them. A tent made of the same chain as their over armour, but with an incredibly durable frame that could anchor into virtually any surface - the demo they had been show had involved pitching the tent hanging from the side of an overpass. Chad really hoped he never needed that feature. A grappling gun and winch system capable of lifting 800 pounds. A broad spread solar panel to give them limited electricity. Long range comms gear, still limited by line of sight though, there was a repeater set on the ship and they had repeaters in their gear as well, 5 each. Getting out of comms range was something all of them dreaded.

At 20 Chad was a child of the post zombie world. He actually had the distinction of having been born the day the dead came to life. Zombies had always been a fact of life for him. He wasn't born in New Hope either, his parents had made the trek from Maine with him in tow when he was only days old. It had taken them four years, and his mother didn't make it. He didn't remember her, and his father hadn't been able to hold onto any pictures. Sometimes he imagined what she might look like, especially in moments of fear or stress - like the one he was in at that moment.

They were supposed to head out shortly after first light, taking a ship to Sydney. Bennett Matheson, the overall commander, came in. His gear was just a tiny bit shinier than the rest. He was a tall, fit man. Dark black hair and pale skin with piercing blue eyes that made you feel like he was seeing inside your soul, finding all of your secrets. Bennett intimidated most people. "Alright men, what we are doing here is new. We aren't just going to be stripping the land, we are going to try and reclaim it. In the process, we should get any of our people who are still alive back, but the end result should be a place that we can take back, that we can build on. This mission today could result in you having a place to live, to raise children, to grow crops. We aren't just fighting for our missing people, we are fighting for our future as a species. That is all. Get locked and loaded and head out."

They started out into the early morning air, fully equipped and loaded. The ship was waiting, an unimpressive vessel, just a small fishing vessel, but enough for the short voyage to Sydney. Chad hoped, desperately, that he didn't get seasick. He had never been on a boat before, and until this moment seasickness wasn't on the list of things he had worried about. The close smell of the area below decks, the mix of salt and old fish, mixed with machine oil, just that smell was enough to almost put him over the edge. He was jammed next to another member of the force, he thought it was Johnny, but it was damned hard to tell them apart in full gear and he didn't want to turn his head to check the name tag, afraid that would be enough to make him puke.

The boat was moving, swaying just a little underneath him. Every swell, every motion, threatened to make him puke. Wayde was talking, saying something about keeping in close contact with the rest of the team, but Chad just couldn't absorb it, he was too miserable.

Just as Wayde finished the guy next to Chad whipped off his helmet and puked all over the floor. It was Johnny, an older guy who Chad barely knew. That put Chad over the edge, because of course it did. He didn't manage to get his helmet off in time and was suddenly looking at a face shield covered in dayglo vomit. The smell set him off even more, and in a moment his stomach was empty, but he was still dry-heaving. The ship finally started moving. Over half the soldiers in her belly had just emptied the contents of their belly in the hold.

The voyage took two agonizing days. Most of that time Chad was too sick to be aware of time. He just lay there, wishing for death. After the initial cast off, they were allowed to go to cabins or above decks. Being above decks was a mercy at first, but as they continued the weather got choppy. Still nice, sunny skies and warm temperatures, but wind and chop on the water. The boat kept making these hopping motions, each time it sent Chad's stomach to his throat.

Finally, they made it to Sydney harbor. The late afternoon sun was beating down on the blue water, everything was green and alive on the shore, much of the city had fallen back to nature, there were trees everywhere. The ruined buildings were covered with crawling vines, pulling apart now ancient concrete. There was a scar on the landscape, where the scavengers had erected a fence. From their vantage point, they could see where the fence had been pulled down in half a dozen places. Zombies still roamed the ruined city, clumped in both small and large groups.

Never Meet Your Idols

Tamra Duchene was furious. She had just read this week's script, and once again she got to stay home and support her man. Vivian was supposed to be tough, a woman who stood up to the world, who made sure her voice was heard, at least that was how the part had been billed to Tamra when she was given it. Now here she was, a year and a half later, and all Vivian did was bake and make sure the home was in shape for Jonathan, the brave ship's captain who ferried the scavengers to and from their zombie-infested destinations. She was surprised they hadn't saddled her with a couple of kids to take care of. They probably hadn't done it, so she could still parade around in a bikini. The role had no damned meat to it. She was an actress, damnit, and good at her job.

Tamra threw her long blonde hair into a ponytail and threw on some sweats. She was going to have it out with Carter once and for all. She might be a blonde, but she didn't have to be relegated to playing one and nothing else for the rest of her damn life. Even here, even in this world with a total of one television channel and only three scripted shows.

She stormed into Carter's office. He was in a meeting, but she didn't care... until she realized who the other person was. Naomi Carvery was the last person she expected to see. A genuine hero and one of the leaders of New Hope, one that many people felt was the only true leader in the entire council. That was enough to slow Tamra down a touch. Still, she was one of the top actors in the world, hell, she was one of the only actors able to make a living at it in the world, and in a way, this made it all the more important. Naomi hadn't made the impact she had on New Hope and the world at large by staying home and supporting her man. She did stuff, changed things.

"Carter, this script is shit. I need something more, Vivian needs something more. She needs to be able to stand on her own two feet, and I am sick of being a fucking Peggy Lee song!"

"Tamra, calm down. We can talk about this later. This meeting is important."

"Let me talk to her Carter, I think she needs a bit of backstory, a bit of why she's written that way." Naomi turned to face Tamra, still sitting.

"Okay, she's all yours."

"Thanks, I think we need privacy for this one. Do you mind fetching us a coffee?"

It might have been phrased as a question, but it was clear that Naomi was giving an order. Carter sighed and stood up.

"Thanks, Carter, you're a good one. I take mine dark and sweet, just like me." Naomi winked at him.

"Alright, Tamra - coffee?"

"Double double, please. Thanks."

Carter walked out, casting them a look. He didn't seem all that happy about being kicked out of his own office.

"Tamra dear, please take a seat."

She did as she was told.

"Now look, the world has changed. Yes, women need to be seen as strong, but not the way men are. There just aren't that many people left, and we can have children, they can't. We don't need that many of them to get us pregnant, but we need a lot of us. This is virtually the only thing Barbara and I agree on. We need young women to have babies, to make family the priority."

"That's... what?" Tamra was having trouble making sense of what she was hearing coming from Naomi.

"Yes, it's not Carter's fault. He actually wanted Vivian to become a scavenger herself, Barbara and I talked him out of it. The fact of the matter is that your uterus and vagina are too important a set of resources to risk out there, and we need women to realize that. You do realize this show is pure propaganda, right? It's there to help shape attitudes. Vivian is brave, she sacrifices herself for the good of her husband and of society."

"How the fuck can you of all people believe this? We moved so far, things were getting so much better for us, now you are trying to throw us back to nineteen fifties housewife attitudes?"

RESOURCE ECONOMIES: RECLAIMING THE ZOMBIE APOCALYPSE

"No, probably more like Victorian-era attitudes, maybe even Medieval. We don't know how many people died, but it was north of ninety percent. I don't want to create laws restricting women, but I also need them to have babies and to raise those babies - it has to be them because we need someone to be out there risking life and limb to get us the resources we need, and it can't be the women. I'm sorry, I know this sounds regressive to those of us who were born before the zombies, who have memories from back then, but it's reality."

Tamra was more than shocked, she was shaken to her core. Naomi didn't say that sort of thing in public, in fact, she was one of Tamra's idols. Tamra had been ten years old when the world fell apart and was one of the few who was from Charlottetown when it changed to New Hope she was already there. Other than having hair that was more blonde than red she embodied the island girl image to a T. Pale skin, freckles, petite but fit. A bit of red hair dye and she could have played Anne of Green Gables perfectly.

Tamra thanked Naomi and muttered something about trying to do better at her role, then hurried out, feeling sick. She almost collided with Carter as he walked back in with coffee. She wasn't crying, no way. Her eyes were just watering a little bit, nothing else. She never did get her coffee.

A Pleasant Jog

Tyson was running again. It seemed like all he ever did was run. He found a place, got to stay for an hour or two, and then he had to move. Once he managed to stay out of sight for a full night, but by morning the zombies had found him. He had no idea how the hell so many zombies had made it here. Sydney was supposed to be low activity. It was an isolated city on the northern edge of Cape Breton Island, and even before the world died the population had been low.

His main goal was to stay alive, while he did that he kept his eyes open for any sign of his crew. Two days ago, he had found the remnants of a fire, evidence that at least some of them might still be going. He thought it had been a week. He had a cough that was worrisome. He was spending a lot of time in the dank underside of half dead shells of buildings, dealing with a mix of industrial materials and mold. His teeth felt like they had grown moss, and his face was a constant mass of itches. Water was scarce, he was finding pools of rainfall whenever he could, but he wasn't getting enough. His arms and legs cramped as he ran, a symptom of dehydration. He was so very, very hungry.

He had to make a decision, and soon. It was either stay in the city and try to find the others, maybe have a chance of rescue - something that felt less and less likely each day, or break into the countryside and see if he could lose the zombies there. There was less cover, but a higher chance of getting clean water, maybe even some food. He had earned decent marks in foraging class, and this environment should be similar.

A road out of town was ahead of him. He could see green growing countryside, something even more wild than the vine festooned buildings surrounding him. The pack of zombies was a few minutes behind him. He decided to go for it, try to find a place he could lose them at, then maybe an abandoned country house. He headed along George St. as fast as he could still manage. He wasn't going that much faster than the zombies at this point, and every step was agony.

The neighborhood had turned to suburban residential, small houses along the road. Nothing he could use yet. The zombies were still too close. He didn't seem to be picking up more though, now that he was out of town. He tried to pick up the pace, but his legs wouldn't do it. He settled for the same loping run he had maintained for the last several hours. He had always hated running in school, but nobody got to opt out. If your legs worked you ran at least five kilometers every day while in school, and a lot more on a pretty regular basis. He was thankful for that now.

Finally, he saw a road that had a steep rise in it, somewhere he could lose his escort if he managed to move fast enough, at least with some luck. He took a left and sprinted, finding a last bit of reserve somewhere deep inside him. He was hours past hitting the wall. Over the rise he saw the best possible case, there were several houses - doors and windows missing of course, but lots of potential hiding places, and a road that curved out of sight quickly. He ran for a small house with the door still partially intact, hanging in the gaping doorframe. He vaulted over it and skidded to a stop.

He turned into the first room he could find, anything to make sure he was out of sight of the doorway before the zombies caught up. Then he hunched down, making sure he was out of sight of the empty window frame. He was lying on broken glass, some of it cut his hands, but he didn't care at that moment. He was spent, all the pain did was bring the world back into sharp focus. He crouched low for hours, not daring to put his head up to see if he was in the clear.

Finally, the daylight started to fade. One thing about being so dehydrated, his bladder wasn't forcing him to move. Of course, his thirst did that in the end. He cautiously stood out of his crouch. His back was cramped in a dozen places and the hollow pit of his stomach sent stabbing pain through his entire body. He needed water. There was just a little light left, but enough that he could see the road in front of the house. It was empty, he had managed to give the zombies the slip.

Tyson walked to the back of the house, sure enough, there was a well out there. It was overgrown with vegetation and half fallen in, the access way rusted shut, but it was a well. A well meant there was clean water, if he could just get at it. He went back into the house and found a bunch of old rusty tools, in what had been the garage when this place was a house. He set to work trying to get the access way pried off quietly.

Looking Out Over the City

C lyde looked down at the city. Strangers had come, they always came. His sons had been right to cut the fence, the strangers would learn not to come.

Shorefall

C had stepped on shore, bow at the ready. There were dozens of zombies in sight, none in effective range yet, but that would change fast. They were closing, shambling in towards them. He fixed one in his sights, signaled to the others that it was his. The rest of the team did the same, and as the zombies got in range arrows flew out towards them. The zombies dropped rapidly. Not every shot hit, but most did. The team was well trained and well disciplined. They picked off the last few almost instantly.

The shore secure, it was time to set up a safe perimeter. Wayde went first, followed by half a dozen men hauling lengths of fence. They were going to use some of the buildings as a wall, with the lengths of fence filling in the gaps. They found a good site in a few minutes, picking of an astonishingly large number of zombies as they worked.

Now that Chad was on land he felt better, still weak and ill, but recovering. The voyage had been one of the most brutal experiences of his life. Apparently, he wasn't great with ocean travel. He helped set up a fenced corridor between the base camp and the dock, then he helped haul gear up the corridor. The way they laid out their camp meant that somebody could see every section of fence at all times, after all something had caused the one the scavengers were using to fail. Chad was happy he had an early watch. It meant he waited longer until he got to eat, his stomach probably wouldn't have held food that soon after making landfall anyway. First though, they had to fetch as many arrows as they could.

Chad had only fired two, and he was able to find them fairly quickly. They had his signature tag on them. Both of them were intact, he had more ammo to work with.

Watch was uneventful. He felled five zombies, each one with a single shot. They let them get almost to the fence before dropping them when the numbers were small like this. Finally, his shift was done, and he got to eat.

His stomach had settled enough to handle the food, and nothing in his life had ever tasted as good as the bland stew they were eating.

This was likely to be the last cooked meal they had while on mission, so Chad savored every bite. He wanted to bolt it all, but his stomach was still too delicate for that, so instead he sipped it from his spoon slowly. Finally, he finished and retreated to his tent, completely exhausted.

Girl Power and the Zombie Apocalypse

After Tamra got herself together she decided to do something about it. Maybe Naomi was right, maybe they would have a better chance of surviving if women just bowed down and decided that they were a walking baby incubator, but who the fuck decided that the human race should survive if they were going to act like it was still the 1800's?

She knew people in the salvage operations, a lot of them. There had to be a way she could get to Sydney, prove that women were more than decorations and wombs.

She grabbed her jacket and headed out into the city. New Hope had been a very small city before the zombies, back when it was called Charlottetown. Now it was a bustling metropolis, the largest, most important city in the world. The downtown core had electricity most of the time. The crowds were thick, wall to wall humanity. Tamra headed for the docks, time to call in a few of her contacts. She had her hair tied back, a ponytail, sunglasses, and a ball cap. Without that she couldn't walk anywhere in New Hope, it was constant requests for autographs, getting stopped every thirty seconds. Sometimes she wished she had never become an actress.

The part of the docks she was heading for was much less populated, a run-down part of town that most of her peers avoided at all costs. She wasn't afraid though, her family was well enough known down here, and nobody was going to risk crossing her brother.

She got to Billy's office in the early afternoon. He was in a meeting with one of his people, it looked like a pretty intense meeting. Tamra felt bad for the guy sitting in the hot seat. Billy might be good to her, but he wasn't a nice guy, not at all. Finally, the door opened, and the young man Billy was talking to came flying out, landing in a heap on the floor.

"Fuck you, you little shit. I find out you're shorting me again you are dead, fucking dead! Oh, hey Tamra - just give me a sec, I think I broke a chair."

"No worries, I don't mind the couch."

They went into Billy's office, light filtering through windows long gone yellow with filth. The place was a relic of the past, a hundred years old at least, and it looked it.

"Hey sis, how's show business?"

"Fucking bullshit is how it is. They want me to be the good little wifey, stay at home and look pretty while the big strong man saves the world."

"Fuck 'em. You don't need 'em, you can always come down here and work with me."

"You know I can't do that, your guys wouldn't get any work done, they'd be too busy staring at my ass all day."

"You make a good point. These guys are fuckin' animals. What can I do for you?"

"I need to make it over to Sydney. Show those fuckers how tough a woman can be."

"That's a pretty fuckin' stupid idea. Nothin' over there but zombies and wrecked buildings. What's getting eaten going to show them?"

"The reclaimers are over there right now, trying to take the place back. They don't know shit Billy, you know that. They think they're tough, but they haven't lived the life we have. They think being soldier boys is going to get shit done."

"Okay, but what the fuck do I do if you get eaten? Fuckin Tony will kill me."

"You let me worry about Tony, I'll make sure he gives his blessing before I head over. The important thing is, can you get me there?"

"Sure, but you'll owe me."

"Fuck you, who hooked you up with Kaitlin? If anything, you still owe me."

"Alright. Look, we have a supply ship slated for three days from now. I can make sure you are on board and that you have a clean way off. I'm going to set up a way back for you as well, you best get your ass on it."

"Thanks Billy, tell Kaitlin I said hi, and give Jr. and Simone a kiss for me."

She headed back out into the heat of the day, the smell of the dock washing over her. It felt like home. She might be the princess of the island these days, but that wasn't how she'd grown up.

The Blessed

The sunset was amazing. Junie thought about how much prettier sunsets were these days. When he'd grown up there was always light somewhere, even as remote as his home was. Now though Sydney was dark, and the sky could be itself. He was worried about Pa. Pa was supposed to be back by nightfall, and here the sun was down almost full over the horizon. Maybe Pa got grabbed by the strangers, the interlopers. Fucking New Hope, all those people thinking they were the rulers of the fucking world. Well, they would learn. Fucking right they would.

He turned back to the village, so serene against the highlands. The little houses all painted and tidy, the church white against the darkening sky. The family had a bonfire going, a celebration of the late summer. The faces of the blessed showed through the gaps in the tight fence of the pen. The blessed were reaching for them, as always, trying to consume them. Sometimes Junie envied them, they didn't have his turmoil, they knew their desires - he was always conflicted. Pa said it was a sin, some of the things he wanted to do, and Pa knew about sin. Pa had read the bible, all of it, even the lost books that talked about the time after the blessed. He had even written most of it down. Junie knew that he would have to read those books once Pa passed on, but until then it was Pa and only Pa.

Evie was looking so pretty dancing around the bonfire. He wanted her, right now - but he knew that he had to wait until they were properly married, had to wait until her thirteenth birthday. It was so close. He had watched her for years now, as her limbs got long and smooth. Now, here she was dancing around a fire in a tiny white shift, almost a woman, almost his.

He longed to join the dance, like he used to when he was little, just let go of his cares and spin wildly around the fire, under the stars, but the blessed needed handling and he was the oldest unmarried man, he needed to lead them.

RESOURCE ECONOMIES: RECLAIMING THE ZOMBIE APOCALYPSE

Junie grabbed a gaffe and got ready by the gate. Once he saw that all the other boys were ready to go he opened the gate. The three-blessed stumbled out, arms reaching for them. All four of them struck at once, sinking the heavy hooks into the flesh of the blessed, pulling them into the firelight. Once the blessed were properly burning they let them go, let them wander as they would. The family avoided them, skipping out of the way as the blessed burned and then finally fell, the fire granting them the peace that death had withheld so far.

After the blessed fell they had a feast. They had captured one of the strangers from Sydney, a big guy with lots and lots of meat on him. They portioned out his meat among the members of the family. Junie sat down next to Evie as he ate, looking at her skinny legs poking out from under her shift. Just a few more weeks now.

Conspiracy Theories

The command tent was larger than any of the other tents. Bennett felt bad about occupying it, but in the end, he needed the space. He had the map table set up with him, all the situation maps laid out. It didn't actually leave a lot of room for him to move about. He started the day with his usual routine, push-ups, crunches, squats, stretching - post workout of course, wanted those muscles warm before trying to stretch. Then he headed out to join the men for breakfast.

The food was cold and bland. They were strictly on a no fire rule until they had more area secured. Already the zombie activity was severe. The fence they erected was solid, no sign that the zombies were going to be able to make it through. They were starting to build up a bit on the southeast corner, a mass of rotting bodies slowly building up, ignoring the number that dropped. It was inevitable, at least with these fences.

Bennett gave his morning address to the men. "You know your jobs. We have a bunch of z's building up right now, but nothing to worry about. Take care of them, then head out. Four man squads, do a grid search, eliminate any zombies you run into. Make sure you search every building, we want our people back. Make sure your end points are clear. Get to it."

He wished he had Naomi's gift for speaking. He always felt like he failed utterly to inspire people. His mind was better suited to tactics, to managing the day to day, than to scenes like this one. He wished there was some way to just offload those parts and do what he was good at.

The men headed out and Bennett went back to his tent. Right now, the maps were pretty useless, pre-zombie relics with modern features drawn on them in pencil. He had small black squares to represent his men, and white ones to represent zombies. The white ones came in three sizes, basically they amounted to one, a few, and holy shit. There were more holy shit sized zombies than he would have liked by far. He also had blue ones to represent any of the scavengers he managed to rescue. He wasn't holding out huge hopes that he would get to use any of those.

Wayde came in with a squad member in tow. "Hey boss, Johnson just finished inspecting the first quadrant of the fence. He found something interesting."

Bennett waited, fixing the trooper with an expectant look. "I don't have all day, out with it. What's going on with the fence?"

"Sir" the soldier stammered "the fence appears to have been cut, using tools."

"Are you saying people did this?"

"No sir, I mean, I'm not drawing conclusions, but the links have been cut clean, would require wire cutters or something like them. Not sure the average zombie has th... the brains to manage it. Sir."

"Okay, thanks for the report. This changes things."

Bennett allowed Wayde to show the young man out. When the man returned they got together to discuss the new situation.

"So, if humans did this that means someone else is here, and whoever it is isn't friendly."

"Yep. That's my assessment too sir."

"How do we deal with that? What kind of options do we have? Everything we have done in terms of security is predicated on the idea of a mindless enemy. If we are fighting people, we have to completely and totally re-evaluate our strategy. I have a few contingencies up my sleeve for this sort of thing, but I'm not happy about it."

"Nope, me neither. Do I tell the men or wait for more intel?"

"Tell them. I don't want to pretend I'm in an old movie, get the men killed just because we don't want to share info."

"Good sir. Anything else?"

"Yes, scouting is going to have to change. We should pull the men back in for today, send them out again as soon we know exactly what we are doing. Also, I want some form of longer range optics, binoculars or something. I'm going to call home and see what they have available."

They discussed a little more, trying to come up with solid plans, but in the end, they gave up because they didn't have enough information to come up with anything concrete.

The discussion with New Hope wasn't much more useful. The only thing he managed to get from them was that he would get a half dozen pairs of binoculars when the supply ship came, in several days. He almost smashed the handset on the radio in sheer frustration.

Hit the Road

They were stuck waiting. The men were busy, but it was all busywork, nothing valuable, nothing with a goal. They reinforced the fence, started clearing the rubble from the ground, started clearing brush, basically making the small base camp a more permanent place. Chad was working next to Johnny, clearing land. They had picks and shovels to work with. It was too hot for their armour while doing this kind of work, so they were in their basic uniforms. Nobody knew who was trying to kill people from New Hope here, or even where the other people actually were.

"Too fucking hot. I didn't sign up for the reclaimers to spend my time doing construction work. Fucking hell."

"Yeah man. Kind of fucked up. Who the fuck would be trying to kill actual people?"

"No clue. Something wrong with them. Fuck 'em. Let 'em come, we got the guns, we got the gear, we got the training. We'll fuck 'em up."

Chad wished he felt as confident as he pretended to be. He was new to all of this. He'd dropped zombies before, but never a person. Truth was he would rather dig than fight at this point.

The day went quickly, then the next, then the next. Bennett Matheson kept them a little bit updated, basically telling them he refused to force them out into the field with inadequate gear. Finally, the resupply ship came. It stopped just off shore for a few minutes, for no reason anyone could discern, and then continued until it reached the dock. That meant more heavy labor, more hauling crates of supplies through the city, over uneven pavement and fallen buildings. The labor was backbreaking, and the weather had turned. It was still summer, still hot, but the rain was pouring down, punishing them. Clearly a storm was coming in.

After they got the new gear up to the main clearing they set up the new mess hall and communal meeting area - a large tent, capable of holding most of the force at once. Setting it up in the high winds and heavy rain was punishing work, mostly performed in silence because they couldn't talk above the wind.

Then the gear tent had to be set up. They were settling in for a much longer time period, with an eye to eventually making this base permanent, which meant setting up long term infrastructure. The gear tent was a middle ground, a staging tent where materials could be stored as they shored things up.

Finally, days after they were supposed to start, they were brought into the mess tent and given a second - and final - mission briefing. Bennett once again talked to the entire group. He seemed less awkward this time, probably because he was exhausted and too dirty to care if he made a positive impression. "Alright men, as you no doubt have heard, the zombie incursion on our people here was the result of human action. Somebody cut the fence, and given that fact, probably lured the zombies inside. So, that adds a new wrinkle to our mission. We need to keep an eye out for enemy combatants now. There are people here, and they don't seem to like us. Ideally, I would like one or more of them to question, but look out for yourselves first. Take one if the opportunity comes up, but don't feel bad if you have to shoot them in the head." His shoulders were slumped, and his voice had a resigned quality.

It wasn't until early the next morning that the teams finally headed out. Chad was again partnered with Johnny. It seemed that it was a simple matter of who they were next to on the boat that decided the teams. They also had a heavy gunner named Tim and a comms officer named Michelle. Michelle handled the big radio, the one not limited to line of sight. Johnny was in command.

The day was miserable, the storm was still in full force, forcing the resupply ship to stay docked. It was the worst possible scenario for the reclaimers, visibility was low, they were wet, they were wearing heavy gear. Johnny was lead, he had slightly longer in the force than any of the others. They were sent southeast to scout.

The going was agonizingly slow. They walked silently in the pouring rain, keeping their eyes alert. Their helmets theoretically allowed them to talk to each other, but the pounding rain was so loud against the unyielding steel shell that they had to shout despite using radio to talk helmet to helmet. The rain drowned out almost everything.

Chad was the first one to spot the horde. A hundred zombies, maybe more, closing on them from the northeast, cutting off their route back to base. They had been walking for a couple of hours, seeing only the occasional single, easily picked off, when suddenly the large horde came out from the rubble. Still a long way off they were in the worst place they could be. It was by far the most zombies they had seen since reaching Sydney.

They started heading back, hoping to get past the horde before being completely cut off, it was quickly apparent that wasn't going to work, so they turned and headed back south. Johnny said "We need to get out of sight of the horde. Once we get far enough south we turn east and try to get around them. Not getting stuck out here, it's not an option."

They broke into a light jog, moving much faster than the horde. Michelle called out "What's that? southeast of us? Fuck, is that another horde?"

Of course, it was. No way was this luck. Something was pulling zombies toward them. The west was the harbor, a dead end - the north and south were both blocked, so they started running east.

A Pleasant Swim

The trip to Sydney was pleasant until the last day. The boat crew treated Tamra with the respect her brother had insisted on. She had some incredibly high-end gear with her, thanks to her contacts. The best piece was the rifle, an Accuracy International L115A3 AWM sniper rifle. She had learned to shoot as a child on the island and had a gift for it. The gun itself was an extremely rare piece, an old-world military relic from another continent. She also had a small inflatable boat, something she could use to sneak off the boat before it docked. Other than that, she had rations for a week, a pair of heavy duty boots, and some basic survival gear.

The weather turned bad the day they made landfall, so she had to slip off in rough seas with high winds. Nothing she wasn't used to. Her family had survived the zombies without ever leaving Prince Edward Island, one of the very few to do so. They did it by being hard and doing what needed to be done. Part of why she didn't believe that her character should be relegated to being the good little wife. Every woman in her family had survived hell and kept going. She'd be damned if her daughters (assuming she ever had any) were going to be relegated to second class citizenship. She slipped into the choppy sea and gave the crewmen a wave. The one advantage of the weather was that it meant she would have an easy time reaching the shore unobserved.

She made landfall near the south end of the harbor and started looking for a place to set up a home base. She knew she would have to be on the move but having a safe place she could flee to if she needed was one of the first things she had learned from the zombies. That and she needed to get her zodiac out of the water, it was a tough craft but there was no way she could keep it secured in this weather.

She found a semi-collapsed dock with a mostly intact building next to it. She wasn't sure what the building had been in the old world, now it was just a shell, all the glass long since shattered, the furnishings and finishing destroyed, but it had stairs that were intact, more than one set of them, and a good perch on the roof where she could scope out the city. She got the zodiac secured above the high tide mark under the ruined dock, and then set herself up in the shell of a building. It was tall, five stories at least. She had never seen a building that tall.

The view from the roof covered most of the downtown core, although her view of the reclaimers camp was obscured. She used the scope on her gun to get a better look at anything that caught her interest.

She decided to leave the next morning, which gave her a day and a night to get her home base set-up, make it ready as a backup location. First she set up a small camp inside the fifth floor, hidden from view but with access to the rear stairs, then she set up a route she could use to get from the camp to the front stairs, something that would make sure she wouldn't fall through the floor - much of it was unusable. She had to re-enforce a few spots with some of the better boards she was able to find. She used a tarp as a lean-to against a wall, setting up a small sleeping area underneath it. She had a minimal camp mat and a sleeping bag inside of it.

She knew she needed fire, but also that she needed to keep any smoke out of sight, so she had a small rocket stove. It burned so hot it burned up almost all the carbon in its own smoke, making it effectively a smokeless heat source.

Her night was spent resting, alert for any noises. The solitude was both the best and worst of it. Since she had become a star she hadn't had much time to herself, something that the years before had been full of. She had time to reflect. Since her meeting with Naomi she had been running full tilt, taking no time to think. Now that she was resting and by herself doubt started to set in. Was she doing the right thing by coming here? Was it too much for her, a survivor, but self-taught and essentially untrained? Was, god help her, Naomi, right? She rejected that last thought almost instantly. It didn't matter if Naomi was right in an abstract sort of way, that would mean living a life that was unacceptable for half the population for the near future. Sometimes a person just has to take a stand.

Morning came finally, and Tamra headed back up to her lookout perch on the roof. She could see the troops starting to head out from the reclaimers base. One quartet was heading her way. She decided to try keeping up with them, staying out of sight but shadowing them, when the time was right she would let them know she was around.

She followed them in the scope, and with her eyes, as they came closer. Then she was the hordes approaching, seeming to come out of nowhere. There was no sign, no warning, then there were hundreds and hundreds of zombies, coming from the north and the south. At least the east seemed to be clear. She grabbed her rifle, handgun, and machete and headed down to try and catch up with the reclaimers. She could see from her perch where they would have to go to be safe, and her secrecy wasn't worth getting four people killed.

Star Power

Tim noticed the blonde girl running along behind them first. She was moving fast, much faster than they were. The girl was wearing an olive drab tank top, a pair of camo pants, and heavy boots. Her hair long and pulled into a pony-tail, peeking out from under a baseball hat. She also had a large rifle slung over her shoulder. She was running at a pace that wasn't quite a sprint, but too fast to sustain. Tim nudged Chad and pointed back, Chad nudged Johnny and Michelle. They slowed the pace to let her catch up. As she got close Chad recognized her. Terry was a big fan of Homefires and made him watch every episode before she dumped him. That was Vivian running towards them. He liked her way better in camo than he ever had in those silly sun dresses she was always wearing on the show. What the hell was she doing in Sydney?

She yelled "follow me, I know how to get past the hordes" and kept going past them. Despite the fear, Chad appreciated the view. No question that she was the best-looking woman he'd ever seen.

The girl led them between buildings, down alleyways, through parking lots, until finally, they found themselves at an old school. She led them inside "We should be all right in here until the horde passes."

"Holy fuck, you're Vivian!"

"No, Tamra. I just play Vivian. I'm way, way cooler than she is."

Chad thought she might be telling the truth. Johnny motioned for silence, they all shut up.

One thing about hordes, you needed to stay out of sight until the horde passed. You also needed a good, strong building, just in case they noticed you anyway. This place was solid, a fortress. They were in the swimming pool building, an empty pool, dark and musty, occupied the center of the building. There was a set of fire doors, still mostly intact, too rusted to open ever again. The building was almost windowless, just a small set of windows around the top of the high walls.

They waited several hours. The sounds of the rain on the roof were so loud they couldn't have heard a horde if it was right outside. After a while, Chad offered to see if he could spot anything outside.

He headed into the main school building and headed for the upper floor. The stairs were in pretty bad shape, but he stayed next to the wall and headed up. The top floor was a ruin, holes in the concrete, showing right through to the floor below. The roof let in water in hundreds of places. Chad got to a street side window and looked out. The horde was nowhere to be seen, but he spotted a human shape, moving furtively from doorway to doorway. The shape was clearly alive, but not one of theirs. It looked like a large man, but the silhouette wasn't smooth, like the man was dressed in rags.

Chad headed back to the group to give them the all clear. Finally, they were in a position to question Tamra.

"What the fuck? How did you end up here?"

"Decided you folks might need a hand. Wasn't doing anything more interesting."

Chad didn't question her any further, there didn't seem to be any point. They left the school, walking in silence. Chad quietly told Johnny about the figure he'd seen, and the direction he had been moving in. They headed that way, looking for signs of other people. They found tracks fairly quickly, large boot prints in the snow. Whoever it was they were making no attempt to conceal their presence.

Production Problems

"Where the fuck is Tamra Duchene?"

Everyone could hear Naomi. People in the next building could hear Naomi. She wasn't angry, she was furious. She had taken on the production of Settlers as a personal project, and it was working. People loved it, people were desperate for drama, for escapism, and Settlers provided it. The men were stronger, braver, better than real men. The women were more beautiful, more patient, sexier. It was everything that they wanted the world to be. The moral decisions were simple, t complex enough that people thought they somehow were important. The whole thing was a propaganda piece, that was obvious to anyone who was paying the least bit of attention - not that anyone was, but it was a well written, well-acted propaganda piece. Even Barbara Miller was on board, and she hated spending resources on anything. Now the female lead was missing. What the hell was the woman thinking?

Maybe it was time for an off-camera collapse, maybe a hospital stay. Vivian was too important a character to just write out, at least until they had confirmation that Tamra was dead. Of course, even if she was alive, Naomi was going to kill her.

Teddy was sitting there, all ready to shoot, makeup on. This was supposed to be a major tear jerker homecoming, with Vivian throwing herself all over Johnathan, who had been presumed dead. Instead they had to deal with shooting without Vivian, and with Teddy the half-wit trying to roll with the punches, something he was chronically bad at doing.

The worst part was now she had to deal with Barbara complaining about the budget. The old battle ax might be on board with the project, but she could find a reason to complain about everything. This meant major script changes, major changes to the shooting schedule. Thank god there were no other shows to compete with Settlers.

Rude Awakening

Tyson was moving again. The small house had been a godsend, a place to get his wits together, a place to figure out a plan, and most importantly, a place with water. The well had been hard, extremely hard, but at least it had turned out the water level was high enough for him to get water without needing a vacuum pump. Now he needed food. He hit the road, making sure he was still alone. He started early in the day, as per training. They used to think traveling by night was the best option, but the zombies didn't necessarily move by sight, sometimes they didn't even have eyes. They shuffled along guided by some combination of smell, hearing, sight, touch, and who knew what else. Humans on the other hand would sometimes walk directly into a zombie if it was dark enough. Better to move when your dominant sense was still in play.

The road was overgrown, to the point where it was barely a suggestion of a road, but it was still less dense than the growth around it. Tyson walked along occasionally stumbling on a bit of asphalt that was still intact. The sun was low in the sky, finally clear and blue after days of rain. It already felt hot, the kind of summer day that make you want to just laze by a river. Tyson was listening intently at first, but as the sun started to get warmer his attention started to wander. He started to think about home, to wonder if he would ever make it back. He saw movement, a sudden blur, that snapped him back into reality. A deer, if it had been a zombie he could have been screwed. He started trying to pay more attention. The land here was beautiful. Heavy forest on either side of the road, places that nature had reclaimed from humanity years ago. The road, once a testament to our power over the world, now reduced to patches of rubble and a narrow path of shorter undergrowth.

The zombies had done a number on the road itself, trampling down the brush - on the one hand it made walking much easier, but on the other hand it made things nerve racking. It also made him miss the human foot prints in the trail, at least until he found their source. Jack was standing there, right in the middle of the path. Emaciated, beat to hell, but alive. As soon as Tyson saw him he started running. They gave each other a big hug, uncharacteristic for their normal gruff manner with each other. "Holy shit, you are still alive. How are you still alive?"

"I ditched the horde, hid in an abandoned house for the rain. Just you left?"

"Yeah, I got to watch the rest of the crew get torn to pieces, barely managed to escape. Believe it or not, I climbed a tree once I got out of sight. Took the horde hours to pass. Though I was going to fall near the end, even though I was wedged decently. I figure another half hour and I would have gone down. Haven't eaten much since... well, you know?"

"Yeah, same here. Did manage to get a well, the drinking water helped a lot - and I know for sure it was clean. We are going to need to get someplace tonight, water and food too. Soon as possible."

The pair kept going, eyes out for anyplace they could use for shelter. It wasn't until late afternoon they spotted a place. A mostly fallen down farm house, but it had an apple orchard in the back. In the decades the orchard had been untended it had overgrown, but there were still apple trees. Most of the apples were too green to be eaten, however a handful of early ripening apples were there, gleaming red and green on their branches. Tyson and Jack set to work, harvesting as many as they could.

The house had a fireplace, still mostly intact - the chimney looked like it was in desperate need of a mason, and the room it was in only had three quarters of a roof, but it was better than anything else they could find. They built a fire and roasted any apples that were close, eating all the truly ripe ones - but slowly. It was hard, almost impossible once the first crisp, juicy, tart yet sweet mouthful hit, but they both knew the consequence of eating fast while this hungry and dehydrated. It had been grilled into them for years in school.

They made sure the firelight couldn't be seen from outside the walls, and then set up a small sleeping area in the limited shelter afforded by the ruined structure. Both of them knew they should set watches, but neither one of them had the energy to do so. Exhaustion overcame them, and they fell asleep.

Tyson woke up to find a man crouching next to him, leaned over him, and poking him in the shoulder. "What? Who the fuck?"

"Wake up shithead. It's morning."

"Sorry - what? Who are you?"

The man was big, broad shouldered and tall. He was dressed in layers of rags, and the smell coming off of him was almost on a level with the zombies. Tyson could barely breathe when confronted with the horrid stench. There was something wrong with this man. He had close cropped blonde hair and angular cheekbones that suggested starvation, despite his overall size. His teeth were rotted nubs, black or grey and foul. He had a large smattering of freckles across wind burned skin. In the end though the smell was the one feature that stood out most about him. From his face he was young, probably late teens or early twenties, despite the horror of his mouth.

"Junie." the man said, with a snarl. There were a dozen other men with him, all dressed similarly. One of them had Jack pushed up against the wall, a blade to his throat.

Mapping

It was a clusterfuck. They had sent out a dozen teams, and only five had made it back by nightfall. Yes, the teams were supposed to be autonomous, yes, they were able to operate on their own for extended periods - hell, they had assumed that at least two or three wouldn't make it back by that night. This though, where were they? The teams that did make it back reported no major zombie sightings. The odd one here or there, but nothing else. Bennett was worried, far more worried than he was letting on. He kept his demeanor cool, business like, relaxed even but inside he was a mess. These people had come here on his orders, and if something catastrophic had happened it was on his head. He had decided that this was worth the risk, partially for the sake of the missing, but mostly because he believed in the reclamation project, that humanity needed to take back as much of the world as they could, and soon.

There had also been no sign of the salvage crew. Nothing at all, which was bizarre. There would normally have been bones, scraps of clothing, something to indicate the dead. The blood made sense, with the heavy rain. Maybe some of the other teams had discovered something, but one of the teams that made it back was the team that had been surveying the location where the salvage team were working when the zombies attacked. None of their gear was there either. The only sign of them was the broken fence.

Bennett updated his map. There was still a lot more city that hadn't been ruled out than that had. The only groups that had made it back had all been north of the camp or straight east, any movement south at all and the group were gone. That was a problem, a major problem in fact. Bennett decided that in the morning he was going to send the remaining groups to the south. Nobody was answering comms either, which was even more concerning. They all had long range radio, and they were all trained to use it even if the official comms officer was disabled. There should be no situation in what the comms people didn't answer at all.

Fun and Games with Clyde

Clyde was proud of Junie. The boy had done well. Two of the outsiders captured, a useful source of information and extra food stores for the winter, if neither of them could be convinced to join the family - truly join the family in their heart and soul. Some folks were just so blinded to the truth that they just couldn't see at all. The darker skinned one was fighting something hard, two of Clyde's boys had black eyes from keeping him restrained. The other guy though, he was docile as a lamb. Clyde didn't trust that one at all. When the darkie broke he would be broke for good, the ones that fought always were. The red fellow seemed like maybe he was playing a game, pretending to give up but just waiting for a chance. Clyde was going to give him a chance, let him think the opportunity came, then slam it shut in his face. It was his favorite game.

"Alright boy. I can see I ain't gettin' nothin' from you. Seems like you ain't gonna be useful. Let's see if the oven can loosen you up."

The red guy didn't say anything back. Just sat there, silent as hell. Clyde had two of his boys grab the guy and haul him outside. The dark one started bucking, trying to get free from his bonds. "Fuck you. You fucking touch him, I will kill you motherfucker!"

"Shut up boy. Wait, no. What's your names - both of you. You don't tell me I drop him off the cliff. We got a big cliff."

"Jack. I'm Jack, you sick fuck. My boy, that's Tyson. You let us go you might get to live. Keep fucking with us and my people are going to rape your ass with an assault rifle."

"Yep. Reckon they will. Just soon as they find us, except they probably don't reckon how many of us there are, how good our setup is. I reckon that we end up with good eating this winter."

Jack, the dark guy, suddenly went pale, skin turned to ash in an instant. Probably had the old-world thing about eating people. Didn't matter to Clyde. They tasted the same whether they hated him or loved him. Still, always good to get new blood in the family. The more of them the happier Jesus would be when he came down and handed over the earth to Clyde and his.

Outside Tyson was screaming. The oven was an aluminum box made from old roofing material, with a door on it. Now, Tyson hadn't talked when they threatened him, when they beat him, when they threatened Jack, pretty much nothing had scared him - but apparently the box oven was just too much. Maybe he was claustrophobic. Clyde headed out of the prison hut to check things out, put a little more pressure on the boy. It wasn't Tyson screaming. Tyson was standing tall, glaring at the boys, blood streaming down his mouth. Tommy-boy was curled up on the ground, one hand clutched in the other. There was a finger lying on the ground between them. The screams were coming from Tommy-boy. Clyde walked over and smashed Tyson in the stomach. Tyson folded. He wasn't soft, but Clyde was a big, big man. Tyson was making retching noises as he lay there on the ground, trembling and weak. Clyde had some respect for him, but he was still from off island, not a member of the family. Strong as he might be he was still not part of the family, he still wasn't saved. Clyde kicked him in the ribs. Tommy-boy wouldn't be able to do full work in the next harvest, wouldn't be able to handle a net the same, hell, if he couldn't keep up he might just end up having to go in the pot.

You've Got Me in a Box Here

Tyson got up from the dirt, his ribs felt broken. He coughed up blood, spilling onto the hard-packed dirt. The people around him were dirty, horrible, the smell was unbearable. He didn't think they bathed. Many of them seemed to have birth defects, either physical or mental. The place itself was bizarre. A series of small houses around a giant cliff face, hundreds of meters tall. The houses were poorly constructed and mostly on the edge of falling apart, held together with tar paper and random bits of wood. It was clear that they had once been real houses, poor but decently built. The intervening years had not been kind to them however. There was also a pen full of zombies, crudely built but strong with high rails and a heavy gate.

He was still being held by three people, large men dressed in layered rags despite the heat. They were dragging him to a small box on the ground, rusted corrugated aluminum sides and a wooden door with a small slit in it. They shoved him down while the big one who seemed to be the leader looked down on him. The big man spit on him as he fell to the ground "You fucked up Tommy-boy. He can't work right then we have less hands to make sure all the mouths get fed. You have to pay for that shit. Gonna spend a few days in the oven. If you ain't dead by the end of it maybe we figure out a way, we can use you to make up for the work Tommy-boy can't do. You gonna be so fuckin' sorry you did that to his hand."

In Tyson's mind he told the big man to go fuck himself, that it was all his own fault - in reality he didn't do any of that. Instead he let them push him into the box without a sound.

It was hot, unbearably hot. The floor of the box burned his hands despite his built-up callus. He pulled of his t-shirt and put it under his hands, trying not to let his back touch the top of the box. He curled up as best he could, slowly getting his body used to the temperature. Initially it hurt every time a piece of his bare flesh touched anything, but slowly he got used to it. It reached a point where he could bear it, just. The pain in his ribs wasn't getting any better. There was nothing he could do except endure, so he did. As time went on the thirst became stronger and stronger. He started to feel cramps in his arms and legs, growing stronger and stronger. Every time he thought he might sleep another cramp hit and he was woken.

Night fell, the temperature however didn't go down for a while. The heat had built to the point where it hurt to breathe. Slowly, slowly the temperature started to decrease, but that didn't suddenly replace the water missing from his body. He heard life going on outside the box, people talking, then music came on. Crude music played on simple instruments, someone was calling a square dance. He was drifting in and out of consciousness, never able to fully sleep, but not fully awake either.

The sounds of the party started to ramp down outside, and things got quiet, silent even. The temperature kept dropping, until it was cold. Now the metal was conducting heat away from Tyson 's body. He started to shake at some point during the night and couldn't stop shaking - his limbs were heavy with exhaustion. He heard the insects start to chirp shortly before the slit in the door started to let in light. The heat started to go up almost instantly. At first, he welcomed the change, but soon enough he was starting to be overcome with heat. He was thirsty, incredibly thirsty. Eventually he did black out.

Camping with Friends

They found tracks pretty quickly after the rain stopped. Whoever the large man had been he wasn't being careful about being followed. The foot track ended at a set of tire tracks, an actual vehicle. Michelle tried raising base on the comms unit, but the signal couldn't get through. They thought about heading back to home base, but Chad did a bit of scouting and discovered that there was a large horde in the way. Instead they just started following the tracks.

The tracks led out of town, they would have been unable to follow footprints by this point, there were hundreds of them - clearly a horde had headed this way. The sheer number of zombies in this town was staggering. Tamra was tired, and the heat left her feeling like she could just lie down and sleep - the smell of clover was all around, a gentle buzzing of insects, but distant, not the oppressive sound of flies crawling on skin, more the gentle background drone of life, of nature carrying on with what it was doing without human intervention. The light filtering through the trees was green and yellow, bright blocks and brief moments of shade.

The tire tracks led to an abandoned farm house with an apple orchard. They headed inside, trying to figure out who this might be. "Looks like a bunch of people were here" Tamra said.

"Yeah, two of them didn't leave willingly. You can see where they were dragged." Chad pointed to a set pair of long drag marks.

Johnny said "Well, not zombies then. Maybe that's our guys."

"Hope not. Whoever it was looks like they might have been in rough shape" there were traces of dried blood next to one of the drag marks, someone had been bleeding, probably not much, but some.

"Alright, we need to try to get hold of base again. Michelle, you think you can get on top of this place? Try getting a line of sight if possible. If not, I guess we keep going and try again at dusk."

Michelle headed outside. Tamra could hear her climbing. She decided to follow the larger woman, maybe use the scope on her rifle to try and get a better view.

The climb was hard, the farmhouse was falling apart, most of it didn't want to hold her weight, but she managed it after a while. Michelle was already on top, perched on a small patch near the chimney that looked more solid than the rest. "Hey, hold on a sec. Let me do my thing before you get up here. This place probably won't take both of our weight."

"No worries." Tamra held tight. Michelle was doing something with the radio. Finally, she sighed in exasperation "Alright, it's all yours. Can't get a good line of sight, guess I'll try a bounce when there's less solar."

She climbed down past Tamra. "Careful, the climb down's a bitch. Stay close to the chimney, the rest of the roof is pretty much done."

Tamra did a quick scan of the horizon, starting with the direction it looked like the tracks went in. There was nothing visible. A more details scan though showed dust, not too much of it showing above the trees, down on the ground it would be thick though, chokingly so. She focused her scope on the spot. Despite the tree cover in a few minutes she was able to catch a glimpse of the source of the cloud. It was zombies, a lot of them, hundreds at least - headed their direction. They were still a long way off, probably an hour or two at least. She spun and checked the town side. Yep, there was a horde coming from that direction as well. That one was a bit further, maybe three hours at current pace, but it absolutely cut off the town side... they had to run now, before they were in sight of either horde.

Tamra climbed down as fast as she could and ran into the building "Two hordes, closer one is an hour or more away. We need to book, fast. east and west are both closed off."

"Okay, anyone see a clear path north or south?" Johnny asked.

"There was a route South seemed pretty clear. Just a couple minutes west from here. Next one I saw north was about an hour ago. Not a good option." Chad replied.

"Alright, looks like we are heading for southern climes. Grab your kit and move your ass, quietly if possible."

They moved out, taking the first road south. It was a small road but in better repair than most. Twenty years really did a number on most roads, the fact that there was still asphalt visible at all was a minor miracle. They walked in silence, looking for anywhere that was hidden enough for them to hole up while the hordes passed. It was Tamra who spotted the cave. She gestured to Johnny, then showed it to him through the scope. It was a bit off the road, and well hidden. Hard to tell how deep it went, but it looked reasonable. It was on a medium sized hill, so they started towards it.

The undergrowth made for slow going, thorns gripped Tamra 's pants every step, branches ripped at the skin on her arms. The soldiers didn't seem to care, probably because they were wearing armour, the titanium mail of their clothes was far too strong for something like thorns. Tamra wished desperately that she had something like that. Maybe making her own way here hadn't been such a good call.

Eventually they reached the cave, sweaty and tired. The cave entrance turned out to be about seven feet tall, and wide. They pushed inside, into the darkness. The soldiers pressed a button on their helmets and then moved into the cave confidently. Tamra couldn't see anything. She didn't want to speak, just in case the zombies were close enough to hear, compromising their hiding place, but she was getting left behind quickly. "Uh, guys... I can't see shit here. Help a girl out?"

"Sorry, forgot. We all have night vision." Chad grabbed her hand, startling her. He led her deeper into the cavern.

The going was slow. The soldiers had extremely good night vision, but the environment was dangerous. Just after the entryway it opened up, a chaotic cavern full of random rock formations, dripping water formed pools everywhere. The air had a foul, wet stench to it.

They kept trekking, deeper and deeper. After a few minutes Tamra said "Guys, there's no way in hell anything is seeing us this far in, I'm going to pop on a flashlight."

The group killed their night vision so Tamra could use the flashlight. The cavern filled with a dim, feeble light. It was massive, hundreds of meters across, with dozens of side tunnels within sight of where they were. So far, they could still make their way back, however all of them knew that getting lost was a real possibility if they strayed too far. The place was awe inspiring, crystals in the rocks reflected even the dim light of the flashlight back at them, creating a multitude of small light pools. There was a stream running through the cavern just ahead of them.

They decided to camp out for a bit, re-group after the panic introduced by the two giant hordes, give them enough time to head in a different direction. Seemed like since they had arrived in Sydney most of their time was spent hiding out, holing up somewhere and hoping that the horde headed in a different direction.

Tamra found herself sitting next to Chad. The young soldier had very kind eyes when they weren't hidden behind a mirrored face shield, and he seemed to have more of a sense of humor than the rest of the unit.

Johnny said "Alright, who wants some grub?"

"Hell yes, I'm starving. What's on the menu?"

"Normally we'd be on cold rations, but this place is big enough we can risk the cook stove. We get to heat up our ration packs."

They set up a small alcohol stove and started cooking the aluminum packets on top of it. Tamra had some rations of her own, a little higher end than the unit's. She said "Fair's fair. You guys can have some of my kit if I can have some of yours. Trust me, this is to your benefit"

"Thanks. Sitting in a cave with a fucking movie star. Who'd have ever thought? My Mom would be all over me for my manners" Michelle took a portion of Tamra 's meal for herself, about a fifth of the apple crumble.

Sitting together in the feeble light of the stove and the flashlight, cool because of the layers of earth above them, out of immediate danger and finally able to talk, they started discussing the mission and the plan.

"Okay, so clearly I need to re-think some details on this plan. We're going to be gone a while I think. Michelle, you think you can get a message out to base?" Johnny said.

"Don't know. The hill here is pretty tall, but we've been going down for a while... might be a lot of land between us and base camp."

"Okay, Chad - you're our resident scout. I think we are going to hole up here for a little bit if the situation doesn't change. Tomorrow AM you get to do some scouting, earn that big pay check. Try and see if there's any high points around here with a better chance at a signal. Hell, maybe somewhere you can dump a repeater."

"Ten-four chief. I'll find it if it exists. That assumes of course I don't get eaten as soon as I poke my head out."

"Yeah, that brings me to my next point. Tamra, I have no official authority over you... but how good are you with that rifle of yours?"

"Good. Very good even."

"Alright. Would you be willing to place yourself under my command for the time? It means following orders, no matter what they are."

"Yep, you got it. I may have been dumb enough to come out here without the gear you guys have, but at least I'm smart enough to work with the team." she said with a self-deprecating smile.

"I want you to cover Chad in the morning. Set up on the top of the hill where Michelle is trying to get a signal from. Keep an eye on the young fellow in your scope. See any zombies trying to eat him, put one in their skull. See any humans that look hostile, put one in their shoulder or leg if you can, somewhere a bit more vital if you can't manage that."

"Can do chief."

"That's what I like to here, a can-do attitude. You would have made a good reclaimer if you weren't so damned busy being a TV star."

"Not sure I made the right choice... I though what I was doing mattered, but now I'm not so sure. You guys, coming out here and risking everything, much respect."

They ate the food and then set up tents. The tents weren't to keep out the elements, the titanium weave of the fabric meant that they were almost impenetrable once set up, a good secure shelter. There wasn't enough room for two to sleep comfortably in a tent, and Tamra didn't have one, but they needed a watch schedule anyway, so they just rotated with one person up and about the whole time. It was easy enough watch duty, with only one was in to the caves that they were aware of.

Separated

Morning dawned in the cavern without any visible change. It was Chad's watch, so he was the only one who saw the forest slowly emerging from the dusk, emerald green and full of life. The birds started their morning chorus, filling the air with life and noise.

"Hey people, time to get your asses out of bed. It's morning."

Tamra was the first one to come out, mostly because she emerged wearing just a tiny pair of underwear and a tank top. Chad turned bright red and turned back to watching the entrance. Tamra just laughed as she pulled on her cargo pants.

Outside of the cave it was starting to warm up, the bright summer day just getting going. The recent rain storm had brought even the yellowing grasses back to life and filled everything with green. Chad started out to scout the area as soon as he had a quick bite to eat. The sun was only a couple of fingers above the horizon, creating long shadows.

First, he headed to the top of the hill they had camped underneath, to give himself a broad view of the area, looking for other high points, and also trying to see if he could spot the hordes.

The dense forest meant that spotting the hordes was near impossible, and the mountainous terrain limited his view plane. He did spot a high peak nearby, dominating the landscape. Not something they had been able to see from the forest floor, but clear from his current nearly barren hilltop. Everything about Cape Breton was foreign. PEI, and even more the area around New Hope, was flat. Most of it was cultivated, with only small stands of trees. Cape Breton was overwhelming outside of Sydney, mostly forested, dense cover was everywhere as soon as the buildings ended. Peaks and valleys constantly broke the land, almost like the place abhorred flat ground. It was lush though, so much life this time of year.

The peak looked like it was fairly close, maybe an hour or two distant. Chad checked the short range comms gear built into the suit "Johnny, can you hear me?"

"Yep, you're good."

"Alright, heading to the peak slightly west. Will check in once I have more."

"Is it clear for Michelle and Tamra?"

"Check, sorry. Send them up."

Chad started down the hill to the east. The top of the hill was relatively clear, basically it was a large piece of rock. However, the sides of the hill were rough going. Lots and lots of undergrowth, tangled and wild it caught at his legs as he tried to walk. He pulled out his machete and started swinging at the brush. It helped, but the going was slow, and soon his arms were suffering, the repetitive motion of chopping the brush taking a rapid toll. Amazing, one swing was nothing - he didn't even notice it. By the time he had swung a hundred times it burned. By a thousand, his arm was rubber and his face was dripping with sweat. Part of him wanted to chuck his armour, drop the heavy helmet so he could get air in easier. He almost did, but then he thought about the horde, about images he had seen as a child of people torn apart and partially eaten, and he decided to endure the heat.

The forest was thick in the way North American forests are. Most of the growth was low, near his feet, or far enough above his head to be irrelevant. It was hard to see very far, the thick trees limited him to a few feet, and only the compass in his face plate display kept him in the right direction. He had expected the woods to be silent, like it was out in the countryside in PEI, but it wasn't. There were sounds everywhere. He kept catching glimpses of movement through gaps in the trees, something was out there, maybe a lot of something. It got dark in the deeper woods. Ahead he could see a pool of light, gleaming and golden. It was so bright he couldn't make out detail, so he moved ahead as quietly as he could, moving slowly and carefully.

Finally, he reached the edge of the pool of light, staying the shadows. It was a clearing, just a natural break in the tree cover. A small field of flowers and grasses, and a family of deer, contentedly munching the brush. They were beautiful creatures, lithe, strong, graceful. There was a buck with them, antlers raised, looking around. Chad didn't want to disturb them, so he carefully moved around the clearing, keeping low and quiet. That was partially responsible for him finding the zombie before it found him. It was snarled in undergrowth, able to move but not to make any progress at all, still putting one foot in front of the others, or at least trying to. The thing was old, decayed to the point where he had no idea if it had even been a man or a woman. All of its clothing had rotted off, probably years ago, except an orange toque, probably some sort of synthetic material. Even that was dirty and full of holes, with small wisps of grey hair poking through. The thing heard Chad moving and turned its sunken eyes in his direction, opening its mouth wider than possible for a human, desiccated lips over nubs that used to be teeth... it pulled towards Chad, using feeble arms to grasp at the nearest tree in an attempt to dislodge itself. Chad was a child of the zombie age, but the horror of the walking corpses had never left him. This one was the worst he had ever seen, probably the oldest he had ever seen. He overcame his revulsion and stepped forward, machete held high. The creature reached for him, yearning evident in the tension of its body, the strain put on every muscle, even if the things face had nothing but wide mouthed slackness. Chad brought down the machete on its head, breaking its skull with a single practiced move. It dropped like a wet sack, empty and void finally.

The sound of the struggle had spooked the deer. Chad saw them running off into the deep woods. He was sorry to see them go, sorry for intruding on their idyllic life.

It wasn't immediately clear when he hit the base of the higher peak. There was no instant change in terrain, just a gentle upslope, one of many he had hit during his trek. It became clear quickly however, as the going started to get harder.

The tree cover started to get thinner as Chad got higher. This peak didn't get above tree line, but it did get high and the trees became sparse. Chad was near the top when he heard a loud crack ring through the air. He turned to see the source and saw a zombie falling over, it's head destroyed. Once he made it to the top he looked around. Sydney was still out of sight, too high above them. He could however see something, through a break in the tree line. There was a horde, heading toward them somehow. The timing didn't work, not really. The horde they have avoided the day before should have caught up and passed them a long time ago. This group was close, close enough that he wasn't going to make it back to home base.

"Hey, Chad. You have a bunch of zombies incoming. Not sure how many, but way, way too many. Everyone should get inside, I'll catch up afterward. Oh, Tamra thanks for watching my back, nice shot."

"No worries. Heading downside. Leaving a repeater here, keep in touch okay?"

Chad found a solid rock and set his back against it, sat down to wait. Nothing he could do at that moment. About an hour into the wait he heard a scream over his headset.

"Johnny, anyone, what was that?"

No answer. He tried again, several more times. Still, nothing. He needed to get down there.

Captured

Tamra was bored. That wasn't something she could have predicted when she set out. Boredom while sitting in a cave with an army of zombies passing outside. It was dark, and because of the proximity of the horde they weren't using lights. Every sound was amplified, echoing through the cavern, making it hard to determine where it came from. She knew the reclaimers were watching the entryway, weapons ready, it didn't make her not terrified as she huddled there in the darkness, but the terror lost out to boredom, which eventually lost out to sleepiness. She woke as her head slowly drifted down, startled, then she drifted off again. Eventually she fell into a sound sleep.

She woke to pain. Someone let out a scream, stifled quickly with a thud. She couldn't tell who it was, and she still couldn't see. There were strong hands holding her wrists, so she started to scream as well, and felt a boot impact her stomach. The air rushed out of her stomach in a gush, leaving her unable to speak or breathe. A torch flared, and the cavern was flooded with firelight. There were men, dirty and disheveled, most missing teeth. The stench of the man who kicked her flooded her nose, a mixture of rot and decay that was overwhelming. It was like being in the company of one of the undead, but the way the man was moving it was clear he was still living. All of them were clad in rags, layered so that almost no skin was visible. They were figures of nightmare, somehow more disturbing than the actual zombies. All of them had at least some rotting flesh sewn to the rags they wore, almost like talismans. The one by Tamra had a hand hanging from a chord around his neck, half rotted and wet. The man reached down and grabbed her, pulling her up and over his shoulder. She flailed her fists at his back, but with the angle she couldn't generate any force at all. He casually walked deeper into the cave, as she tried to struggle out of his grasp.

She was able to see the rest of the group, all being dragged or carried out. They all had their helmets removed, and she was pretty sure Johnny was dead.

That amount of blood on him was too much, surely, for anyone to survive losing. The others were bound and gagged, leaving her the only one with their hands free. She wasn't sure if she should be relieved or insulted by that. A moment later one of the men grabbed her head, while she was still hanging upside down, and shoved a stinking filthy rag into her mouth, then bound her hands with layer upon layer of rotting cloth. Each layer would be easy to break through, but all together they might as well have been iron bands.

It seemed like they were walking deeper into the cave for hours, then they found themselves emerging into mid-afternoon sunlight. Tamra's eyes burned with the light for a moment, until she adjusted. She was in a dirt clearing. The man who was carrying her dropped her to the hard-packed earth, knocking the wind out of her again. At least she could see her attackers clearly now. In the full light of day, they were worse. There was nothing, not a single detail, that looked like civilization, or even sanity. Every one of them had a wooden cross around their neck, crudely carved and assembled. Some had barbed wire stringing the chains, others used leather chords. Several had barbed wire wound around their limbs, the points digging into flesh. Worse than any of that, some of them had red rimmed eyes and twitching muscles, couple with random bouts of laughter or tears.

There was an overgrown dirt road leading out of the clearing, and an aging pickup truck, the body made more of rust than steel. The truck had a bizarre contraption welded to it, a giant canister with flames periodically shooting out of the side. The men were loading something onto the truck, but it was hard to make out exactly what it was.

One of them bent down next to Tamra and attached a collar to her neck, clicking a padlock closed on it. She heard locks closing on what she assumed were the rest of the team. There were only three, and she saw a couple of men lifting Johnny into the bed of the truck, pitching him casually. He was limp like a sack.

The men lifted Tamra to her feet and attached a chain to her neck. The other end was attached to a ring in the back of the truck. Finally, Tamra was able to see what was in the cargo bed. It was a number of things in sacks, and a bunch of dead bodies - none of them except Johnny fresh.

The rest of the team were attached to the truck as well. The men spoke a language that none of them recognized, although some of the words did seem to be English. They were joking around with each other, and with some of the gestures thrown Tamra's way it was clear some of the jokes were crude ones at her expense. Finally, one of the men got in the cab of the truck and started driving. The chain around Tamra's neck suddenly pulled taut, forcing her forward. The truck was moving slowly, a bit more than a fast walk... still making it hard for Tamra and the rest to keep up. They had to hustle, waking faster by far than was comfortable. Within a few minutes she was drenched in sweat, she could only imagine what the others must be feeling. They didn't have their helmets, but they still had the mail outfits, much heavier than her tank top and cargo pants.

The ragged men kept up with the truck, those that weren't riding on the walls of the cargo bed. They seemed to take turns ranging off to the sides, probably scouting. The one thing that Tamra kept in her mind was that Chad wasn't with them. The young soldier seemed competent on a level that most people weren't. He moved so quietly, so well, Tamra couldn't help but think he would find them, might even be following them now. She hoped, prayed that was the case.

Logistics are a Bitch

Most of the teams had checked in. Three were missing though, and no radio contact from them at all. It was within parameters, but many of the teams that had checked in reported numbers of zombies that were way, way, above estimates. Not only that, the zombies seemed to show up in a less than random way. There were very few individual roamers, and the hordes almost seemed coordinated. The map in front of Bennett was busy now, they had spotted at least three hordes, each one with over a thousand zombies in it. One of the teams that had reported in was pinned down in an old mall, surrounded by a horde that seemed to be sitting on the spot. Bennett was trying to come up with a way to move them out, but no luck so far.

The others seemed to be in decent shape, nobody was in immediate danger, and nobody had any results to report so far. One team thought they had seen a human in the city, but it was during the rain storm and they didn't get a clear look, so it could have been a roamer.

How the fuck did this city have more than three thousand zombies wandering around? Twenty years ago, there had been thirty thousand, but the island was very sparsely populated and twenty years of zombies wandering in random directions should have resulted in hundreds left, not thousands. Something was drawing them here, keeping them in the city core. So far there was no living population, which was the usual thing that would keep zombies around. It didn't make any sense.

"Wayde, I need some way to get my people out of the mall. Pretty much open to anything at this point."

"Do we have any safe way to draw them off? What's the terrain like?"

"Same as everywhere else in this fucking place. Ruined buildings and roads that are more grass than pavement. It's a bad spot though, lots of open space around the mall, most of the buildings that are there are long and low - not giving much of a view block. Sound will carry well there too."

"Is that a race track or something?"

"No idea. A big dirt circle, no idea what it might be. Horse racing maybe?"

"Yeah, that's a shitty spot. Enough city left to keep us from using the forest, not enough city left to use it. It's a big fuckin' horde too. Maybe there's something we can do with the lake back there? Set up a boat and pull the horde in, haul ass in a zodiac?"

"Less than ideal... it's a small lake. The bigger one to the northwest though, maybe there's something with that one."

"A hell of a haul for the men... getting all the way over there while drawing the horde. Might be the best way to it. I'll get them to scout it. How long do you think the folks in the mall can hold out?"

"They said they are good for a few days. Still have roof access, enough rations to last them a little bit. The mall itself is probably going to fall, but so long as they can stay on the roof they will be fine. Water might be tight. Many, I wish we had helicopters."

"Yep, or wings... maybe a plane with napalm. We don't. All we've got is my men, not many of those either."

"We'll make it work. Start by getting a zodiac to the big lake. We need to find our missing guys too. There's enough of them that it merits some work... but has to wait until we get the folks off the roof."

They talked logistics for the next little while. There were a million tiny details that needed to be taken care of, supply lines to be managed, construction to shore up, etc. Bennett had managed to convince Naomi to send a few dozen general laborers to help get the compound fixed up, but that meant feeding them as well.

It wasn't like the expedition was a failure, but it was not smooth in any way. The reclamation part was going better than the rescue mission, that was certain. Of course, that was Bennett's real priority, as much as he did want to find the missing salvage crew.

The Eye of the Storm

The cavern was empty, but there were tracks leading deeper in, many of them. Most of the cave floor was rock, but there was enough dirt to leave traces and Chad was good at finding those traces. He followed the signs, including small amounts of blood that had dripped to the ground here and there. The blood looked black in the false green of his night vision.

It took several hours for him to make his way through the cavern. The going was slow, sometimes there was no sign for a long time, and many branches or cross paths. In the end though, he came out into early evening light. He was in a small clearing, empty but full of tracks. There were pools of blood on the ground, and even some tire track. It looked like a large group, most walking along with the truck.

The tracking this time was easy, but the sun set, and he didn't feel safe continuing into the night. His gear was gone, other than what he had on his body, so he climbed a tree and set himself up in a v between some branches, lashing himself in with some paracord. It was hard to sleep, his head wouldn't let go wondering what had happened to his team, and to Tamra.

The morning dawned early, birds singing, sun rising, another beautiful day. Chad let himself down and started moving. He needed to drink something, and his stomach was complaining about lack of food, but he needed to move more than he needed anything else. The tracks were clear, there was no question that whoever had his party had taken them this way.

Hour after hour he trudged. The tracks were getting fresher, he was catching up. At one point he saw where they had camped for the night, not as much ahead of him as he would have thought. Then the sound of the truck started echoing through the quiet air. He knew he had to be close. He started moving more carefully, he didn't want to just run into them unprepared, and he didn't want them to know he was there. The path he was following was clearly a dirt road, and still relatively well traveled, not nearly as overgrown as any of the other roads he had seen since arriving on the island. He could see the road continuing some ways ahead and uphill, tracked a fair way to the left.

There was a small deer track off to Chad 's left, it looked like there was a chance that he might be able to cut across, getting ahead of the truck. Worth a chance at least. He started down the trail, moving fast. The trees were close, branches whipping the face plate of his helmet, snagging at his armour, trapping his ankles, he didn't slow down, adrenaline flowing now that he could hear the truck, had a goal in sight. He pushed, hard, breath running ragged and heavy. There was a beeping in his helmet, a warning that his heart rate was well above safe levels. He ignored it, pushed even harder. He finally reached the pass, no recent truck tracks in it. He found a bush with a clear view of the pass and lay down. He realized that his vision was starting to go black around the edges, starting to blur, losing the ability to focus. He forced himself to breathe deep, in through his nose, out through his mouth.

After a while Chad 's breathing stabilized and his vision cleared. Around that same moment the truck came into view. It looked for the most part like a standard pickup truck, an older model with a lot of rust damage. There was a monstrous contraption just behind the cab however, belching smoke and fire from time to time. It appeared to connect into the fuel tank. The other strange detail was the line of people chained to the back of the truck, stumbling along. The chains ran around their necks, secured to heavy steel collars. He could see Tamra, Tim, and Michelle but no sign of Johnny. They were surrounded by people that looked like the worst dregs Chad had ever seen. There were zombies that looked more put together than these people. All of them were armed, most with bows, spears, makeshift swords, etc. Only a few of them had guns, and those guns were clearly stolen from the captives they had chained up.

The odds were too high for him to take them out, but the group was moving slowly, Chad was confident he could keep up with them, trail them until he could figure out where they were headed. He figured he had a decent idea what had happened to the scavenging party. Some of the captors had muscle twitches, Chad recognized them as being signs of cannibalism.

He kept them in sight, traveling far enough behind that he wouldn't be seen - at least he hoped he wouldn't. He kept a close eye, looking for any opportunity to free his team.

The truck stopped at nightfall, and the captors set watches. Despite the issues with their appearance they set disciplined watches, sharing around captured helmets from the team. No opportunity overnight. At some point Chad slept for an hour or so, hiding under a thick clump of bushes.

Morning dawned gray and damp. The clouds were close overhead and the winds were high. The rain started around ten in the morning, a driving steady rain blanketing the landscape in water. It got harder to walk, and the truck seemed to be having problems. They set up a tarp over the contraption, which seemed to be running the truck. From time to time they would put wood in either a lower hopper that seemed to be a firebox or an upper hopper that had hoses coming off of it. The issue seemed to be that they needed the fire to last in the lower hopper.

Eventually they reached a spot where they were facing open water. A thick cable ran across, attached to a flat-bottomed barge. The winds were extremely high by this point, and there was thunder booming through the air. Chad watched as they tried to wrestle the truck onto the barge, a task that was made nearly impossible as waves crashed over the ramp. Chad snuck down to the barge in the confusion, slipping briefly into the water. It was cold, shockingly cold. He hated the water, was developing a deep distaste for the ocean. Still, he could lose them in the passage. There was a pile of rope and detritus on one edge of the barge. He snuck between two large coils and buried himself under random crap, hoping and praying that they wouldn't need to move any of it.

Finally, they got the truck loaded onto the barge and cast off. Chad was still secure where he lay, although he was wet and cold, waves bringing frigid salt water over him every few minutes, rain pouring down on the tarp above him, flowing through in dozens of places. He was shivering, missing his waterproof tent, and sleeping bag more than he ever imagined he would. The trip across the short straight would have normally taken a few minutes. It took almost an hour. Once the barge docked he slipped off the side, not lifting the tarp, just sliding his way out.

Chad thought he was cold before he hit the water, thought it was as bad as it could get. He was wrong. It was all he could do to keep moving, barely keeping his limbs moving. There was a gap in the vegetation next to the ramp, he slid his body up it, limbs numb and unresponsive. This was bad, he was hypothermic, needed to do something to warm himself up and fast. He looked around, seeing if there was anything he could use, while still only feet away from the people who had captured his team. There was the shell of a building that had an opening near the ground, maybe a shelter. He crawled on his stomach, more slither than anything and made his way to the opening.

Once inside things got marginally better. He was still freezing, but there was no wind and he was mostly out of the path of the rain. The building he was in was about three quarters collapsed, however there was an old wood stove, and a pile of near desiccated firewood next to it. Part of his carried kit was a canister of cotton balls coated in petroleum jelly, and a fire steel, everything needed to start a fire. The risk was high, incredibly high, but he knew he had to take it, it was that or die. His hands were shaking so badly it was almost impossible to get a spark, but eventually he did. The fire bit hungrily into the cotton balls, eager flames consuming the soggy white mass, looking for more sustenance. Chad put one of the desiccated logs on the fire, a small one, propped so it didn't smother the eager flames. After a moment the flame between to lick greedily at the wood. In moments Chad had a larger log on as well, warmth flowing out into the room. He moved as close to the fire as he was able, terrified that the smoke was visible from outside. It was quickly apparent that he needn't have worried. The chimney wasn't working, and the remnants of the room quickly filled with smoke.

There was a gap in the wall, near the ground, the smoke started flowing out of it, leaving Chad able to breathe if he stayed low. It was worth it for the heat. He waited until his body recovered, the shaking a thing of the past. He was tired, through his entire body, limbs lead, eyes trying to drift shut of their own accord, but he couldn't let himself sleep. First, he had no idea what was going on outside. Had they stopped once they crossed or were they still going? Could he catch up? The air was warm enough that now that he was reasonably dry and out of the immediate danger caused by the seawater he should be fine outdoors. Of course, maybe they had seen the smoke emerging from the building and were waiting just outside his bolt-hole, guns at the ready. Nothing for it but to head outside and see, carefully of course.

Crawling out was harder than crawling in had been. It seemed like a million pieces of rubble were digging into his skin, trying to hold him back. The armour helped of course, but it wasn't very well padded - a compromise reached to allow the reclaimers to work in the summer heat. Chad managed to push his way through and out into the clean air. The rain was welcome now, still cold but not frigid and it meant relief from the smoke. He suppressed a cough as best he could but lost out to the urgent need his lungs had to purge the carbon. He was racked for a moment, his body trying to double up on itself, a harsh racking cough splitting the air. He was sure that if the captors were still there they would have heard him, were probably coming to get him. That fear was quickly allayed as another rumble of thunder rolled through the landscape. Out here visibility was measured in feet, in fact he could barely see the building he had just left, and the rain was drowning out any sound less than the thunder claps. They were in a full-on summer storm, an epic blow coming from the south. The winds almost knocked him over, and he saw trees lashing the ground, branches pushed down. Given the weather there was no way they had continued on.

Despite the weather, Chad began to move through the small town, more a village than a town, and not occupied for twenty years. It took him just a couple of minutes before spotting the truck. The vehicle was under partial cover and had tarps tied down to it. The tarps were flapping in the wind, despite being pulled as tight as possible. Chad had never seen a storm this bad before, and it had come in so quickly. The truck was next to a mostly intact house, a small place with thick, sturdy walls. It was an old design, predating most of the construction around it, and more solidly intact than the rest. He guessed that was where the group was holed up, so he started towards it. The walking was nearly impossible, he was knocked prone more than once, and in the end resorted to crawling on hands and knees, the only way to be sure he wasn't knocked over again.

The small building had holes where the windows had been, giving him a view of the interior. He was careful, poking his head just over the sill, staying back a ways. The window he picked was sheltered by the next house, not so much a structure as a pile of rotting building materials, but it blocked the wind.

It was hard to see inside, so Chad flipped on his night vision, casting the interior into a green false light. He could see Tamra kneeling on the ground, hands and feet bound. Michelle was lying next to her. Tim wasn't in sight from his vantage point. There were at least a dozen captors around them.

RESOURCE ECONOMIES: RECLAIMING THE ZOMBIE APOCALYPSE

Despite his armour and weaponry, Chad was confident he couldn't take more than a dozen men by himself, especially since at least four of them had weapons stolen from his comrades. Still, this storm seemed like it might be the best opportunity he was going to get. He decided that it was more a matter of creating an opportunity than looking for one, and he had an idea for how to do that. The truck, with the tarps. After surveying the scene as best he could he crawled his way to the truck. There were five tarps total, and they were all well lashed down. A couple of minutes with a knife and the tarps started to come loose, however, at just that moment everything stopped. The storm didn't start to taper out, it just went dead calm. The rain vanished, the wind died completely, everything was calm. He could see clearly, and what he could see was a wall of water to the north, and another, further away, to the south. The barge was gone, ripped from the cables that had held it in place. His hiding place had further collapsed, the ceiling falling in some time while he was searching the town. He rolled under the truck, just in time. Two of the captors came out to look around, not really paying attention to the truck, focusing on just looking around in wonder.

The southern wall of water was closing on them, moving slowly. Chad realized that this must be a hurricane, that they were in the eye of the storm. Perfect. As soon as the weather hit again the tarps would be pulled off the truck, loudly. He wasn't sure it would be enough, but maybe it would give him an opening to free his companions.

After the two men went back inside Chad moved into a better position, between the two buildings where he had started. The wind hit, hard. It was almost instant, going from calm to full hurricane in less than a minute. As predicted, the tarps ripped off the truck, slamming into the side of the building on their way past. The captors flooded out, trying to get the truck secured again. There were still three inside, but Chad figured that this was the best chance he was going to get. He fired in through the open window, catching one of them in the torso with his first shot. The other two turned, unsure where the shot came from. Chad fired off another round, dropping a second man. His third shot went wide, the man moved too quickly, and Chad wasn't able to get a clear bead. He dove through the open window, landing hard on the floor. He looked up at the barrel of a gun, pointed at his head. He thought to himself "Well, fuck. That didn't work out" and then the gun barrel swung off target, just as the man pulled the trigger. Tamra was behind him, standing but still chained, her body still moving from the shoulder check she had slammed into her captor. As he fell to the ground she kicked him in the head, again and again. The kicks were still raining down as he came to a rest, still, on the floor.

"Holy shit, where did you come from?"

"Been following you guys for a few days now. Couldn't get near you until now. Let's grab..."

The door flew open and several of the men came in. It took them a moment to register what was happening inside. Tamra took that brief pause to run, full tilt, to the window. Chad turned and dived with her, out into the storm.

Naomi and Barbara meet

It seemed like all Naomi did these days was wait and sit in meetings. She almost missed being out in the world, back when her and Jasper started all of this they still did stuff, still took action. Here she was, waiting to start a meeting. Fucking Barbara was the reason of course. Back dealing bitch was late again. Everyone thought she was the new messiah, just because she'd come all the way from Pittsburgh solo. Sure, it was a hell of a feat, but it didn't mean she knew shit about how to run things.

Sometimes when Naomi was angry she felt like she was still the bitch from the projects she'd been when all of this started, before she made her own journey through hundreds of klicks worth of zombies. Hell, sometimes she wished she was still that girl. She'd take Barbara by the hair and smash her face into the boardroom table until she decided to go along with Naomi's plan. If it was just a philosophical difference it could have been overlooked, worked around, but not now. Naomi 's husband was in Sydney, in the middle of one of the largest hordes of zombies they had seen since PEI had been cleared. If something happened to Bennett because Barbara wouldn't commit the resources Naomi might forget that she was a community leader for a little while.

Finally, the older woman arrived. She had a couple of decades on Naomi, and she seemed to think that entitled her to run the show.

"Sorry to keep you waiting. Had a meeting with the dockworkers union rep. Hard to believe we still have to contend with unions. Someday I'll decide if I hate them or the zombies more."

"We need to get supplies to Bennett. They are dealing with way more than we ever thought."

"Of course. We need to get our boys whatever they need."

What? She had to be up to something, her attitude completely changed overnight.

"Alright, that's great. Let's get thing moving."

"While we're on the topic... I found Tamra Duchene, well, sort of."

"What do you mean, where is she?"

"Sydney. She made her way over on a supply run. I took the captain in for questioning this morning. Did you know her brother runs the dockworkers union?"

"Didn't know that, but it makes sense. Her family was here before first night. There's a lot of them too. French and Irish, go figure."

"Yeah, they are pretty much the Irish mob."

Naomi had suspected as much, Tamra was a decent actress, and pretty, but she had come a long way since she got the role. At the beginning some of the scenery was more emotive.

"So, where did she end up?"

"Jumped off the boat before it docked. She had a zodiac with her, some supplies, a big gun. The captain has been co-operative, at least since we gave him some gentle persuasion."

"Don't tell me your methods, I will sleep better not knowing."

Torture was one of the areas they disagreed on. Not the moral justification, the effectiveness. Many years before Naomi had been on the receiving end of torture, not an experience she would repeat. It hadn't made her say anything or taught her a lesson. The man who tortured her was dead and buried, but his face still haunted her memory. In the end she didn't like torture morally but was not tied to any moral stance if it worked. Barbara on the other hand believed in it. Sure, it could get intel, but it wasn't reliable. Might as well just guess, a torture victim would tell you anything they thought might get you to stop, true or not. Better to build trust, at least that's what had worked for Naomi for the last two decades of running a city and a small country behind the scenes.

"So, the silly twit. All right, we roll with it. How about we make a public proclamation that she has gone to Sydney to help out with the recovery efforts? Should drum up some patriotic fervor."

"Exactly what I was thinking. We can get people on side, really get them focused on the Sydney project. The only down side is that we might have to rethink Tamra a little bit on the show, make her more active. That is assuming she makes it back alive. I'm guessing she went off based on your talk with her?"

"One would have to assume. She seemed to accept the reasoning at the time, but she's a good actress these days, I suspect she just went along because she didn't want to let me know what she was planning."

"We do have to do something about her family of course."

"Of course. I'll get my people to take care of that. When we are done her brother will still have his title, but nothing else."

"Are you sure you can handle that? I mean, on top of all your other responsibilities. It's a lot to take on. If you need me to lend a hand I can, of course only if you need it."

Fucking bitch. Tamra had cost her, more than she would ever know. This power struggle between Naomi and Barbara had always been close, and this incident could leave Barbara winning. The Sydney mission, it had to succeed. Right now, Naomi was very worried about it failing, and with Barbara giving her the resources she was it meant Barbara was confident in that end. If it failed Naomi wouldn't be able to claim Barbara had sabotaged it, although Barbara waited until failure looked likely before offering those resources. Bennett had to pull this off, had to make a win out of it. If not, they were handing power over to Barbara wholesale. The woman could play the game, that was for sure. You wouldn't think it from looking at her. Barbara was tall and thin, a quiet mousy woman with graying hair and granny glasses, she looked frail most of the time. She was smart though, smart, and dangerous. People tended to forget that.

Her trip on first night was a legend, bordering on myth. It was made worse by her appearance, the tiny woman who made her way on foot, starting out unarmed and alone. The longest solo journey to New Hope anyone had managed. Never mind that Naomi was one of the founders of the city, that without her and Jasper this place would be nothing but the undead wandering through empty streets.

Tyson escapes

Finally, Tyson was taken out of the box. He wasn't quite dead, just close. Junie pulled him out of box and dropped him on the ground. Tyson didn't notice though, he was unconscious. He had a moment of awareness when they dumped water on him but lapsed back into unconsciousness instantly.

By the time he finally came fully to consciousness he was back in an old hut, chained to a wall and lying on a dirt floor. There was a pounding sound, driving rain and shutters slamming open and shut in the wind. Every part of his body was sore due to the beating before he got put into the box. At least one of his ribs was broken, and there was a dangerous looking swelling in his left arm near his armpit. His arm was stiff and very, very hard to move.

Tyson needed water, badly. It wasn't that he was thirsty, it was that every cell in his body craved liquid, of any sort. The inside of his mouth felt like dirt, ash, glue, all piled on top of each other. There was a puddle of water on the floor of hut, rain coming in through the shutters. He was just close enough to stretch to it. He buried his face in the puddle and drank deep, his mouth filling with dirt. He didn't care, the water was so good, so sweet. He drank and drank and drank, until the cramping hit. He was already close to doubled over so it didn't take much to put him there. It hit lard, like a hammer to the gut, almost enough to make him throw up, but he swallowed and swallowed until the impulse passed. He wasn't going to give up a single drop of liquid.

The rain was coming in fast, clearly the shutters weren't meant for this level of storm. One of them ripped off, flying into the sky. He never heard it land. The others seemed strained to their limit, smacking the frame of the house over and over again. This place was little more than a shack, a tin roof on top. It might not survive the storm. Once the cramping passed Tyson started pulling at his chains, bracing his feet against the wall. Every pull sent shocks of pain through him, his vision tinged with red.

RESOURCE ECONOMIES: RECLAIMING THE ZOMBIE APOCALYPSE

He felt something crack, a sudden loosening of the chain. At first he wasn't sure if it was his shoulder or the ring the chain was attached to, but after a few minutes the pain in his shoulder faded back to excruciating and the extra play was still in the chain. He tried again, and again, and again. The ring finally gave, ripping from where it was anchored in the wood. Now he just needed to stand up. His first attempt went badly. He got to his knees and then feel flat, laid out in the mud. At least the mud was wet. He spent a few minutes just relishing the feeling before he tried again. His ribs were fire, a burning knife trying to cut through him.

Standing took what felt like hours. "Fuck. Alright, I'm proper fucked. No way about it. I stay here, the crazy fucking cannibals torture me then eat me. I go out there the zombies eat me, or maybe a bear. Fuck it... I'm going with the zombies."

He was aware that he'd probably lost his mind, talking to himself like that.

The hut had a door, possibly the sturdiest part of the whole structure. He didn't bother with it. He looked out the window and couldn't see anything. Even the closest houses were lost in the storm. Time to go. He crawled gingerly out the window, arms still locked together, trailing the length of chain. Sure, he was going to die, but at least he'd die on his terms not theirs.

The hut turned out to be a way away from the rest of the village, an empty field between them. On one side, the giant cliff led down to crashing waves, violent surf that would tear a man apart today. On the other side forest, mostly evergreens, swaying with the wind, some touching the ground. There were constant cracks as tree limbs fell, or even entire trees. The wind was so strong it was close to picking Tyson off the ground, rain lashing his body repeatedly. His clothes were reduced to rags, covered in mud, torn almost to shreds. He pushed through the storm, slowly walking to the forest. "Fuck, I'm not going to survive long enough to get eaten by something. Fuck it. Got to do it." he kept saying over and over in his head. Finally, he reached the trees and slipped between them. He was safe - or at least safe from the villagers, what had they called themselves? That's right, the Family. Not creepy at all, inbred freaks.

Once he made it into the woods the wind was less severe. It was still lashing at him, but at least the trees provided some small cover. The trees inside were less blown, less likely to fall. Tyson started to move forward into the deep woods. What little daylight he had was giving him enough light to move. Of course, the rain was still streaming down his face, but slower, less severe. The tree canopy above him helped. His feet were bare, they had taken his boots at some point. A million sharp sticks and stones pushed into the bare souls, which were slowly going numb from the exposure. Every prick was that sickening feeling that happens when your flesh is halfway to losing feeling. A pain that is both dulled and amplified, that seems to last forever. Still, better than being eaten by cannibals.

He had no idea where he was, just that it was somewhere on the shore. He wasn't even certain it was still Cape Breton, given how long he'd been unconscious. Nothing for it though. He didn't know if Jack was alive or dead, let alone how to save him if he was alive, still, nothing for it though. All he could do was try and walk to somewhere, preferably far from Junie and Clyde and the rest of the fucked-up hillbilly clan.

He walked until he couldn't walk anymore, then he crawled. The forest floor was strewn with pine needles, undergrowth, not much in the way of animals though. They were probably all hiding from the storm. The cold was seeping into his bones, slowing him, leaving him incapable of thought. He was about to fall over in despair when he saw a small shelter, an overturned tree on the side of a small moss-covered hill, there was space under the roots. It was dirty, smelly, but shelter, a place to get out of the rain for a few minutes.

Tyson moved to the shelter, crawling across the forest floor. Finally, he reached the hill, curled up. His body fit, he was able, just barely, to curl up so that he was completely out of the wind and rain. It was a tight fit, he practically had to go full fetal position, but it was worth it.

Hours passed, his body was warming slowly. The ground was covered in moss and leaves, giving him something to protect his body from the ground. The storm died off, just as night was falling. Tyson slowly pulled his body out of the shelter. The forest was still, full of warm air and soft breezes. Through a patch in the canopy above Tyson could see stars, clear and vibrant. The air felt tropical, humid, hot. There were downed trees everywhere, fallen branches. His entire body ached, and he had nothing, no tools, no weapons, not even real clothes - the rags he wore did almost nothing to protect him from the elements. He was terrified the religious fanatics would find him.

Time to get moving. That little cave was not going to be a valid option for long.

He started walking, the moon casting silver light on the forest floor, shadow branches forming patterns on the ground. Things were not where they seemed to be, it made the walking hard. His feet kept hitting ground that was at an angle he couldn't see. The exhaustion was starting to hit, dragging him down. His brief sleep in the cave provided no real rest, his body was using calories keeping itself warm, and now he was in full crash mode, his body getting shocky and faint. He needed someplace more secure to lie down, someplace where he could sleep for a few hours. The calm, silent forest and humid air was making him feel even sleepier.

Looking around there was nothing obvious, no abandoned houses or the like nearby. There were however broken trees and branches everywhere, left over from the storm. The ground was wet, which was a problem, he couldn't afford to get cold again, not enough reserves on his body. He needed something now.

One of the overturned trees looked like it might work, secluded and hidden with thick branches, and still a lot of canopy overhead. Tyson crawled in between the branches, dragging a couple of pine boughs behind him. He got himself covered, and arranged some leafy boughs arranged underneath him. It was warm enough, and since he was on a slight slope dry enough. With enough layers on top of him he eventually fell asleep, if not warm and comfortable, at least close enough to start to recover.

Chad and Tamra escape captivity and follow their captors

Chad and Tamra were in the midst of the storm, running as fast as they could. The wind was whipping their breath away, streams of water covering them, soaking them to the skin. They held on to each other, afraid they would lose track of each other if they broke contact for even a moment. It slowed them down, made them less able to move freely, didn't seem to matter though, nobody was chasing them. Tamra's captors didn't seem to want to brave the storm.

They managed to get far enough away from the town, deep into the dark of the storm. The wind kept trying to knock them over, slamming their bodies again and again. They passed into a bit of shelter, a small defile in the rocks nearby. As the storm passed they heard the rednecks starting to search for them. The defile was poor shelter, decent for wind but not great for hiding. "We have to move, no way I'm getting grabbed again."

They peeked around the defile cautiously, making sure they were relatively clear. None of the captors seemed to be close at that moment. They sprinted for the tree line nearby, heading into deep woods. After they got well clear they started looking for a place to hide, somewhere a bit more secure.

There was a cabin deep in the woods. It was more intact than most, clearly abandoned but only by a few years. The door was missing, and the windows were just shutters. Chad cautiously peeked around the door frame, checking the interior. The cabin was a rough log structure, logs that were cut in different widths, most with bark still on. The interior was dark, drier than the surrounding woods, pretty much empty. There had been a mattress, parts of it were still left on the floor, moldering and rotten neither one of them wanted to touch it. There was an old pop bottle full of ashes in one corner.

"We need to get back to base. Let them know what's going on."

"Michelle and Tim are still with them, we have no clue where they're headed. We need to follow them."

"They know I'm here, that you're with me. They'll be watching for us, it'll be way harder to follow unobserved."

"We can't leave our people We may never find them again. We need to follow, you have no idea what these people are like. We can't leave Tim and Michelle. We can't."

"Okay. So, Johnny?"

Tamra didn't reply.

They waited out the storm, hoping that the cabin stayed standing. Much to their surprise it did, and the storm ended as suddenly as it had begun. The air that followed the storm was wet and hot, it felt like the air was pregnant with water, like it would just coalesce into pure water suddenly.

"If they are searching they will find this place. We need to move, keep going." Chad said.

They left the cabin reluctantly. It wasn't much, but it was the best shelter they had experienced in days. The woods were dark, close, full of fallen branches, downed trees, detritus left over from the storm. The ground was soaked, in many places the rain formed small lakes, turned level ground to swamp, impassable. The storm had turned Cape Breton into something that felt more like tropical jungle than anything else.

Slowly they wound their way through the dark woods, trying to backtrack to the town, someplace they could keep an eye on Tamra's former captors while not being seen. Tamra was close to collapse, she had been forced to keep pace with the truck all the former day and had been unable to rest while chained up in the town. Her only rest at all had been in the rotten cabin, the storm however had prevented that from being rest, she had spent the entire time tense and terrified, both of the storm itself and of being recaptured. She was shaking, unable to get control of her breath. Her boots got caught in deep mud, and she fell face first. It was a matter of reserves, hers were gone. Her body had nothing left to give her, no matter her will power, her internal fight. She wasn't giving up, she kept fighting to stand, to get back to her feet, but her arms wouldn't co-operate, her muscles didn't accept the commands she was giving them.

Chad lifted her, pulling her to a sitting position. It was the best she could do in the moment. Sitting in a puddle, soaked to the skin, covered in mud and dirt, she started to cry. A quiet sob, but one that wouldn't end, wouldn't let her go.

"I fucked up. I fucked up so bad. I thought I could do this, I could just come over and help, contribute. I can't, I'm no soldier. I need to go home. I'm a fucking actress. What the fuck was I thinking? Oh god, what have I done? Did I kill Johnny? Is it my fault? If you hadn't had to look after me it would have been different."

Chad held her, comforting her. He felt more awkward than he ever had in his life, holding this crying dirty beautiful woman. "No, no it wasn't you. You kept up with us every step of the way, you saved me on the hill earlier, nobody got grabbed because of you."

It was clear that Tamra couldn't keep going, but it was also clear that she needed to. "Alright, Tamra, look, we need to take break. Let's get your butt out of this puddle, get you on some drier ground, take a few minutes to rest up. You need it. I'm exhausted too, I could use the rest"

"Okay. Oh god, I'm filthy."

The moved to the base of a tree, a small rise that was slightly drier than the surrounding area, Tamra leaning heavily on Chad's shoulder. Chad helped Tamra sit down, afraid she would fall over if he didn't. He sat down himself, only then realizing that he wasn't in much better shape than she was.

The planned few minutes rest ended up with both of them falling asleep, leaned against each other. When Chad woke Tamra was already up and about. His body was stiff in ways he hadn't felt before. Sleeping on wet dirt leaned against a tree was not ideal. He did feel slightly better, but still weak. He hadn't eaten in days, and even water had been rare. Of course, finding liquid wasn't a problem right then, the world was covered in it.

They were worried that the captors had moved on, that they might have lost them, but neither one of them could blame themselves for it, they had fallen asleep through sheer exhaustion. The landscape was drenched, but the sun was shining now that day had broken, and the day was hot. Sunlight fell, dappled green through leaves, leaving spots of brighter and darker on the groundcover, now rapidly drying. It was a soft, green world that morning. Many trees had fallen, so the patches of light were larger, the canopy less dense, the walking however was harder. Deer trails now found themselves with trunks blocking them, clearings were random, some were enlarged, some shrunk. In one of the clearings they found a patch of ripe blackberries, a welcome bit of nutrition, tart and sweet at the same time, bursting with juice, the berries brought them back to life. They crammed as many as they could into their mouths. They made a makeshift basket for the berries out of Tamra's undershirt and continued on. Eventually they made it to the town, now empty. Tire tracks and footprints made it clear which way the captors had taken so they started down the road, listening carefully.

It didn't take long. The road had already been in poor condition, but now it was almost completely destroyed. The truck might allow the captors to carry more weight, but in this case, it also slowed them down. Chad heard them up ahead, cursing in their strange language. They were around a bend, just out of sight. The road wound through rock and hills, keeping the view plane short. There were large rock faces on Chad's left, dense woods to the right.

"Let's go up, we can probably get a better view from up there" Chad said in a voice barely above a whisper.

They climbed the rock face, white granite reflecting the bright sun back at them. Chad managed to find handholds and footholds easily, the cliff was pitted and scarred, with bits of dirt and the odd small tree pushing out of it. It was only about fifteen feet up, but by the time they reached the top Chad's hands were raw and bloody. Tamra seemed to have an easier time of it, she scampered up the side of the cliff like a goat, flinging her body from handhold to handhold, moving easily and smoothly.

Once they reached the top they could see forever, the arch of the blue sky contrasted with the deep green of the forest. Off in the distance the darker blue of the ocean met sky, a perfect symmetry. They were on a rocky promontory, leading gently down to the forest floor. Tree cover was scarce, mostly low bushes. It looked like the tree cover had been higher a day earlier, still sparse, but there were a large number of felled trees part way down the slope. Chad and Tamra crawled across the rock to a point where they could see around the curve in the road. The truck, and the strangers, were down there. A large tree had fallen across the road, blocking the way completely. It was a massive oak, hundreds of years old. The strangers were trying to move it and forcing Tim and Michelle to help. They were hacking at the tree, trying to break it into pieces small enough to move, and placing some of the pieces in the back of the truck, on top of the bodies. It seemed unlikely they would be able to move before nightfall.

Chad motioned down the hill, and Tamra followed him down. Once they were further from the strangers they stopped. "We should find shelter, set up camp for the night. No way in hell they get moving before tomorrow. We can use the opportunity to rest up a bit."

"Agreed. We can hole up for a bit, maybe even find something to eat."

"I still have my bow. Saw some rabbit tracks a bit back. If we can find a spot that hides the smoke, we might even manage a bit of meat."

"Oh god, meat. Let's make that happen. I'm so fucking hungry. They didn't feed us, nothing at all."

"For the best. They're cannibals. No way to know what they might have tried to give you."

"What do you mean cannibals? How do you know?"

"The muscle twitches, a couple of them have trouble with balance, red rimmed eyes, classic symptoms of Kuru. It's part of what we covered in training. The reclaimers goals include making friends with the locals, but if they show those symptoms, not a chance in hell... we avoid or exterminate, preference give to the latter. Once a society goes far enough down that road that Kuru becomes commonplace, there's not much chance of redemption for them. A single case, maybe that's an isolated incident - probably not though, usually Kuru involves eating people on a semi-regular basis for a long time."

"Okay, so they're planning on eating Tim and Michelle?"

"My guess, Tim is destined for the dinner plates, Michelle maybe not. They seem like an inbred bunch, new genes must have some value, and women are typically easier to add to the genetic lottery. She's probably planned as a brood mare, at least for a while."

"So, the plan is we find out where they live, we get to base, come back in force and wipe these fucks off the planet?"

"Yeah, sounds about right. If they got hold of the salvage crew, there's not a whole lot of chance we get any of them back."

"Yeah, probably not. God, I can't imagine anything worse. It's not enough the world is full of walking corpses trying to eat us, we have to eat each other too?"

RESOURCE ECONOMIES: RECLAIMING THE ZOMBIE APOCALYPSE

Disturbed, they set to finding a shelter, and to building a smokeless fire. They found a sheltered hollow, a small valley with a decent runoff point, but sheltered enough that the ground was dry. There was a large stump in the middle of the clearing, something Chad could convert to a rocket stove to allow for a low smoke fire. He set to work while Tamra gathered brush to burn. There wasn't a lot dry to choose from, but she got enough that they would be able to start the fire. After that, if Chad got the design right the fire would burn hot enough to dry out anything they added.

The work was hard. The large stump needed to be leveled, and Chad had to carve out a burn chamber in the center. By the time he was done Tamra was back, a pile of small branches and brush in her hands. They got the fire started, a bright flame burning hot enough to burn most of the carbon in the smoke. Chad grabbed his bow and headed out to try and find some meat, while Tamra rested.

This was almost a rest break for him, a relaxing way to use his skills, that didn't involve chasing crazed cannibal rednecks. He settled in next to a rabbit trail and waited. The sun beat down on him, slowly traveling across a blue sky dotted with wispy white clouds, high in the air. There was a small breeze, faintly rustling the bushes. The sound of bird song and distant flies buzzing carried through the day. Finally, he heard a faint thumping sound, a rabbit moving through the forest floor. As soon as he saw the rabbit he drew back his bow, hit the touch point on his cheek, and then let fly. The arrow caught the rabbit through the chest, killing it instantly. It was a large rabbit, but thin, probably in the three to four-pound range. Some protein at least, although too small to make a huge difference. Cleaning and skinning the rabbit took Chad a couple of minutes, then he skewered it and put it over the rocket stove log, turning it as it cooked.

The meat was tough, hard to chew. It was delicious. Chad was shocked at how fast Tamra gobbled the meat down, wolfing it like she hadn't eaten in days - largely because she hadn't.

"Slow down, it's not going anywhere."

"Mm" she was saying something but didn't stop chewing to say it.

"No idea what you just said, don't worry about it though. Doesn't matter. Just don't want your stomach cramping up."

"Just saying it's too good to slow down."

"You have grease all over your chin... actually you just have grease all over. I thought you actress types were supposed to be all dainty."

"We eat between takes. We might have two hours, we might have two minutes. No way to know. If you're dainty on set, you're going hungry. That's why the tables have so much food on them, so you can grab and snack. Trust me, nobody who acts is dainty for very long."

"I didn't know that, thought it was all fun and games."

"Nope, we work really, really long hours too. In the old days most actors married other actors, they were the only people who understood the lifestyle. Nowadays there's a couple dozen of us... I choose to stay single instead."

"Sounds almost like being a soldier. We work the hours they tell us, we eat when they say we can, we sleep when they say we can."

"Good point. Maybe I should be looking at soldiers for my dating pool." she gave him a look, eyes half hooded, head down but meeting his eyes. It was sexy as hell. Chad had no clue how to deal with it. The conversation died off, awkwardly.

After a few minutes Chad stood up "I'm going to, uh, get some, uh, look for some more food. Hell, maybe we can even, uh, have two meals today."

"Okay, hurry back."

Chad was pretty sure she was flirting with him. He'd only ever been with three women, all disasters. Tamra was famous, a TV star, one of the only ones in the world. Her face was one of the best known in the world. Maybe Barbara Miller was better known, but that was pretty much it. Truth was Tamra had been his fantasy girl for a couple of years now, and here they were, in the middle of the wilderness, with nothing, and she was flirting with him.

A quiet moment - Tamra goes fishing

It was frustrating. She was trying her hardest to flirt with Chad, but he wasn't picking it up. Sure, it was silly, even stupid, to be flirting with a guy while in this situation, but she just wanted something, anything, to take her mind off what she had gone through in her recent ordeal. She didn't expect anything to come of it, wasn't looking for a boyfriend, or even sex, not that she would mind, but they would need to find someplace to bathe first, they were disgusting. It was just some harmless fun, a bit of playing while they talked, but he just shut down as soon as she started. Still, she had some rabbit in her belly, thanks to his efforts, and she wasn't on the edge of being used as a brood mare. Maybe she would even be able to achieve her goal, maybe she'd be useful to the mission.

Tamra set about trying to gather some food. She knew there were berries here, although she didn't see any in her little clearing. Probably Jerusalem artichoke, maybe even some apples or something. It was the right season, at the end of summer. As she made her way into the woods she made sure to mark her trail, using a sharpened rock to score the tree trunks, making sure to keep the sun on the same side of her, the basics for finding her way back. The forest here wasn't very dense, the area was too rocky, and it was hard for vegetation to get a hold, leaving the whole area with a kind of park like feel. Tamra wondered if it had been cleared in the past, maybe a part of an actual park twenty years ago.

She ran into a small stream, and had her theory confirmed. There was a foot bridge over the stream, barely held together at this point. The best news was that she saw a trout grabbing insects off the surface of the water, then another. It seemed like the stream was filled with fish. The flowing water glinted in the sunlight, dappled with sparking reflections. After getting a line and hook from camp Tamra set herself up on the shore, waiting for trout to bite.

Clyde discovers Tyson is missing

C lyde walked into the hut, fearing the worst. Ever since he discovered the guards had abandoned their post in the storm he'd been worried, but the storm was too intense, too strong for him to check. Finally, he had the opportunity.

He opened the door, and his worst fear was confirmed. The prisoner was missing. He's managed to pull the ring out of the wood beam it was attached to, tearing the beam up in the process. It must have been an incredibly painful process, tearing his hands to pieces. The guards were going to suffer for this fuckup. Suffer a lot. The prisoner might not be in the oven anymore, but the guards were going to be spending some time there. Maybe they would figure out not to abandon their posts.

"Men, let's go. The prisoner is out there, somewhere in the woods. He's hurt, badly. His hands are in chains. We will find that man, we will bring him to the lord's justice!"

His men came out quickly, the two guards who were supposed to be at the hut looking downcast and fearful, as well they should.

The town needed repairs, many of the houses here hadn't been in great shape twenty years ago, and they hadn't been well maintained in the intervening years. Most of the family were too busy with other tasks, and none of them were experienced carpenters. Most of them weren't experienced at anything meaningful when the dead rose, useless people until the lord god saw fit to deliver them to Clyde to educate, to shape. The new generation though, they had potential. All of this meant that many of the houses had not weathered the storm well, two had completely collapsed, a dozen others had major damage. At least one had a tree crashed through the roof, sitting in the upper floor. That was not one of the worst ones.

Meat Cove was a picturesque town in its day, and elements of that history were still visible. Most of the local economy had come from tourism, people attracted to the town at the edge of the world. Now, the brightly painted houses were dingy, most of the paint years in their past, shingles missing and broken. The newer buildings in town, the ones put together by Clyde and the family were rough, tar paper shacks for the most part, uninsulated and built without foundations. The worst of them had fallen down, and the rest were propped up with years of tinkering, to the point where most of them were bizarre monstrosities. Who knew, back in the early days, that building a wooden box was so much work. All of them had sloped roofs now, but that had taken some learning. In the beginning they hadn't figured out how important the slope was, so a lot of roofs collapsed under snow.

The place was still breathtaking though, giant cliffs hundreds of feet about a raging North Atlantic, with nothing in sight except ocean, for as far as you could see. The cliffs looked like the end of the world, like there was nothing else ever. Once upon a time, at least as far as Clyde knew, the cliffs had been used by the native population as a hunting method, they used to drive herds of animals over the cliffs, then gathered up the animals by carefully winding their way down a gentler path off to one side. It was a tactic that Clyde hadn't managed to replicate, until recently there were no large herds of wild animals. With most of humanity begin gone though, the herds were starting to come back, meaning maybe the family would have access to lots of meat in the near future.

They had lost both fish drying racks, a major blow to the community. Fish was their main source of protein; the sea was giving up far more bounty in recent years than it had for a long time. Another benefit to the reduction of humanity. The cod still hadn't come back, but everything else was at record numbers. Clyde looked forward to the day when eating humans wasn't something they needed to do. A few lean winters had convinced him of the necessity though. It just took a few of your children dying of starvation before you couldn't justify letting a stranger thrive when you and yours didn't have enough. Besides, he had the words of God telling him that he was in the right, that the godly, the good, had more right to that flesh than the sinners who carried it around on their black and decayed souls.

They headed out into the forest, trying to find any trace of the prisoner, a footprint, a drop of blood, anything. The problem was that the man had fled during the height of the storm. Trees had fallen, a huge amount of rain had fallen, all trace of tracks that weren't deep and permanent were likely to be washed away. They spread out, all of them scouring the ground, but nothing. Clyde started narrowing the search, looking in places that were high and dry, hoping that the prisoner had hidden somewhere he would be easy to discover. The man was hurt, badly. His time in the oven would have weakened him, sapped his strength and ability. Clyde was betting on his having taken the easiest paths, even if he didn't mean to.

After many hours of beating the woods the search had to be limited. There was a huge amount of storm damage that needed to be repaired, and the manpower was need there more than here. Clyde kept a few men out, told them not to come back until they had something. He knew that his own experience was too important to the cleanup and repair efforts to stay out. One thing he could do though was leave Junie in charge. His eldest son and heir apparent was a bulldog, the kind of man who took a task in his teeth and worked until it was done. Smarter than the rest of his followers too, able to make decisions just like he would. That was the only thing that gave him peace, that let him relax about the family and what would happen to it after he was gone.

That was going to be sooner than the rest thought too. He had noticed the first symptoms recently. Just a couple of muscle twitches, but enough that he knew what was happening. Soon he would be a wendigo, no longer a flesh and blood man, but a spirit of rage and destruction. It happened to people here, out in this remote place. Always had from what he'd been able to find out.

The camp grows.

Naomi was coming to Sydney. Bennett was overjoyed, a visit from his wife was amazing news. The shopping mall rescue was still top of his mind of course, but other than that things had really come together. There was still the matter of the missing salvage party, and one team of four still out there out of communication. Overall for an operation this size that wasn't a failure though.

The operation was about to kick off. Bennett discovered he had been holding his breath, waiting. He had a high vantage point, looking down at the operation through binoculars. His men were close, ready to start making noise, ready to draw off the zombie horde around the building. Finally, his clock ticked to the minute in question, and then the men stood up and started firing rifles into the horde. Normally firearms were used as a last resort, but this time the goal was to attract attention. A half dozen zombies dropped, then the horde turned, en mass. Even knowing the measures in place, it was terrifying, thousands of undead corpses staring hungrily at a dozen soldiers, a literal wave of appetite crashing towards a few brave souls. The men turned and ran. All of them except one managed to overcome the fear and run at a slow jog. One of the group, Bennett couldn't tell who from where he was, took off in a full sprint, clearly, he had lost it. Bennett hoped that he managed to pull it together before he collapsed.

There weren't enough zombies following. There were still several hundred trying to climb the shopping center walls, apparently something in their primitive brains remembering the prey up above. "Wayde, check the numbers"

"Right, too damn many sticking around. Any ideas how to fix it oh glorious leader?"

"Grenades maybe? It's a big one off, not a repetitive pattern. Should draw them."

"If we drop it in the front ranks could thin them a bit too, worth a shot at least. I'll call it down"

Wayde radioed the men on the ground "Drop some 'nades into the front rank. We need more following you."

The men below complied, three of them pulling pins and throwing small oblong objects. Grenades weren't all that effective against zombies, they tended to keep going, just with a few more holes in them, however all the man had been issued them, mostly for situations like this. It wasn't part of the standard kit - most of the grenades left in stores were pre-first night relics, more than twenty years old. Sometimes the stability wasn't what they would have liked. Three explosions hit in sequence, dropping a handful of zombies, most of whom either got back up or kept crawling forward.

Many, many more of the zombies from the lot turned and followed. It was down to about a hundred around the building. If they could get the horde far enough they could deal with that number, it was just a matter of time. Guns would be out, but they all had lots and lots of arrows. The compound bows they carried were better than a crossbow in well trained hands, even if not as effective as a rifle.

The men were keeping ahead of the zombies, although the one sprinter had slowed too much. He needed to get moving again, the group had almost caught up. Bennett nudged Wayde again.

"Yeah, I see him. Jones, get your ass in gear. I don't give a shit how tired you are, shouldn't have taken off like a fucking rabbit. Now either you get your ass in gear or your ass is dinner."

That did it. The guy was moving again. It was working, they were getting enough of them! All they had to do was hold them until the lake. Once they hit it, the boats would take them out of range, and to safety far faster than the zombies could catch. Part of Bennett wished he could be down there, felt like a coward for sitting on the high ground and watching. He knew it was irrational, that he could contribute nothing to the run. He was older than these men, and not as fit. His real value lay in his experience and being able to pass the benefits of that experience to these younger, fitter models. Didn't mean it didn't feel like cowardice to be sitting half a mile from the action watching in his binoculars though.

Wayde nudged him this time, pointing him slightly to the west of the group. Fuck. It was another small group of zombies, closing in from the side. How had they missed them in the scout? It was only a couple dozen, but enough that they might slow his men while the zombies behind caught up. Had to be dealt with, and fast.

At least this was something he could do. He took his long-range rifle and sighted one of the zombies in the second group, one near the back. A single shot dropped it. Other shots rang out, from all over the landscape. No one place had enough shots to bring the horde, and with the way the shots echoed across the landscape they couldn't even pinpoint what direction to move in. It was an old and well-established technique, but it did mean that they each only got one or two shots. The small group was down to half a dozen zombies, a manageable number. Jones hit them first, swinging his machete. Clearly, he hadn't recovered from his run, his swing was wild, totally off target. Against a human it would have been fine, but he just bit into the zombie's arm, a bit above the elbow. It was such a bad angle it didn't even sever the arm, rotten though was, just stuck in the bone. Bennett had a feeling Jones wasn't going to be with the force for long, some people just weren't cut out for the field. The soldier managed this one though. He slammed the zombie in the chest with his shoulder. It clamped teeth down around him as it fell, but the armor did its job. Jones would survive a little longer. That machete was gone though.

The rest of the squad fought through the zombies, dropping them quickly, not dispatched, but down was as good as dispatched for the purpose of this mission. By the time they stood the squad was well clear. Bennett managed to breathe again. Only another half click to the lake, and then they were clear. The zombies were out of sight of the mall, the team was weaving between buildings, making sure there were as many obstacles between the zombies and the parking lot as possible, to make sure they couldn't see as the remainder of the force picked off the remainders of the horde.

There was no single position that would allow Bennett line of sight for the whole mission, and no time to move before the team was supposed to be on the water. He had picked the viewpoint that gave him clear line of sight for the longest period of time but was now regretting his choice. What if they stumbled? What if there was another group? Anything could happen, and he had to rely on other eyes to let him know about it...

Finally, the signal came, the group had made it to the zodiacs, they were on their way. Apparently, it was all of them, even Jones. Time to mop up the rest and bring his men back to base.

Bennett still longed to be down with the men. It was still dangerous, still a hard slog. The men waded in, a triple line. The first rank closed, loosed arrows, took out a vast number of zombies. Second rank did the same, then third. That gave the men time to draw a new arrow and fire. Not quite the slow line by line of musket fire in the old days, but a similar concept. Wave after wave of zombies fell, by the time the last few reached the human forces there were only a few dozen remaining, the men drew machetes and went to work, pushing the zombies back and slamming the short, heavy blades into their skulls. All told it took about fifteen minutes to clear the lot. Several of the men grabbed ladders and placed them against the building. The troops from the roof climbed down, tired, thirsty, grateful.

It had been a clean op. One of the cleanest of Bennett's career. Simple and direct, politics left miles behind. As much as he wanted to see Naomi, practically craved her presence, he dreaded the politics that would come with her. Still, better than leaving her home to deal with them without him. Their last radio conversation had hinted at some sort of trouble with the council, something with Barbara probably - wasn't it always? How in the hell had she become such a thorn in their side? This woman was one of the saviors of their civilization. She practically taught them how to combat zombies.

Naomi travels to Sydney

Naomi took to the sea quickly, she hadn't been on a boat until she was in her twenties, but it was as natural as breathing to her. Sure, much of her childhood had been spent in the water, spending as much time in the community pool as she possible could, and not just so she could show off in her bikini. There was something about the water she found calming, natural. Maybe in a different life she would have been a sailor. The small fishing boat sped across the sun dappled waves, bow breaking in choppy surf. The wind was light, and welcome in the late summer heat. The captain walked up to her "Mam, you should get ready. We're almost there, just another fifteen minutes or so."

"My stuff is all packed up, and it's way too nice to spend any more time than I have to below decks. I don't get to get out on the ocean much these days. Back when Jasper and I first founded New Hope I spent most of my time sailing around, checking the coastline for other survivors. Jasper always wanted me to stay in the city. I couldn't do it. That's how I found Bennett you know?"

"I didn't know that. Figured you for more of a landlubber type."

"Yeah, I didn't get to discover the sea until everything changed. My childhood was spent as far from the yachting life as is possible. It was after... sorry, I tend to go on. I'll let you get back to your post."

"Thanks mam. It's interesting, and I would love to hear about it some other time, but we're coming into some trickier waters right now, I probably should focus on that."

She knew he was being polite - indulging a woman who was lost in memory, old, in spirit at least, before her time. She turned her focus to the view out the front of the boat. They were going as fast as the old boat could manage, speeding past tree lined shores, green and verdant. The harbor came into view, a narrow path between ruins, overgrown with vines, trees breaking their way into the landscape, pushing concrete out of the way.

The harbor was long, extending deep into the land mass, wharves dotted the sides from time to time, all collapsed or on the edge of it. Near the end, once the harbor was narrow enough to swim across, she spotted the repaired wharf the reclaimers were using. It was obvious they had been working hard. Barrier walls surrounded the wharf, leading right into the water, giant sheets of steel that sloped outward, keeping the zombies at bay. Most of the material used in them was local, built on the spot from what they could strip out of the ruins. The wharf itself was new material, right down to the support pylons. Built next to the remnants of the most intact wharf from the old city, still on the edge of collapse.

The area around the wharf had been expanded, a few hundred meters across now, and it was a beehive of activity. Workers carried building materials, putting together more panels, stacking salvage for the dock, some of them seemed to be putting together the framing for a building, something smallish, maybe the size of a small house. Since the original team of one hundred and twenty soldiers had come over there had been a steady stream of support personnel, more every day it seemed. Right now, the town was at six hundred give or take. Mostly men, mostly rougher types, construction workers. Most of the food was still being delivered by boat, pulling from New Hope. There were plans in place to extend the corridor to an empty field, start doing some farming there. Naomi hadn't seen it yet, she confidence in Bennett's decisions about that sort of thing. If you couldn't trust your own husband who could you trust?

They docked, the captain was very good. There was a small bump, barely noticeable, and then lines were being thrown to the crew on the docks. Bennett was standing on the dock, waiting for her, looking dashing in his all black combat armour, helmet tucked under one arm. She did love that man, sometimes she forgot exactly how much. He'd been her constant companion for more than a decade. He'd even accepted her closeness with Jasper, something very few men would have been secure enough to do. Somehow, he could see that they were both tighter than a romantic relationship could ever make them, and not in any way heading towards a romance.

She ran to him, forgetting dignity, forgetting that she was a leader, just wanting to hold her partner, the person who grounded her, who made all the struggle worth it. They held each other, wrapped in each other's arms, holding as tight as they could. She pulled her head back slightly, looked him in the eyes, and then started kissing him, like a sixteen-year-old, no shame at all.

After a few minutes they finally parted. "Well, good to see you too!"

"I missed you. Damn I missed you."

"So, what's the good word from our government? Do I get what I need for this mission?"

"Yeah, anything apparently. Barbara went all in. I'm still trying to figure out how that can fuck us."

"Yeah, that's terrifying."

"Well, at least it gives us what we need to manage here. I think it might just be public sentiment... there are a lot of people right now looking at this project as a way to get out of New Hope, and to maybe find some real hope, some chance at a reasonable future. New Hope just doesn't have any reasonable way to expand at this point. People want a frontier, some way to have a better life than they have right now. That was what New Hope was all about when we founded it, when we renamed it. Now though, it's a trap for most of them. No way to leave, no real way to improve their situation. Maybe she just figured out that if she fought it even her reputation wouldn't save her from the repercussions."

"Politics. I'm not convinced though. That woman seems like the sweetest lady on the planet, and she's a hero to most... too bad they can't see that she's a snake."

"More like a shark, a predator that just keeps going because it doesn't know any other way to exist. Enough about her though, how are things here?"

"Troubling. We have confirmation that the original fence was cut, and there's been a number of sightings of people, but always far off. No contact with them at all, at least from most of the teams. One team is missing though, no contact from them since they hit the field. It's been weeks now."

"That's not good. The storm set you back much?"

"No, not too bad. We were pretty battened down, and it did help clear a few of the abandonments... sped up the demolition process."

"Okay, so now my brave soldier, take me back to your tent. There is ravaging to be done."

"Don't worry, I'm going to ravish you right. Right and all night long."
They started walking back to the camp, hands clasped together.

Tamra and Chad make it to Meat Cove

Following the captors took over a week. By the end of it both Chad and Tamra were on the edge of collapse. The truck never went very fast, but it did stick to roads, while they had to shadow from the cover of the forest. The major saving grace was the vehicle kept getting stuck in mud, and often the captors had to clear trees or large branches that had fallen in the storm. Eventually the truck made it to a ramshackle town on the edge of a cliff. There was still a sign that said Meat Cove, a pre-zombie relic that somehow was still standing.

Chad felt like the name was a bad omen. There was a sense about the place, a spiritual weight that he couldn't easily put into words. It felt wrong, deeply, deeply wrong. The view didn't help much. The town consisted of a few remaining pre-zombie homes, all in disrepair, and a bunch more shacks that looked like they were slapped together in haste by people who had no clue what a house was supposed to look like. Nothing about the place was okay, nothing felt like human civilization. Chad had heard about places like this, small communities that made it without contacting the larger world, leaving themselves open to hordes, surviving by a combination of luck and determination. Most of them were bad places, isolated largely because they didn't play well with others. Most ended up turning to cannibalism or piracy at some point - some to both.

They found a vantage point that let them see at least a part of the town without being obviously visible. It was risky; however, they didn't want to take the larger risk of not knowing what happened to Michelle and Tim. The truck pulled into an empty area in the center of town and all the captors got out. Several people from the town were already milling around. One very large older man seemed to be the leader. He was at least six-foot-five and broad. He was barking orders to people, pointing out where they should go, etc. Eventually he walked over to the to truck and grabbed Tim from where he had fallen to the ground. The big man picked Tim up as if he was a doll, throwing him over one shoulder after unchaining him. He headed to a small hut, dumped Tim inside and came back for Michelle.

"At least we know where they are. Probably going to be well guarded though. I'm not sure if we should try to get them out of head for base and come back in force."

"I'm guessing they get eaten before too long. I don't want to leave them alone. You don't know what it's like, these people are animals, not even human."

"Okay. We'll try to get them out. We need a plan though, we can't just go running in, and I doubt we'll get another hurricane to help us out."

"No. We need a plan, you're right. It might take a few days though."

"Yeah, we need to figure out shelter as soon as possible. I'll scout around. You keep an eye on the town, see if anything changes. Don't stray though, I don't know if I'd be able to find you if you did."

"I'll be here. Hurry back though, I don't like being this close to them without cover."

Chad headed into the woods, looking for potential shelter. He wasn't certain he agreed with Tamra, but he wasn't ready to fight her on it yet either. Better to try and come up with something that accomplished her goal, and to leave if that failed.

The woods were dense, filled with fallen branches and thick undergrowth. Despite the sunny day it was dark on the forest floor, although there were sun dappled patches wherever the canopy broke. The air was still tropical, drawn north by the hurricane. He was sweating in minutes. Visibility was terrible, opening up occasionally, but for the most part it was limited to a few feet in any direction. Sound was muffled as well. It felt claustrophobic.

He was on edge, nerves firing rapidly. Every sound made him jump. He was starting to get used to the feeling, it had been going on for so long. At first, he thought he was hallucinating when the figure stepped out from the trees, one arm held high in the air, the other one also held up, but pressed close to his side, not very high. He had matted hair and beard, dried blood over much of his clothing. What little of his skin could be seen under the dirt looked pale. He was obviously a big guy but seemed shrunken in on himself. Chad leveled his bow at the man. "Don't move"

"Thank god. I thought I was dead, but here you are. I need help"

"Alright friend. Slowly now, turn around, let me make sure you have no weapons."

The man turned, he was unarmed, and looked like he could barely stand. His feet were the worst of it, bloody and black. He moved with kind of a hunched shuffle, never lifting his feet far from the ground.

"Who are you friend?"

"Tyson. Was one of the members of the salvage team in Sydney."

"Shit... I can't believe we found you. We'd given up hope completely."

"Here I am, at least mostly."

"Put your hands down. Look, my unit got taken by the psychos in Meat Cove. We're trying to figure out how to get them out right now."

"How many of you?"

"Just two of us, me and Tamra Duchene believe it or not. I'm Chad."

"Fuck. Look, I'm in bad shape. Got beaten pretty bad. I don't know if I'm going to last a lot longer."

"Where have you been hiding?"

"I managed to find a small shelter, underneath a few fallen trees. It's just over there. I saw you and headed your way. The uniform you know? Let me know you were from home."

"Okay, show me. Then we should grab Tamra. I've got basic battlefield training, I'll do what I can to patch you up."

Tyson led him a few hundred feet deeper into the woods. The shelter was rough, crude. It was using an overturned tree as the main structure. It was also well hidden, Chad didn't think he would have noticed it had he not been guided. It was just a bit of shelter, and the smell was horrible. "No latrine then?"

"Nope. Until today I probably couldn't have walked to it. Believe it or not I'm in much better shape than I was. They fucked me up."

"Yeah. Okay, we probably can't stay here for long, but I'll bring Tamra back and we'll work something out. Sit down, before you collapse. I think we still have a bit food too."

Chad headed back to where he had left Tamra. He realized he hadn't asked about the rest of the salvage team. Tamra was waiting where he left her, he didn't think she'd moved a single muscle. He let out a soft whistle to make sure she knew he was there. When she turned he beckoned her to come over. He whispered to her "I found one of the salvage crew. He's in rough shape, not far from here. We need to look after him. We'll come back as soon as possible."

"Alive? Okay, of course."

Minutes later they were at Tyson's side. He was in terrible shape, near death in Chad's opinion. Chad started checking him over, while Tamra gave him some water. They decided that food had to wait for a little bit, at least long enough to make sure he could keep down the water. Poking around Chad found a broken rib. The feet weren't as bad as they had looked. It wasn't gangrene setting in but was severe bruising and masses of dirt. His arm on the other hand was bad, possibly bad enough that it would need to come off... not something Chad was remotely trained to do.

Chad was pretty sure they needed to make the shelter a bit more secure if Tyson was going to survive. He left Tamra to get Tyson cleaned up and started scouting for materials he could use. As much as he wanted to focus on the town this couldn't be ignored. He didn't have the first clue how to save Tim and Michelle, but Tyson was very much in his power to help. The shelter needed to be water tight, or at least as close to it as could be, and they needed something to keep them off the ground. Maybe enough space to move around a little so they could treat Tyson as needed. All of that without making it visible from the outside. Chad started gathering fallen branches, focusing on pine boughs as much as he could. His gloves kept the sharp needles from being a problem. After a couple of hours, he had a bunch, and started to weave them into each other, creating a new roof above the one they started with. It was a good day's work, and at the end of it he had something that was well hidden but gave them ample space inside. Next came a platform. Most of that he built out of the original shelter, with a few additions. It was a lot of labor, he worked well into the night, using the night vision built into his helmet to allow him to keep going long after anyone else would have been forced to abandon the project.

Part of the urgency Chad was feeling came from Tyson's weakening condition. He had taken a turn for the worse and was feverish. They didn't have appropriate medicine, all of it was in the medical kit, which was in the survival pack, so in the possession of the Meat Cove people. The best they could do was to make sure Tyson's body was as capable of healing itself as possible. Keep him sheltered, dry, hydrated, provide food as he could eat it. That meant work, a lot of work. Fire was another concern. The shelter itself was a wigwam style, decent for fire but they needed the fire to be smokeless, stealth was critical. Chad had used a log-based rocket stove in the past, but that wasn't going to work here - the log tended to get consumed by the process. Instead he decided to build a simple rocket stove out of mud. That meant digging, and lots of water. He kept going, his eyes starting to fill with grit, exhaustion setting in. He wished Tamra could help out, another pair of hands for the work would make it much faster, but she was needed at Tyson's side, monitoring his condition. Her bush medical knowledge was comparable to his, although a little folksier in origin, but he had a larger frame and more strength, making him the better choice for the hard slog of cutting, digging, shaping, carrying, all the things needed for building this basic shelter. Normally he would have created something far cruder, a simple a-frame they could use to reflect body heat, with a fire outside the open end. The wigwam was really meant for a long-term solution, something you would build as a hunting lodge and leave in place for example. Still, if Tyson survived because of it then the effort was a very small price to pay.

The rocket stove was arduous work. After he had the stove itself built he created a chimney for it, mostly a heat flow system. It was a long mud bench, cured in phases by burning brush in the stove itself. Eventually though, shortly after daybreak, the damn thing was finally complete. They had a source of heat that they could use for cooking and for water purification. The shell of the reclaimers helmets was created with the idea that all the contents could be removed, and it would double as a pot - so that's exactly what Chad did. He grabbed water from a nearby stream and boiled it, then he cut open the wound in Tyson's arm, a small cut to relieve some of the pressure. The wigwam quickly filled with a sickly-sweet smell and pus began to drain out. Tamra boiled some bits of cloth pulled from their clothing and added some mint leaves to create a poultice. She dried the strips and then used them to pack the wound. Tyson was coherent enough not to scream, although they did have him bite down on a stick as they made the cut. All of his wounds were worrisome, but his arm was by far the worst of it. "You're going to make it. You survived this long. Just stay strong. We'll pull you through it." Tamra was talking softly the whole time. Finally, Chad gave in to exhaustion and fell asleep, leaving Tamra to take care of Tyson by herself for a while.

When Chad finally woke it was late afternoon. Tyson was sitting up, still looking green, but alive. Tamra wasn't there. "You're alive!"

"Yeah... not feeling great, damn my arm hurts. Tamra thinks I'm going to get to keep it though. Better than I could have hoped for. If you two hadn't come along when you did..."

"You are the mission, you and your team. New Hope sent a hundred and twenty of us, plus support staff, just to find you guys."

"Makes a guy feel loved. Tamra stepped out to gather some food once she saw I was conscious. Man, that woman is something isn't she?"

"Yeah. She wasn't supposed to be here. She just came over on her own. She's tough as hell."

"Damned right. Easy to look at too. Something between you two?"

"No."

"Then you're an idiot, no offense. She looks at you like she wants something to happen. You don't take advantage of that, I'm going to." Tyson said, there was a smile in his eyes as he said it though.

"She's a freaking celebrity. I'm a nothing, why would she go for someone like me?"

"Well, let's see... you just worked around the clock until you literally collapsed to save a random stranger. Seems to me like you might just a decent person. Who knows, maybe she likes decent people?"

"Seems unlikely. Who likes decent people?"

"Fair enough. Guess I'm going to have to go for it then. I'm a complete asshole."

"Now, now. I didn't say that. Mostly I just have to work up to it. Honestly, I'm not that experienced with the ladies. I know, I know... it's shocking with my rugged good looks, but I've only really had one girlfriend."

"Nothing wrong with that. This woman though, she's something else. Anyway, how the hell are we gonna get your people and get back home? No offense, but you don't strike me as the Rambo type."

"Who the hell's Rambo?"

"Sorry, I have a thing for pre-zombie cinema. Rambo was a character in one good movie and a bunch of crappy ones. Sort of a super soldier who takes on armies by himself. Not that you aren't good at your job, but you seem kind of like you might be a normal human."

"Oh, yeah. No, I'm not taking on a redneck cannibal horde solo."

"You forgot religious fanatic."

"What?"

"Religious fanatics. They believe they are gods chosen, some shit like that. Tried to convert me in between the beatings. Odds are good they give your people time before they kill them. Last I checked Jack was still alive too. I hope he still is. We kind of need to find that out, by the way, he's my best friend."

"Alright. Anything you can tell me would help, I need to know how they do things, how the village is laid out, where they keep prisoners, all of it. The more I know the better my odds of not getting us all killed."

"The big guy, Clyde, he's the leader. Some kind of prophet figure. Nasty guy, seems to be a true believer from what I can tell. Most of the higher ups seem to be his kids. One really nasty bastard they kept calling Junie. That guy gave me the creeps. Had to be the sleaziest motherfucker I've ever met. They like to torture people, really make em suffer. I spent a few days in a hot box, because I didn't want to find God, and I wouldn't tell them shit about our people. They didn't even bother asking me much after they took me out, I think the questions are more a game than anything else. Also, they keep a bunch of zombies in a pen in town. They have some sort of weird religious thing with them. Not sure the details. I don't know a whole lot though, I was mostly kept chained up in a hut. Only escaped because of the storm."

"Yeah, they had Tamra for a bit. I managed to get her out because of the storm too. It threw enough chaos into the mix to make a bunch of stuff possible."

"Yeah, maybe something in that idea might help us," Tamra said, entering the shelter. "Also, you guys really suck at keeping a lookout."

"How long you been outside?" Chad asked.

"Long enough... I got some berries. Also, if we get out of this alive you and I are going on a date. If we die first though I'll let you off the hook."

They kept talking for a while. Chad got over his discomfort quickly when he got into the details of trying to rescue their people. There were a lot of factors to work with, and a lot of unknowns. In the end, they decided to sleep on it, give Tyson another day to recover his strength before they risked having to run for their lives. The shelter was cozy, dry, and warm. Chad couldn't help looking at Tamra, the whole conversation was lodged in his mind. He knew it was stupid, he was fighting for his life and the life of his team, and he was obsessing about a girl. Also, he hadn't taken any action. That was a bit disappointing, she had removed any and all doubt, and he was still paralyzed with self-doubt. What exactly would it take for him to make a move? Did she have to perform a strip tease and then jump on him? What was wrong with him?

Where Did Everybody Go?

The villagers were beating the bushes looking for them, Tamra, Chad, and Tyson could hear them, but they were snug and secure in their shelter. It wasn't perfect, and they knew it was going to be days before Tyson could really move on his own, so they kept shoring it up. Tamra and Chad flirted more, a lot more. Chad was sure she'd heard his conversation with Tyson, that she knew he was into her. He kept finding excuses to touch her as they worked. Both of them were filthy, sweaty, they didn't smell very good. Bathing was a thing for more civilized humans, but he didn't care. He still wanted her, every glimpse of her pale skin, it set him on fire, filled him with need.

Other than that, those few days were physically hard. Chad spent almost every hour cutting down branches or pulling off deadfall, making sure to take only things that were concealed, that wouldn't be easily noticed. He knew that if their shelter was going to work for what he had planned it needed to be solid, the best shelter he had ever built in his life. It needed to be hidden, deeply hidden, and it needed to be secure. It was going to be his base of operations as he tried to create enough chaos in Meat Cove to keep the villagers on edge, to create an opportunity for him to rescue the rest of his team. Right off the bat that meant it had to be zombie proof, hard to achieve with what he was working with. It would also need to have other escape options because no good to be able to weather the zombie storm and at the same time not be able to leave until they starved to death.

Tamra was a trooper, working as long and hard as Chad did. He looked at her with new admiration. Calories were low, very low, and that was taking a toll on the two of them. Not to mention what they did have, they gave to Tyson.

Conversation was also at a low. While the villagers had thinned out, they were still present, which meant everything had to be done quietly. It was something Chad had trained for, working in silence. The ever-present zombie threat meant noise was often the enemy. Complete silence was impossible, but the woods were never completely silent anyway. What mattered was ensuring that none of the noise sounded like human activity, that noises happened once, and were only repeated at irregular intervals.

The shelter took shape over three days, and by the end of the three days they had stopped hearing signs of the villagers searching for them. It was time to start putting the plan into action.

Chad waited until after dark and put his helmet back together. Okay, so they wouldn't have a pot for the night, that was okay, he needed it more that evening. He snuck through the brush until he could see the town. It was quiet, but there was still movement. Chad waited, patiently, to an outside observer he would have looked like he was calm and cool. Inside his stomach was filled with butterflies, having some sort of butterfly jamboree. He got his materials ready, some bundled tinder he'd been drying by the stove for three days. It was dry as bone and reduced to thin wisps. There was a lot of it. He'd spent most of his free time working on it. Once all the people had turned in, except a couple of guards, Chad started crawling on his belly into the camp. Night vision gave him an advantage that was almost impossible to overcome. He could see exactly where the guards were, plain as day. They could only see him if they got lucky.

Chad found an older building, looked like a food storage building. He set up a fire bundle against it, and then moved on. It would be the last one he would light. He found another good target, set up a bundle there. He had three with him, and he wanted to use all three. The third was a house, he felt a little bad about that, but then he thought about the villagers eating his team mates, he thought about Tyson's condition when he found him, he thought about all of that and started the third bundle on fire. It was a concealed flame, designed to take a couple of minutes to really catch. He went back to the second, carefully, trying to move slowly and deliberately despite his heart pounding at a million beats a minute. He was sure the sentries would be able to hear his heartbeat, that he would be caught any instant, but he kept going. Finally, he made it to the first, that one was just a straight light. He set it on fire and then crawled, hoping he would at least be a few feet away before the sentries spotted it.

He did better than he anticipated. He was almost to the woods when the cry came out. "Fire!"

Chad hopped up and ran, hoping the light of the fire would keep him concealed. Once he was in the cover of the forest he stopped and looked back. Nobody seemed to be following him, so he started moving slowly, deliberately. Looking back occasionally, the village was in chaos, people grabbing buckets and trying to put out the fires. The fact that were three fires would make it clear to them that somebody had started the first. That was okay, that was what he wanted. He wanted them thinking there were a hundred men in the woods if he could manage it, set up a good state of panic.

It was a starting point, a way to create panic and confusion. Enough panic and confusion and the opportunity to get his companions out would present itself. Not only that, by keeping the villagers off balance they would be too busy to deal with the prisoners. At least that's what Chad hoped.

The walk back to the shelter took a very long time. Chad stopped every few meters to check his trail, erase any sign he'd been there. All of his training was coming into play, and he was making some of it up as he went along. After what seemed like hours he stumbled on the shelter. If he hadn't known exactly where it was he never would have seen it. As he crawled through the opening he found himself facing an improvised spear in the hands of a gorgeous redhead. "Oh, thank god!" Tamra said, dropping the spear and pulling him inside. "I was so worried."

Chad pulled off his helmet, his face covered in a huge grin despite the severity of the situation. He pulled Tamra to him and gave her a kiss, deep and long.

As they pulled apart Tamra said, "Well, about time. I didn't think you were ever going to do that," then she kissed him again.

After a few minutes, Tyson cleared his throat, "Ahem, uh, look, I'm happy for you guys... but there's not a lot of privacy in here."

"Uh, yeah, uh, sorry," Chad was turning red.

"So, you lit a few fires, got them freaked out? You know that's not going to work again."

"I have a plan for keeping the chaos going. There's a bunch more of that kind of sabotage I will be doing. The punchline is I take out the zombie paddock while I get the team out. That's got to happen after you are well enough to move Tyson. I want manpower, not that we will have much. I suspect that the prisoners won't be in great shape."

"Why didn't you just grab them now?"

"It's one thing to sneak into the village, the prison had a bunch of guys guarding it, not like the village as a whole. I'm not, what was that name? Right, Rambo. I'm not him, I can't take out four or five guys solo. I need to set up a situation where I have the opportunity. I'm going to get them walking on eggshells, and then I'm going to give them something to actually react to."

"Okay, fair enough. I just hope they don't eat your friends, or mine, in the meantime."

"Yeah, me too. I know it's a risk, I know that a lot can go wrong. Thing is, it's just me and you two."

Tamra said, "Glad you finally realized I'm in the mix here. I'm a very, very good shot. I can help out, nothing causes chaos and confusion like a sniper."

"Yeah, that's actually one of my ideas. Take out a few villagers from range, maybe do two, move on and wait a few days, take out one or two more. Keep going like that, never from the same spot."

"It's a good plan, there are a few limitations. The most obvious one is that we only have so much geography to work with. The cliffs mean we can only approach from two sides, although I think we have enough coverage for two sides."

"So, you have no issues with shooting the villagers?"

"I lived through first night, the years between. I may look like a movie star, but I didn't grow up like a princess. I had to fight my way through the world when I was young. People forget that because they see me on TV all the time. I didn't have it easy either, my family went through all the same things everyone else did back then."

"Right, got it. Sorry." Chad finally noticed that Tamra looked distinctly unhappy, her eyes flashing with anger as she talked.

"Yeah, it's okay, just don't forget again okay? I like you, I'd hate to have to shoot you."

"I'd hate to have to get shot. Don't worry, I won't forget again."

They went dark again, staying silent and waiting for the searchers to miss them. The shelter was so well concealed someone would have to be inches from it to see it. It looked like a pile of deadfall, and not even a hollow pile.

The only risk was someone seeing the paths in and out, but they were taking care to limit that. The next day was spent hunkered down, not speaking, not moving unless they needed to. They burned the stove for half an hour, giving them twelve hours of heat. It was agonizing, the wait. By the end of the day, all of them had to use the washroom desperately, all of them were sweltering with heat. Turned out the shelter kept itself warm with three people even without the stove. They were dripping with sweat, dehydrated, starving. The sounds of searching kept going outside.

Sometime late in the evening, the sounds vanished. Chad gave it a little bit longer, then he gave the all clear.

They let Tyson go first, his physical condition meaning he was in the worst shape of the three of them. He hobbled out of the shelter and went as far as he could, then he peed for the first time since his escape. His body was still so weak he could barely stand. After he was done Tamra took a turn, then finally Chad got to. It was heaven after the day they'd had. As the pressure released Chad thought about the pre-zombie fiction he'd read. Hell, some of it was even about zombies. They never talked about the pain of a full bladder, how hard it could be to stay hidden when you desperately needed to go. Of course, his armor had options, but those were long since used up and now he was in the same boat as anyone else. Just another way people who'd never been in true fear for their life got things wrong.

It was time for the next phase. Chad wasn't sure which one to go with. They had a handgun and Chad's rifle, not the kind of gun that was ideal for distance shooting, but Tamra was confident it would do the job. Chad wished they had more guns, especially the heavy sniper rifle Tamra had been using before they were captured. It would make life so much easier, so much better.

Oh well, wishes weren't worth much. They found several good vantage points, high ground around the town. Tamra picked one for today and set up, Chad's rifle supported by some rocks, a compromise for the fact that it was an assault rifle, not a meant for this kind of work.

Chad found a spot on the other side of town and set up his handgun. He didn't expect to hit anyone or even anything. The plan was just to cause confusion, make it harder to tell what was going on. A few minutes after he got set up a shot cracked out. He fired as soon as he heard it, not even bother to really aim, just firing in the general direction of the village. As he did he spotted a woman, middle aged and heavyset, falling to the ground, her skull missing a large section. Well, Tamra was cold blooded as hell. Chad was pretty sure he would have aimed for a man instead.

The town erupted, everyone running, not knowing where to run. Tamra took another shot, and Chad followed her example. Another person dropped. Jesus, she just shot a kid! Chad fled back into the woods, getting a distance, then starting to obscure his tracks.

Tamra reached the shelter before Chad did. She was already inside when he got there. He could see right away that she was shaking, her eyes rimmed with red. He had been ready to start yelling at her but seeing her in that state changed his mind. He came over and put his arms around her. "Oh god, oh god. What did I just do?"

"It's okay, it's all right. Just breathe."

"The kid. He had the shakes, red eyes, all of it. I know it was the thing to do, but he was so small, so innocent."

"Fuck. Look, if had the symptoms, if he had kuru, he was already dead. There was no person left inside. You did him a mercy."

"I know, in my mind I know, but it's not that easy to actually do."

"Yeah, I believe you. I wouldn't have had the courage to do it. You are amazing. So strong."

"Next time I don't shoot the head though. If I hit the body it's a zombie in the middle of the village, that ups the chaos factor."

"Yeah, good call. Sorry I didn't think of it."

"Well, we did it in episode nineteen. Not me of course, I'm the good little housewife, but my husband," Tamra was starting to breathe normally, starting to recover from what she had to do.

Trouble at Home

"**S**till can't find them. The storm totally messed up any trace of the missing squad or the work detail. I'm pretty sure they were taken, but everything is so messy, it's almost impossible to even figure out where they went before they were taken," Wayde looked down. It was a weird thing to see on the large man, a sort of half shuffle in his step. He looked almost sheepish.

Bennett said, "Look, it's not you, not your fault. Nobody could possibly do a better job. You've protected this installation, and all the people in it as best anyone possibly could. The storm wasn't something we could have predicted or dealt with. Whatever these people we keep seeing, that's also something we couldn't predict. We were ready for zombies, as many of them as we might run into, but not for this."

"Yeah, I just feel like I need to do something. I want to lead a team myself, get out into the wilderness and take a look. I know it's probably useless, but I just need to do something."

"Alright, give me today, I have a large task queue that I need you for. After that, I will give you your reigns, let you take a team with you."

"Okay, I'll give you today. I guess it won't matter at this point. I just hope they are still alive."

"You and me both. Now, get to work... figure out who you want for your team and be ready."

Wayde left Bennett alone with Naomi. "He's a good man, but this is hard sauce for him."

"Yeah, for me too. I don't know how to let it go. Things are going well here, but I don't think I can accept that things are in such a state of uncertainty. I don't expect to know everything about a situation, but missing teams and mystery people, that's hard to manage or deal with, for all of us. Wayde is just less able to keep that inside. Or at least with me he is, I don't think the men see it."

Naomi started rubbing Bennett's shoulders. "It's okay, I get it. Hell, I'm the one who put this shooting match together. You think it isn't everything I can do not to grab a weapon and hit the road. It's torture. I just don't know that I would be any good at it. I haven't been in the field in years."

"Yeah, I'm in the same boat. I'm an administrator now. I want to be a superhero and rush off saving my people, but I would suck at it, and I'm decent at running things here."

The two of them talked over the problem, how to find their people, how to allocate resources. It was boring, it was detailed, it was planning. Bennett was once again astonished at how quick Naomi was at picking up tiny details. How quick she was. He'd never met someone with a mind for logistics like hers, she knew details he'd mentioned once in passing, she knew details that somebody had mentioned three tables over at dinner.

As they talked they heard a commotion, then a loud bang, and a bunch more bangs. Weapons fire was going off like crazy. The two of them rushed outside. Bennett grabbed someone running past. "What's happening?"

"Sir, another horde. Huge, larger than what we've seen before. No idea how there are this many zombies. Need to get to the fence, it's enough that we could be in danger inside."

"Fuck. All right, guess I'm active duty again."

Bennett and Naomi ran for the armory, grabbed rifles, and headed for the wall.

The horde looked to be ten thousand at least... maybe even more. Bennett started shooting, picking his targets. So, did Naomi. Neither of them was a great shot, but passable, and in an environment like this it wasn't hard to hit something. Everyone else on the wall was doing the same as them, firing shot after shot into the horde.

The bodies started to drop. Bennett's hearing was starting to go, and the area by the wall was filled with an overwhelming smell of blood and gunpowder, the sharp, acrid smell filling everyone's nostrils. It was a welcome relief from the scent of rot and excrement coming from the zombie horde. No matter how many times Bennett was around that smell it would never get comfortable. He fired and fired and fired some more. As night started to fall the horde was still there. Runners were bringing ammo up, fresh clips by the dozens. Bennett wasn't sure they were going to have enough on hand.

After the night got too dark only the soldiers wearing NVG's were still able to shoot, so the volume of fire dropped off. Bennett had someone bring up floodlights, and once they were going he kept shooting.

By the morning most of the horde was gone, and so was most of the ammo. The ground outside the camp was piled half a dozen deep in corpses. Nobody had slept. The few stragglers against the fence were deemed not enough of a threat to waste limited ammo on. Bennet grabbed Wayde, "Sorry man, you have to wait until this is cleaned up to go. Take a few squads, head out, machetes in hand. Take out the remainder. I'm going to order another ammo shipment."

"Yeah, I feel like this is deliberate. Somebody is managing these zombies, making sure they mass where they don't make life easy for us. After I get these ones dispatched it's time to start hunting whoever is in charge of them."

"Yes, but with some rest first. Somebody managing a horde like this, they will be dangerous. No point making a mistake because you haven't slept. After these are cleared you will wait a day, at least rest a full night."

"Of course. I'm not a complete idiot, just mostly."

The team went out, machete's in hand. Despite what Bennett said about rest he sat on the roof of one of the shipping containers watching the teams. One of the soldiers got swarmed, pulled down. Wayde ran over, slamming zombies off the man with his shoulders, decapitating one after the other as they were sent flying. The last few were down on the ground, he kicked on so hard it was lifted into the air, his titanium blade slicing through its head as it fell. The last zombie came off the soldiers and the man stood up. There was a conversation and then the man walked back to the wall. Bennett came down to meet him. "Hey son, how are you?"

"Bit shaky sir, my armour held. Nothing got through, but damn, I thought I was done there."

"Glad you made it. Come on inside, let's get you a cup of coffee and something to eat. You must be about ready to collapse."

Bennett watched, anxious, but the rest of the operation went smoothly. Finally, eventually, all the zombies at the wall were gone and the team came in. Bennett pretended he'd been doing other work, hurrying back to his office before they came back. No point in letting Wayde know he'd wasted the whole morning watching the big man and not taking care of other duties.

There was a lot of work that hadn't gotten done because their focus was on the horde, which Bennett suspected was the point, but he still had to catch up. He went back to his desk and started on it. Wayde came in, looking grey and exhausted. "Sir, I need to catch some sleep."

"Of course, you should do so as soon as you grab a bite to eat. Scratch that, shower, then food, then sleep."

Wayde headed off for the mess hall, and Bennett realized that he was probably in about the same state. Despite not being out there he'd denied himself sleep for just as long. He needed rest, desperately, and he needed it now. Bennett made his way over to his bed, in the back of the command tent. A perk of the job if you could call it that. Naomi was already there, sound asleep. Bennett lay down next to her, snuggling up to her slim body.

Next thing he knew he was being shaken awake by Naomi. "Hey, time to get up."

"Uh."

"No, for real. You've been asleep for like fifteen hours. There are things needing to be done."

Bennett registered fifteen hours and hopped out of bed, as fast as he possibly could. "Fifteen hours? Holy shit. That's not acceptable."

"Relax babe, your boss isn't going to say anything, and the camp held together okay. I would have let you keep going, but you are needed. I woke you as soon as that was true."

"Yeah, I guess so. So, boss, what's the emergency?"

"No emergency, I'm just trying to convince Wayde to wait at least another few hours before he heads out. It's too soon and he's too tired."

"Yeah, well, good luck with that. The man is not exactly what I would call amenable to suggestion."

"You're his boss, you make him listen."

"Okay, but I already gave my word. I'll do what I can. You're right, he does need to be convinced of it, for our sake as much as for his."

Bennett walked outside, following Naomi. She led him to the armory, where Wayde was getting his kit together. The large man looked like a stiff breeze would knock him over. His eyes were hollow and glassy, and he was swaying slightly as he stood. "Wayde, no. Absolutely not."

"Look, a deal's a deal. You promised me."

"Nope, look, right now you probably couldn't take me in a fight. Me. So, you have no chance if you go out there. You will get eaten alive long before you ever manage to find anyone, and if by some miracle you aren't eaten you will fall off a cliff or something. Either way, you need at least another twelve hours of sleep before you are of any use to anyone. So, fuck off, stop being a martyr and accept reality."

"Okay."

"Okay, you won't go?"

"Okay, if you can take me in a fight I won't go. I'll sit down like a good boy and listen."

"No, I'm your CO, this isn't negotiable. You do what the fuck I tell you. Go back to bed. Also, you just offered to fight me. I suspect your judgement isn't what it should be."

"That's. Wait, yeah, that's a good point. Okay, fuck it. I'm sorry sir, I'm not myself right now."

One crisis averted. Time to move on to the next one. Bennett went to check out the perimeter. The smell of the zombies was a serious issue, but he had no idea how to deal with it. The camp was filled with the stench, it was nauseating everyone, and the risk of disease was huge.

"How the fuck do I deal with this?" he muttered under his breath.

Naomi looked up at him, "What was that?"

"Nothing, just, how do I deal with thousands of rotting corpses? We can't leave them there. The smell, the risk of infection to the living. I have no idea how to deal with all of these bodies."

"Yeah, that's an issue. I mean, a big fire maybe?"

"No way, this is what, ten thousand people. It would have to be a volcano, a forest fire. I don't know how we can deal with that. It's already started too, you see the crowd of crows?"

"It's called a murder."

"What?"

"A group of crows is called a murder. It's a murder of crows."

"Oh, yeah, biggest murder I've ever seen."

"I know we have to deal with it, and I'm not doing much better in that regard than you are. It's too many to burn, we sure as hell can't bury them, no real idea how to get rid of them. Might be easier to move the camp."

"We don't have the resources. It would sink this project, we'd be done."

"Yeah, that's true. I don't know. Maybe we can't do this. Maybe this place, with whatever is going on here, is just too much for us."

"Wait, I have a thought. There's an agricultural supply warehouse, still reasonably intact. Lye. If we get enough lye maybe we can saturate the bodies. Dissolve the bodies."

"Yeah, that's a lot of lye, and it's a risky operation. I mean, our armor is good, but it's not proof against that. Also, the air quality will suck."

"It's that or let ten thousand corpses rot next to us."

"Okay, yeah, the lye might be the best option."

Bennett got a squad together to investigate the warehouse. It was already on the list for potential salvage, this just moved it up the queue to the top. It was a fairly intact building and not the kind of building where much looting would likely have taken place. Nothing really edible, nothing really immediately useful. Long term incredibly useful though.

The squad came back saying there was a huge amount of lye, pallets of it. Maybe even enough to do the job. There were sprayers as well, intended for use with insecticide, but they would work when the lye crystals were mixed with water. It was a few days' work to get it all together. Ammunition was also a major crisis. They had almost no ammo left. Of course, another horde showed up before the ammo did. This one was smaller, quite a bit smaller. Only a few hundred. They showed up a couple of hours after Wayde took his squad to search. Bennett was standing on the wall, surveying the surrounding area, when the call came out. "Zombie, lots and lots of them!"

Bennett and Naomi ran as fast as they could to the section of the wall the call was coming from. Bennett had a moment of panic when he saw the horde, they were coming from a narrow gap between buildings, and the end wasn't in sight. A moment later the horde ended, it was a huge group, but manageable. "All hands, we have to take this horde out, fast as we can. Armour and machetes. Right now."

Even Bennett and Naomi went out this time, leaving only enough on the wall to keep watch. Bennett hadn't been in the field in years, he wasn't used to the grind, the proximity of the dead. The group of them stood in the narrow path, swinging machete's repeatedly. As they were taking out the group a bang followed by a shout came up from inside the wall, "Breach, we have a breach."

Bennett ran in, getting the man next to him to take his spot. It was instantly clear where the breach was. There was a steady stream of zombies coming in from a hole that was blown in one of the walls. Somebody had opened a path, leaving zombies to come inside. "We need some men inside the walls, right now!"

As the zombies started shambling around the camp, a steady stream of them coming towards him, Bennett raised his machete, again and again, swinging at slow moving corpses. The first strike split a rotted skull in one, brains and viscera leaking out onto the creature's shoulders as it fell, then into the hard-packed dirt and broken asphalt of the enclosure. His blade stuck for a moment, just a moment, but it was almost too long. He managed to get it raised barely in time to take down the next zombie, a strong sideways strike that took the dirty corpse's head off. He couldn't tell much about the original owner of the head. It was probably a woman, based on the breasts that showed through rotted clothing, but it could just as easily have been a fat man, the state of decay was too far along. He moved to the next, an overhead strike down into close cropped hair above grey, empty eyes and gnashing teeth full of filth.

There were dozens in his line of sight, and more every moment. There was no way he could win here. Not by himself. A minute, another zombie down, and then he felt hands grabbing at his back, pulling on him. He turned, there was a large zombie, in life this man must have been enormous, a wall of muscle. In death, it was weak, slow, but still stronger than the rest. Bennett swung his blade down on the creature's arm, cutting it off. The other hand still gripped, still pulled, and now there were more hands. He was being pulled down, losing his balance and his grip on his machete.

A Hunting Trip

J unie looked at the swarm around the camp. Luring zombies was hard work, but they'd made an art of it. Fresh meat, preferably human, provided the right smell. Moving in rapid ways, staying in sight but avoiding repetition. He'd had to move three hordes in, a hell of a lot of work, and balancing the two hordes so they didn't join up but hit at almost the same time, he didn't think even his dad could have done that.

The invaders were going to pay, this was his island, his and his families, and the godless had no place here.

The strangers were skilled fighters, and their armour was formidable, but the big horde had left them depleted, he knew it had. No way they had enough ammunition to deal with a horde that size and have lots to spare. When they started taking the second horde, the smallest one, close range with blades he knew that he was right. Blowing the wall, that was pure good luck. The fertilizer in the agricultural warehouse was what made it possible. He hadn't even thought of explosives, but nitroglycerin was easy, and when he saw the strangers go into the agricultural warehouse it came to him. In a way, they were the cause of their own fate. God provided, as he always did.

Junie found a high vantage point to watch the carnage. He smiled as the zombies poured through the breach he'd made in the wall. That was the only variable he wasn't sure of. He'd had to remote trigger the explosives, or else be caught in the midst of the horde, so they could have turned. They didn't.

The fight outside was going well for the strangers, but that was okay, it was a distraction, a way to deny them their safe haven. The godless got no succor, no respite. He wished he could see inside, but the walls were too high. All he could see was his horde outside getting smaller and smaller. It was the last big one in the area. A thousand or so, should be enough.

Satisfied that things were going as expected he moved away. Even if this didn't finish the issue he had other plans in the works.

A Trip to the Shore

Chad and Tamra were outside the town again. They had varied up their positions. Ammo was low, but there were still a few shots left. If Tamra kept her near perfect record they should be able to hit this place twice more. It was less than ideal. They had managed to take a rabbit with the bow the day before, so they had some food in their stomachs, but not nearly enough. Chad was making sure that Tyson got the most food, followed by Tamra. It wasn't just protecting a pretty girl, he needed her hands steady.

A shot rang out in the still night air, and a tall man in the middle of town dropped, like a stone. The spray of blood was from his chest. A moment passed, and he stood up, turned instantly as those who died by trauma usually did. Another shot, another body, another walking corpse in the middle of the village. Time to go again.

They met up at the shelter, exhausted from the walk through the woods, the sneaking and skulking. The three of them were approaching a level. Tyson was healing from his wounds. He was probably going to keep his arm, although it would never be the same as before, never be capable of hard work. As he recovered, grew stronger, the two of them were growing weaker. Exhaustion, lack of calories, lack of nutrition, lack of bathing, lack of sunlight. It was taking a toll. They would need to act soon, or they wouldn't have the resources left to act at all.

"We need to step up the schedule. I don't think we have all that much longer."

"I can help, I'm recovered enough."

"No. I know you feel a lot better, but you aren't as much better as you think. You getting actively involved would jeopardize all of us."

"Yeah, well, you need the extra hands and I have them, so either you tie me down to this... I was going to say bed, but let's be honest here, it's a bunch of sticks woven together, or you let me help."

"Okay, yeah, you can help. I don't know how yet, I'll figure something out. I don't have enough spare rope for the alternative."

"Also, I want me some payback. I want to make that fucker pay."

"Well, that's not a primary goal. We can make it a secondary, but our people have to come first."

"Of course, man. What can I do?"

"Well, what do you know how to do?"

"I worked reclamation. I'm really good at breaking things, that's pretty much it I think. I know how to smash shit really well."

"Not a useless skill set in this case I guess."

They planned the next stage. Tyson's plan was too crazy for Chad to even think about, plus it would require a lot of gear they had no way to get. He wanted to take out the cliffs under the town, something that would require explosives. After some back and forth, and some harsh words from Tamra, Tyson gave the idea up, realizing exactly how difficult it was likely to be. They settled on a more conservative plan. They would wait until that night and do the same thing they had done twice before, but instead of coming back to the shelter Chad would make some noise, give them something to follow. Tyson and Tamra would make their way into the village and free the prisoners. They were almost certain they were all in the same hut Tyson had escaped from, they kept seeing Clyde and the others make their way into the hut.

Chad went out during daylight, something he'd been avoiding doing, and found a route that would allow him to lead the villagers astray and double back to the village after losing them. It was going to be a long trip, demanding work. He was just starting to head back to the village when he saw a figure standing in the woods, just a few feet away. It was a little girl, one of the villagers.

She turned towards him just as he noticed her, spotting him. She was young, maybe eight or nine from Chad's guess. Blonde hair in pigtails, wearing a gingham dress and black shoes. She saw him and started to open her mouth. Chad ran forward, as fast as he could, taking her off her feet and to the ground, a hand covering her mouth and nose before she could even get the scream out of her lungs. He held his hand there, cutting off her air as she thrashed and kicked. He didn't want to do it, hated himself for it, but he didn't know what else to do, so he kept the pressure on until she stopped moving, until her chest stopped spasming as it looked for air that wasn't coming. He didn't let go until she started moving again, differently this time. Could he lose her? Set her on the path back to the village as a zombie? Another piece of chaos to add to the equation?

Inspiration hit him. He gagged her, so she couldn't bite and bound her arms and legs. He threw the tiny zombie over his shoulder and walked back to the shelter. As he came inside Tamra said, "What the fuck?"

"She saw me in the woods, I had no choice."

"Killing her, yeah... taking her back here?"

"Well, I wasn't going to. Hell, I was thinking of piking her brain, but instead, I'm going to drop her on the path behind me tonight, untied. If I do it right, if I time it so she goes after the villagers it will make it harder for them to follow me, give me maybe an extra couple of seconds to vanish, and it will make them angry enough to prolong how long they try to follow me."

"Yeah, okay, but dammit, that thing stinks."

"Sorry, not much I can do about that."

They rested, trying to take their mind off what they were going to have to do that night.

Finally, night fell and it was time to go. Tyson was moving steadily, stronger than Chad had expected. The three of them found vantage points that did what they needed. Chad a little way away from the village, Tamra and Tyson together. When the shot rang out Chad did his usual counter shot, delayed by a moment, but then he fired a second shot, this one on its own. It was much easier to pinpoint, especially because there was no echo where he was. He waited until he started hearing pursuit, close enough that there was no easy way to avoid it and started running. He ran, full tilt, for a little bit. Paused, slamming the ground so if someone was paying attention the pause sounded like a trip, and took off again. The sounds of pursuit were clear, obvious. He was only managing to stay a little bit ahead of them because this was a pre-scouted route.

The little girl came into sight, tied to a tree with knots that were easy to break, but that she couldn't reach. He pulled the knot free and went up the tree she was tied to. This was the risky bit, the scariest part of the whole thing. There was a large boulder, not exactly near the path, but Chad had tried jumping to it, and he was able to. It was a stretch, near the limit of his ability. If he fell here he was getting captured, and probably eaten. The gap, it seemed so much easier when he was doing it without the time pressure of the villagers. The little girl was heading towards them, not standing at the base of the tree, so that was good at least.

Chad tensed up his muscles, gather himself up, and froze. The rock was so far away, it was so long to the ground. He tried again, but he couldn't make his muscles obey him. He said, quietly, "five, four, three, two, one" and leapt, putting all of his strength into the jump. His body left the bounds of earth for a moment, the apex of his jump feeling weightless, effortless. He kept his eyes on his goal... and realized he was just a tiny bit short of it. He was going to only be half on the boulder when he landed. Panic hit, and he stretched out as long as he possibly could, getting as much of himself on the rock as humanly possible. His chest hit, mostly on top, followed by his chin, jarring his skull deep in his brain. He was rocked, seeing stars, but he started to scramble anyway, pulling with his hands, and pushing with his feet. He slipped, a tiny bit lower, on the edge of falling.

The Raid

Tyson knew he was in worse shape than he had let on. His body was wrecked, he'd always been physically strong. He didn't think he'd ever be able to work again. Was he being stupid insisting on coming along on this trip? He didn't know, maybe, but at the same time he had to do it, had to reclaim some of what these people had cost him, or else this was forever. He crawled behind Tamra, every movement agony, he could feel the bone grating against bone. It was something to be ignored, if they didn't get their people out now they would never get them out.

Tamra. A TV star, maybe the biggest in the world now. That was unexpected. Tyson watched her ass in front of him, crawling through the dirt. He was happy for her and Chad, they were so cute together, but that didn't mean he wasn't going to look. It's not like she became a huge star by being ugly. What the hell was wrong with him? Why was his mind constantly in the gutter?

Oh well, he kept going, the pain in his arm taking his mind off the horniness he was feeling. They made it into the town, not empty quiet, but close. One guard on the prison hut, a good sign that there were still people alive inside. That was something, a starting point. Tamra flowed up in front of him, lithe and fast. She wrapped one arm around the guard's neck and plunged a blade upward into his back, coming up between two ribs. The man let out a soft sigh, Tyson could barely make out the pink, frothy blood that came out of the wound, and then, as he fell, out of his mouth and nose. His eyes were full of panic, desperation, but he couldn't make a sound. He died in silence, clawing at his throat trying to draw air into lungs that were already filled with blood. The night filled with stench as his bowels let go. Tyson jammed a knife into his temple. No good allowing him to come back this close to them.

Inside the hut, there were three shapes, two hanging from the wall and one lying on the ground. Tyson walked over to the one on the ground. Tyson had found Jake. His stomach was sliced open, his intestines spread around him like some sort of grim halo. He wasn't quite dead though, just almost. The smell of excrement was strong in the air, tinged with the dark coppery smell of blood. His friend was going to pass, in moments, and when he did he would turn. Monsters. The people they were fighting were monsters, not people.

Tamra took the other two down from the wall. Both were beaten and bloody, barely able to stand on their own. Tyson said, "I'm going to fucking kill them all. Every one of them."

"He was your friend?"

"Yeah, best friend. We were captured together. I haven't seen him since we were captured."

"You want me to?"

"No, I owe him that much. I'll do it."

Tyson took the same blade he'd killed the guard with and gently, slowly, drove it deep into Jake's skull. There was nothing else he could do for his friend, no other way to help him. He wouldn't be able to burn the body even. Just this, the small mercy of making sure he didn't come back. Tyson sobbed, fat tears dropping into the pool of blood. Then he gathered himself, took a deep breath, and turned back to Tamra. "Let's go, I'll take the bigger one."

The man said, "Thank you, I'm so sorry. So, so sorry."

"Yeah, me too. He was a good man. Now, get your ass moving so we don't all end up like Jake."

The man leaned his weight on Tyson, he didn't weigh much. His gear was missing, of course. Tim, Tyson was pretty sure Tamra and Chad had said the man's name was Tim. They made their way out of the hut, slowly moving through the dark night. The village was so close to empty they almost didn't have to be careful. They walked in shadow though, hiding and moving as fast as possible through open space.

The woods loomed ahead of them, dark and welcome, inviting them inside. They made their way slowly, carefully, when a female voice behind them said, "Stop."

She was speaking quietly. Tyson turned, looked at the woman, a young one, pretty and fair, she looked like she was just entering her teenage years.

Tyson locked eyes with her. She looked back at him, an intensity in her eyes. "Please, please, take me with you."

"What?"

"If I stay here they will make me marry him. Oh god, make me have his babies. Please, please, if you have any mercy, any love at all in you, take me with you."

"Come, keep up. Keep quiet."

The girl trailed along behind them. She was having trouble keeping up, her long dress catching up on the branches. Tamra turned to her and grabbed the hem of her dress, pulling it off the girl. "No time for modesty, move your ass."

The girl turned bright red, but she kept going, wearing a shift that was much more than many women would wear, and a bra that could easily be considered a tank top.

The five of them made it to the shelter. It was challenging work. Getting both the newly rescued prisoners and the village girl to the shelter without leaving a clear path was so very, very hard. Luckily Chad had taught him and Tamra some of the tricks he'd learned in training.

The shelter was there, closed and secure, but tiny with all the extra bodies inside. If they had to stay inside there for long it would be bad. Luckily the plan was to leave the next evening, so only a day of basically lying on top of each other. Hell, it had been small when it was just the three of them.

Tamra looked at the girl, "What's your name sweetie?"

"I'm Evie. Thank you, ma'am."

"Huh, don't thank me yet. We might all get captured."

"If we do kill me."

"Why?"

"I'm to marry Junie. He's cruel, crueler than his father. I hate them all, they are stupid, ignorant. They don't know, I've been reading, my brother taught me. He wasn't supposed to, but he did. They killed him. Found out he'd been reading other books, not just the bible. They killed him and burned all the books. I kept a few, hidden, but that's all. I've read all six of them a thousand times. I hate them. I hate them." The girl's voice didn't rise or fall, and even tone, no inflection at all.

TRAVERSE DAVIES

The five of them made themselves as comfortable as possible and settled in to wait.

Back in the Saddle Again

A last effort. He felt something tear in his stomach, but his body hopped up on the rock, enough of him over that his weight was secure. He slowly, carefully hauled himself up, turned and checked behind him. Nobody had seen him, the child providing the distraction he needed. Now he would have simply vanished, hopefully. He crawled across the top of the boulder, the high ground on the other side of it providing an easy exit. Moving back to the village was still a matter of careful movement, every step was painful, and exercise in patience. His stomach hurt, it hurt a lot. There was a subtle wrongness to his every move.

When he got far enough from the villagers he broke into a slow, loping run. It was hard to manage in the dense forest, but he knew he could do it with his gear, and besides, what other option was there?

The village came into sight in a few minutes. There were still people moving around, but it was close to empty, most of the people had followed him. Perfect. Well, almost. That pain in his stomach was far from perfect, but he figured he'd probably survive.

Chad crept in on his elbows and knees, staying as low as humanly possible. The plan didn't call for him to even be here, Tamra and Tyson had either done their bit by now or they weren't going to be able to do their bit at all. The town was quiet. Chad crept to the fish drying rack, grabbing fish, as much as he could.

The woods were close, he made his way into it and started through the forest to the shelter.

As he crept through the forest he heard something ahead of him. Well, that wasn't good. He was in front of a small bear, a cub by the look of it. So, if it was a baby, where was the mom?

Chad made his way up a tree, staying close to the trunk. He prayed that the mother hadn't seen him.

The bear cub wandered around underneath him, and then the much larger mama bear came through, slowly shambling. She was massive, the largest bear Chad had ever seen. To be fair she was also the third bear Chad had seen, and the cub was number two, but she was definitely bigger than the stuffed bear they had in New Hope.

As the bears wandered off Chad started to make his way down the tree, hearing other noises. Of course, the villagers were passing through now, going back the way he had come from... a half dozen of them. The group were combing the woods, would be for a while. Once they made it back they would probably redouble their efforts. He stayed as still as he could, barely breathing. Not that he could take a deep breath at this point. Damn his stomach.

Once they had faded from hearing he slowly made his way down, moving stealthily through the woods. The shelter was ahead of him. He made a last check to ensure he wasn't being observed and then opened the door. The dark room lit green in his night vision, it was full of people. He let out a breath he hadn't realized he'd been holding. Tamra was there, beautiful as ever. Lying on her was a young girl in a shift and bra. That was unexpected. He whispered, "Hey."

"Hey, you made it!"

"Yeah, barely. It was close for a bit. I met a bear. A long night."

"Find a few square inches of floor and lie down. This is Evie. She's from the village, might hate them more than I do."

"Did Tyson find his friend?"

"No, well, yeah, but not someone we could save. They cut him open and spread his insides all over the floor. Tim and Michelle are in bad shape. We won't be moving fast."

"Wish we could have taken one of the trucks. That would have helped a great deal."

"You know how to hot wire?"

"Not a clue."

"I did it once. Of course, I didn't really, it was for the show. I just took a couple of wires and twisted them together. That was back in the early days when I got to do more than just support my husband."

"I remember that episode. You were wearing those blue shorts..."

"Yeah, figures you'd remember that. Perv." Tamra winked at him.

Chad lay down, his body pressed up against hers and Tyson's. Tim and Michelle were almost on top of each other. The air was close and still. Breathing was a challenge. The six of them made the space in the shelter almost unbearably hot. They stayed there, silent, sleeping fitfully, for the day. The shelter was not quite light proof, very close, but there was just enough light leaking through to allow them to tell when night had fully fallen.

As the light faded they got ready, as best they could. It was a silent process, all of them getting ready to move as best they could. Part of Chad wanted to give Tim and Michelle time to recover, but he didn't want to risk it, didn't want to increase the chances of being discovered, every day left them vulnerable, and he knew they wouldn't survive if they were found. There were too many villagers, and they were too brutal.

They started out into the night, the group sticking close to each other. The night was hot, close, no breeze in the forest where they were. They stuck to rock where they could, trails where that didn't work. Chad went last, trying as best he could to cover their path. It was much, much harder to cover them for a number of reasons. There were more of them, they were all injured except Evie (although Tamra was mostly healed by now), and perhaps most importantly, Chad had picked paths between the village and the shelter very carefully, with a lot of scouting, they didn't have that luxury now. At least his NVG's were still working. Given how much he relied on them it was a miracle, and the battery was almost done, but by using them in bursts he was able to see their trail better than anyone else would be able to.

They needed to make sure they made as much distance as they could before being found, because once the villagers were on their trail it would be nearly impossible to pull ahead. Chad kept them going all night, and well past daybreak. He was keeping an eye out for a secure location. There were only a couple of shots left between the rifle and the pistol, then they were relying on his bow, a weapon intended more for zombies and small animals than humans.

The day was hot, the way Indian Summer gets on the east coast. Flies buzzed around, a constant droning noise. They kept landing on the blood trails on Tim and Michelle's back. The tall undergrowth tugged at Chad's legs, brief moments of resistance. He was grateful for the lightweight steel mesh, even as he hated how hot it made him. He imagined it must be torture for the rest of the group, many of these plants had thorns.

They hit a clearing, long grass summer browned, clover lending small splashes of color to the sepia, the drone of honey bees adding another note to the constant buzzing of the flies. The pastoral scene made him feel relaxed, for just a moment. He felt a wash of well-being sweep over him, a feeling that everything would be all right. The tall grass was much easier to walk through. Of course, it left a trail, broken stalks under their boots, well, for those that had boots. Tim, Michelle, and Tyson didn't have much in the way of clothing.

The far side of the meadow led to cliffs very shortly, a descent of a hundred feet at least. Chad and Tamra probably could have made the climb if they had more rope. As it was there was no chance the group could make it down, so they started along the cliff face, no idea which direction was better. Chad chose the right at random.

After an hour or two, the group was exhausted. They needed shelter, they needed sleep, they needed shoes. Tim and Michelle were leaving bloody footprints behind them, their feet shredded from the rocks. Tyson seemed to be doing better. Evie had fallen to silence a while ago, walking without complaint. It seemed she could keep going forever, she wasn't breathing hard, her footsteps were still light, active. The rest of them though, including Chad, were nearing the end of their rope. Chad said, "I'm going to scout ahead a little, you guys find a spot to rest. As soon as I find a real shelter I'll come back."

"Okay, don't be long. We need to get out of the sun."

Chad took off, moving at a fast walk. He knew that he didn't have a lot left, but at least he had some dried fish. He munched on a filet as he walked, thinking how he hated the taste of seafood, and how very, very badly he wanted to be back home.

The cliff overlooked evergreen forest as far as the eye could see. There were a few lakes dotting the landscape, Chad took compass bearings on them, they were going to be essential if the group wanted to survive. There was nothing obvious in terms of places to rest, but he did reach a narrow defile that seemed to go to the base of the cliff. It was too far for him to scout with his current energy level. There was a small depression in the ground between two trees somewhat close. That would have to be it.

He made his way back as fast as he could. The group was sitting in the shade of a low tree, the tiny bit of shelter not nearly adequate. Evie and Tamra were both in full sun, making sure the rest of the group were as covered as possible. "Come on, I have a spot not too much further. Better shelter, if not by much."

"Okay, come on folks, let's get a move on," Tamra said, standing up. "Not much further and then we can sleep for a little bit."

The group all started moving, slowly and stood as best they were able. They walked on, at the edge of their ability.

The walk wasn't far, but Chad knew that once they reached the end of it, he would have to go out again. They had no water, and they needed it desperately. Dehydration was going to rapidly become an issue. As the rest of the group settled in Chad said, "Okay, I have to go a little further, I need to find some water for us. I'll be back in a few."

Evie said, "No, you shouldn't."

"How come?"

"You are clearly exhausted, I want to be able to contribute. Let me go find water. I can keep going, I'm used to it."

"Okay... I guess. Can I trust you?"

"Well, I wouldn't if I was you, but if you met Junie then you would."

"Who?"

"The man I'm supposed to marry in a couple of days. The only reason I haven't had to marry him yet is that he's out making life hard for your people at their base. I would rather die than marry Junie. I would rather anything than marry Junie. I hate him, I hate him more than anything. I will do anything to keep it from happening." The girl spoke in her usual emotionless monotone, a strange cadence, almost a droning to her words.

"Okay, you convinced me."

Evie took their one small canteen and ran off, continuing in the direction they had been traveling. Chad sat down beside Tamra, intending to keep watch.

He opened his eyes. Evie was standing over him, shaking his shoulder, one hand to her lips. "Huh?"

"Clyde, he's close," She whispered. "Not here yet, but soon, maybe ten minutes and he'll be in sight. Coming from that way, I don't think he knows we're here at all."

"Fuck. Okay, wake the others. Let's move."

The only way to go was down the cliff, hoping that the defile was passable, that the villagers didn't notice them, that they were able to move fast enough not to get caught.

The top of the defile was narrow, they had to move single file. This time Chad went first, bracing himself against the broken rock on one side. The other side was only a foot or two high, and just past that short lip was a drop hundreds of feet straight down. Chad swallowed, counted down from five, and then started to move. He had his back to the cliff face, moving to his side, it was too narrow to walk any other way, and he wanted to be able to lean into the cliff, even if it was an illusion of safety.

Inch by inch he made his way down, the rest following. By the ten-minute mark, he was pretty sure they would be hidden by anyone who wasn't leaning over the cliff. They made decent progress, despite the terrifying height. Chad felt dizzy every time he looked down, his stomach turned itself inside out and he broke out in cold sweat. It was a very, very long way down. At one point he looked down at a falcon flying past. Still, inch by inch, foot by foot, they were making it, and then there was a scream, and Tim was falling. Tim fell out of view in a moment. Michelle cried out, "Tim, oh god."

There was nothing they could do, no way they could save him, or even affect his fall. Nothing to do but keep going. Chad asked, "What happened?"

"His legs just gave out, I think he might have passed out," Tamra replied.

"Shit. Shit, shit, shit."

They kept going, down to five. The path got narrower until it was barely as wide as Chad's feet, and the lip was gone, it was just a narrow strip of rock. By the time it ended they were only a couple of dozen feet from the ground, far enough to seriously injure themselves, or even die, but maybe, maybe, close enough to level ground to be able to climb.

"Alright, I'm going to try climbing this. Take your time, be careful."

He found a handhold that would allow him to turn his body around and started to lower himself off the narrow path. His gloves didn't give him enough drip, so he took them off. No way to store them, since he could only let go with one hand at a time, so he dropped them to the ground below. His stomach churned at how long it was before he heard them hit.

Chad felt below him with one foot, until he found a foothold, slowly putting his weight onto it. Once it was clear that it was solid he started to move his other foot out into empty space. His arms were already starting to shake. He had no idea how he was going to do this, let alone how the injured were going to manage it. His other foot found a foothold, slightly lower than the first, and he moved his hands to the path, one at a time. Every moment he made certain he had three solid points of contact. He kept going, slowly, agonizingly. His arms shook so badly he thought he was going to shake himself loose.

Time stopped having meaning, it was a constant state of move one hand, one foot, search, questing until his limb found a purchase, slowly move his weight down. From time to time the hold didn't hold his weight, and he had to catch himself. He had no idea how far he'd come, but he brought his left foot down, trying to find purchase, and it found purchase well before he fully extended it, not only that, but the purchase was large, uneven, but larger than his foot. He looked down. He was a matter of inches from the ground. He stepped off the cliff face, his entire body shaking, and then lay down on the ground. Looking up he saw Tyson making his way down, the same process he had followed. The larger man lost his grip when he just a few feet above the end, he let out a quick scream, aborted as he landed on top of Chad.

Chad had the wind knocked out of him, he tried to turn over, to catch his air, but Tyson's weight was still on his stomach.

Tyson stood. "Sorry man, I'm so sorry."

"No worries."

The next one was Michelle. Tyson and Chad helped her as soon as she was low enough for them to do so. She was ashen and grey by the time she fell backwards into their arms. Tamra came next, climbing quickly and expertly. Finally came Evie. The girl didn't so much climb as run down the hill, arms and legs in rapid movement every moment. It looked like she would fall any second, but she was fine.

"Holy shit, how did you do that?"

"Grew up in Meat Cove. There wasn't a lot to do other than climb the cliffs."

The Hero Triumphant

The zombies were tearing at Bennett's armour, trying to get into the soft flesh underneath. The armour was holding, but breathing was almost impossible, their weight was on top of him, crushing him. This was it, he wasn't going to make it out of this one. No chance for him to make it. Suddenly the weight on top of him got a lot lighter, then there was a patch of sky visible, the pure cerulean blue marred by wispy white clouds. There were still a half dozen zombie faces, then there were four, then two, then Wayde's wide face, a grin etched onto his features.

"Hey, boss."

"Why the hell aren't you wearing a helmet?"

"Shit, guess it got knocked off. Yeah, that's not cool. You want a hand up?"

Bennett held out his hand and Wayde picked him up, almost lifting him off the ground. Once Bennett was standing he looked around, the inside of the camp was littered with zombies. It was a mix of zombies on the ground, skulls smashed in, and wandering around, chasing the half dozen armored soldiers who had made their way back into the compound. There was something blocking the hole in the wall, not completely, but high enough that the zombies could only get their heads over it. It looked like a piece of corrugated tin roof.

"Looks like I picked a good time to come home."

"You couldn't get here an hour ago?"

"If I did I wouldn't have my special present for you."

"What is it?"

"Let's get this mess cleaned up, then I'll show you."

They set to work on the zombies. Bennett noticed that Naomi was among the soldiers inside the wall, her slight frame and way of movement so familiar to him he would have known her from a mile away.

130

The defenders cleared the interior quickly. Bennett called out, "How's the outside of the wall doing?"

"We are winning out there. Most of the zombies are done. Just a couple dozen left, should be a few more minutes," Naomi replied.

"Okay, so, Wayde, what's your present?"

"I caught one of the fuckers. I have him tied up outside. Ragged looking son of a bitch. I stashed him where the zombies can't get him, left one of the boys on him."

"Alright, what about the breach there?" Bennett pointed to the hole in the wall. It was in fact corrugated aluminum roofing. There were zombies reaching through at them, and there were more zombies behind them, a lot more.

"Well, that's something we are going to have to deal with. The roofing won't last much longer."

The soldiers inside the wall, including Wayde, Bennet, and Naomi, made their way over to the zombies and started stabbing into the mass.

After a little bit there were no more zombies to stab. Wayde said, "Let's go get my gift."

"Okay, maybe we can ask a couple of question."

"That's the plan. He might not really enjoy the questions, but that's alright... I think I will."

"We won't be doing the interrogation, at least not most of it. My girl, she's really good at that you know?"

"Yeah, I can see that. She's an intense lady."

They made their way over the corpses. Each one they stepped over left Bennett thinking, "Well, shit, now we have even more we have to get rid of."

The building across the street was rough, close to collapse, but Wayde assured Bennett it would survive the five minutes it took to get the prisoner. They walked into the dark, musty interior. The first thing to hit Bennett was the smell. Mold and wet concrete mixed in equal measure. It was cold, the day outside had been so hot, but in here it was freezing, and the walls dripped with condensation. The staircase was concrete, probably the only reason it was still standing. It was pitted, scarred, at places, the rebar showed through. The railing was more the ghost of a railing. Strips of rusted metal sticking out from the half-collapsed stairwell wall. Bennett made sure to stick as close to the more intact of the walls as he went up. He had no way of knowing what kind of building this had been when it was intact, something industrial he guessed. They reached the second floor and found the prisoner with one of Wayde's men. The prisoner was sitting against the wall, looking sullen. He was dressed in layered rags and had long hair that might not have been washed since the zombie apocalypse. His teeth were rotted stumps between greying beard and mustache, both long and matted. His eyes had a telltale redness around them, and he twitched constantly as he sat there. The stench coming off him rivaled that of the walking corpses outside.

"Dul ag feck tú féin," he said, snarling.

"I have no clue what that means. You know how to speak English?"

"Níl Tada Níos Measa Na Bód Ina Seasamh," the man replied. Wayde lashed out with a foot, catching the ragged man in the arm. He slammed the man's arm into the wall, there was a crunching noise and the prisoner screamed, incoherent rage and pain. "Answer the fucking questions or I'll beat you down like the dog you are."

"Go fuck yourself," it sounded more like "Go feck yerself" with the strong accent the man had.

"Okay, this isn't going anywhere. Bring him into the camp. We'll give him to Naomi," Bennett said, turning his back on the prisoner.

"You realize that means I have to touch him?"

"Sorry man, don't really see a way around that."

They took the prisoner back to camp. A few of the men were repairing the breach, making sure it would stand if there was another wave. After Wayde got the bearded man to the center of camp Bennett went and grabbed Naomi. "Hey love, I have a job I think you'd be better at than me. We have a prisoner."

"You want me to question him?"

"Yeah. I think Wayde broke his arm."

"Good."

"I thought you were anti torture."

"Oh, I am. It don't work. Not ever. You can beat that man to death and you'll get answers from him, but those answers won't be better than guesses. No, it's good because it was Wayde, and now I can make a show of being the one who cares, I can start getting in his head."

"He's filthy, smells terrible. Hair, beard, it's all awful."

"Okay, I have a plan for that. It's probably a big part of his identity. Shave his head, his beard, cut off his clothes, give him clean ones. Hose him off while he's naked. All of it has to be done before I start talking to him. Get him off balance, kill his sense of identity. When I come in I'll establish a rapid rapport with him. Also, means I don't have to deal with most of it. The teeth... well, it's not like I plan to make out with him or something. Still, something to kill the breath would be good. I want to be able to react as natural as possible."

"Okay, we'll get it done. How long until you talk to him?"

"In a perfect world, three days. In these circumstances, I figure a couple of hours. Let him stew, but we do need fast results."

Bennett went back out, told Wayde the plan. The big man decided to handle it himself. He grabbed the prisoner by the hair and dragged him to where they had an outdoor hose. "We're getting you clean you filthy fucking animal."

"Get the fuck off me."

"Not a chance in hell. Boys, grab his arms."

Two of the men grabbed the prisoner, pinning him to the ground. Wayde slipped his large knife out of its sheath and started sawing at the filthy man's clothing. The ragged and rotten fabric parted like butter before the razor-sharp steel, leaving behind flesh that was pale as the belly of a fish but streaked with dirt and filth. Bennett didn't think the man had bathed in decades. As his clothes fell off he fought harder, straining with all of his might against the men holding his arms.

"Don't fucking matter, I'm a Wendigo, me. I'll eat your fucking SOULS!"

Despite his protests that it didn't matter he kept fighting. Wayde sliced every bit of clothing from his body. Bennett noticed the man was skinny, it looked like he was starving, his muscle mass almost gone, and his belly distended, swollen. After he was stripped naked Wayde grabbed his head. "Holy shit, I've never seen this many lice. His skull is crawling. How do you stand the itch man?"

"Fuck you. Get the FUCK OFF ME!"

"Well, that's not going to happen." Wayde started sawing at the matted hair on the man's head, hauling it off lock by lock. It was slow going, the hair had dreaded, thick ropes fell off to the ground, crawling with small white insects. Finally, Wayde started on the beard. As the man's beard came away he finally let go of the tension in his limbs and collapsed, sobbing, on the ground. After that, they turned the hose on him. Cold water and strong soap. The water ran off his body, black, then slowly turning grey. Clear took a long time. The smell was overpowering, stale sweat and shit. After he was done Wayde decided to be more thorough. He said, "Somebody get me a toothbrush. I'm cleaning this son of a bitch up."

The man lying on the ground had a face that was a mass of wrinkles. His thin frame was wrinkled and decrepit, ancient looking. He was strangely pale and pink but had liver spots all over. One of the troops came back with a tooth brush and tooth paste. The man clenched his teeth together, but Wayde held his nose shut until he had to open his jaw to breathe. Wayde stuck a gloved hand inside. The man tried to bite, hitting jagged, broken teeth on the chain mail glove. He howled, wordless now. Wayde stuck the tooth brush in his mouth and started to brush. After a minute he said, "I used to have a dog with rotten teeth. Thing fought getting its teeth brushed like I've never seen. The smell every time you tried was enough to make you gag. Still smelled better than this though. Damn, how can somebody let this happen to themselves?"

"I don't think they can if they aren't crazy. This man, clearly he's crazy," said one of the soldiers.

His gums bled, not a little. To the point where they had to rinse his mouth out. He winced and cried, after being so strong and violent, it seemed like this was what finally broke him. He sobbed when they were done, naked and bald, blood dripping from his mouth.

They took him, got him dressed in clean, fresh pants and shirt, nothing fancy but soft and warm. They took him to a room they had built in a storage crate. It was meant as a short-term stockade in case one of the men did something too egregious. It was the closest thing they had to a prison though.

After a few hours, Naomi went in alone. The prisoner was tied up, and Wayde had been surprised by how weak he was once they had his clothes cut off. What had looked like a large man was a very weak man, suffering severe malnutrition, but his layers of rags and hair had hidden it well. Naomi stayed in with the man for a few hours. When she came out she walked straight to

Bennett. "His name is Norm. He was a fisherman before the rise. Actually, one of the few original islanders among his people. He's clearly far down the kuru path, and he's going to snap soon. Don't let anyone get near him without armor, but so long as he's restrained he should be okay. He's here following someone named Junie, kind of an heir apparent to the group. They make their base in Meat Cove but consider the island their territory. Crazy religious fanatics, kept calling the zombies 'the blessed.'"

"That's a lot of information."

"I have a lot more. Yes, they have some of our people prisoner. He was part of a group of ten left behind to mess with us. You know, once I started to break down his barriers he remembered a lot about who he used to be, his wife, five kids. They did lobster fishing for a living."

"Don't tell me you feel for him?"

"No, of course not. He's evil, straight to his core, but he didn't used to be, I feel for the lobster guy from before the zombies. Of course, that guy died a long, long time ago, this is just a Wendigo wearing his skin."

"Wendigo? He said that outside."

"Yeah, that's a bit more jumbled, but I think they took native legends around the Wendigo and applied it to Kuru. He's got it by the way, in case you couldn't tell. Probably loses the ability to walk within the next few months, dies not too long after that. It's weird though, usually, with Kuru, they lose the ability to walk first, then eat. Hell, maybe he can't eat because his teeth are so rotten."

"Well, that's a hell of a lot more than we had. So, cannibals?"

"Yeah, for about twenty years now. They have made it into a ritual, makes them closer to the blessed in their eyes."

"So, we need to wipe them out."

"Yeah. No choice really. The number of people who might suddenly develop kuru is far, far too high. No way we can integrate them."

"I wasn't thinking it was likely. So, the next bit, how are they controlling the hordes?"

"Apparently it's pretty simple. They don't do anything mystical or anything like that. It's baiting them with the smell of fresh meat, bringing hordes together, and knowing how to get out. Takes a lot of skill from what

I can tell. Junie's the best at it, even better than his dad, a real psycho named Clyde."

"So, zombie worshipping inbred redneck hillbilly religious fanatics. I think I watched that movie."

"Yeah, you and me both. As to the inbred, he didn't say specifically, but they are an isolated group living far from anyone, with a population in the hundreds, you know there's inbreeding happening."

"Yeah, and every other horrifying thing that those groups usually do. It's pretty distressing, we get wiped out, and this is where we end up when have a clean slate."

"Well, it's not really a clean slate. Too much old hatred made it over. Hell, when Jasper and me came over to PEI we dealt with Robert. Clearly not a true clean slate."

"Yeah, I guess guys like that will always exist."

"I think this Clyde guy might be more dangerous though, guess he's a preacher, got them believing that there's extra books in the bible about life after the zombies rise, books only he has access to."

"I guess we know what we have to do then."

"Yeah, it's going to come down to it. Wipe them out. Can't leave em, can't let that sort of cancer survive. It pollutes everything."

Fox Hunt

Clyde didn't get angry, not ever. These folks though, they were pushing him close. First, they took Emily and turned her into one of the blessed. It wasn't bad being one of the blessed, of course, but it wasn't for the unbelievers to do that to a child. She was such a pretty little girl. He had been thinking he might even give her to Junie as a second or third once she was old enough, but then they had to go and take Evie. Evie, the chosen child. She was so beautiful, and even better she was only barely related to Junie, just a little bit. They would have had such beautiful children.

Sure, the girl was insolent, spoiled, all of that, but nothing a few nights in the marriage bed and some strict discipline couldn't cure. She was tainted now, he was sure. After all, why else would they have taken her? Well, maybe not, maybe they were saving her for someone back at their base, but that just meant he had to find them even faster.

The cliff, it was obvious they had gone down, but he wasn't willing to risk his people like that, it was close to suicide. Sheer stupidity, especially for a man his size. He yelled, "Come. This way. We're going to the base."

It wasn't a terrible walk around. Despite the height of the cliff, there was a reasonable path to the bottom just a little back the way he had come. He led his men back to the route down. There was one woman among them. Someone had gone back to get Emily's mother and father, they only had the one child, so they were on the hunt, as was their right. It was only fair for a mother to get the chance to confront the man who'd killed her only child.

"Clyde, we gonna kill them good right?"

"Damn right we are. I'm gonna see you get the best pieces too. You get the first pick, you and Brother Joseph."

"Promise me. Promise me we make them pay."

"You know I will Sister Rose. Those unbelievers will pay in blood and pain."

Sister Rose was one of his original flock, one of the first group to come with him. She had married Brother Joseph late because for a long time Clyde had kept her for himself. Eventually though as was usually the case he passed her on. She got too old for him. She had born him three children though, before that day came. She was still a decent looking woman and Clyde thought for a moment if he should take her a few more times while they were on the trail, but it didn't seem fair to do with Brother Joseph traveling alongside them. Not that Brother Joseph would mind. He'd think on it as they traveled.

The easy path down the cliff was slow going still, no good taking it too fast. He wasn't worried, he knew how badly damaged the group was. Sure, there was at least one he hadn't had in his captivity, but he was pretty sure from the tracks that it was just one more.

Why did they think they could do this to his people? The arrogance to think they could invade God's Chosen like this, kill their children. Hell, there was a chance that Emily was even one of his - a small one, the timing was suspect, but some. They might have killed his own daughter, him, God's chosen on earth.

The longer they traveled the more he started to feel rage, hate, the need to punish and hurt them.

Once they reached the cliff base he started walking toward where the group had come down, it was obvious where it was, at least to him. There were limited options, limited places it could be. Along the way he discovered the mangled remains of one of them walking around. Tim. That was his name. It had been the only thing he'd even bothered to ask, he didn't really care about the unbelievers, other than that they were invading his island.

"Well, looks like the cliff took care of this one. He's one of the blessed now."

"Should we purify him?"

"No need, it's just one. Snap a collar on him, take him along with us. He might even be useful if we can get him on their trail."

One of the men snapped a leather lead and a gag onto the newly risen blessed. The blessed needed to be revered, but that didn't mean you had to be stupid about it. No sense getting bit if you could avoid it. They started into the forest, following the trail the group had left. They had a bit more of a lead now, but that wasn't a big deal. They'd lose their lead quick enough.

Things Get Hard

As soon as they were able to stand again Chad got the group moving.
They were in shock about Tim but couldn't spend the time to find him.

The thick woods had a trail leading through them, mostly overgrown,
but still remnants, it was clearly a leftover from the old days, small bits of
asphalt showing between the weeds. Chad started moving as fast as possible.

Michelle was having trouble walking. Her feet were shredded, almost
hamburger. She kept stumbling. Chad realized that he either had to deal with
this or leave her behind. He stopped, grabbed some of the cordage he had
and some smooth bark from one of the nearby trees. "Michelle, I'm going
to make you some sandals. They won't be great, but they will be better than
trying to keep going barefoot."

"Okay, yeah... I'm sorry, I'm sorry. I can't keep going like this."

"Not your fault, I should have taken care of this hours ago. I'm sorry."

They got Michelle outfitted with very primitive sandals and were able
to keep going. Evie was inexhaustible. The rest of them weren't. After several
more hours they were all about to collapse, there was no way they could keep
going.

"Time to find a spot to hide in."

Tamra said, "I saw an overturned tree back a few minutes. Lots of space
under the trunk. I think that's the best I've seen so far."

"Okay, take me, we'll check it out."

The two of them walked back the way they had come for a couple of
minutes until they found the tree. There was a large hollow, big enough
for the group. It was dirty, and the smell of earth and mold filled the air
around it, but it was sheltered, hidden, it was the best they were going to get.
While Tamra got the group and brought them to the spot Chad cut soft pine
boughs and covered them with whatever material he could find, something
to keep them off the ground. Then he cut more to cover them with, making

the entrance almost invisible. As he was working the rest came back to him. "This is what we've got folks. Time to take a rest."

They curled up, out of the sun, out of sight, and hoped. Day slowly faded into night, the sunsets were earlier, but still late these days. A stillness settled over the woods, the night creatures making their silent, stealthy way out into the world. Chad woke some time later, after darkness had fallen. He put on his helmet and powered up the night vision goggles, they lasted less than a minute. The batteries were finally done. Well, one advantage they no longer had. The air had a sweet smell, honeysuckle maybe. It was mixed with the dark, decaying scent of the hole.

The moon was barely a crescent, new and faint. Where there were gaps in the dark forest canopy the stars filled the skies, intense and bright. Chad thought for a moment about once, before his birth, humans had gone up there, off the planet. According to his father even set foot on the moon. There were plans to go to Mars. Now, he was sitting in a hole, hiding from ragged men who ate other humans, trying to make it back to what passed for civilization. It was unfair, beyond unfair. He should have been born while humanity was still exploring the sky, slipping the bonds of gravity.

A few minutes of letting self-pity wash over him and he stood up, time to get moving. "All right cats and kittens, let's get a move on."

The rest got up with him, leaving the shelter behind. It was so dark they could only see a foot or two in front of them. Slow going, at least they weren't any worse off than their pursuers. Darkness treated everyone the same.

The biggest surprise was Evie. They had gotten used to her being fearless, inexhaustible. Now she was hanging onto Tamra's hand and almost hiding behind her. Chad figured it out quickly. Poor kid was afraid of the dark. He wished he could pick her up and carry her. Actually, he wished he could throw her in a truck and drive her back, but this was what they had.

They picked their way along remnants of trails, not worrying about erasing their track, not because they didn't want to but because it was impossible in these conditions. Chad was exhausted, near the end of his stamina by this point. He'd been going so hard for so long that there wasn't a lot left inside, but there was also no choice, so he kept going, kept pushing the group to move forward, as fast as they could. At some point he tripped on a rock, invisible in the darkness, and couldn't get up. His face smashed into something hard, again. It wasn't quite exactly on his bruise from earlier, but almost, and it was an even harder hit. He lay there, face down, and started to sob. It wasn't anything in particular, just the cumulative effect of weeks now spent exhausted, terrified, having to make the decisions for everyone, he had no mental reserves left, and damnit, his face hurt!

Tamra came over to him, talking softly, "Come on, I know, I know. It's too much. But you can do this, it's just a tiny bit longer. You can hold it together for a tiny bit more."

"I... I don't think I can."

"You can, because you have to... so you will. Now, stand up. Just get your feet under you and stand up."

"Okay. Okay. Just, give me a minute."

"One. Sixty seconds. I'm counting."

And she did, counting down from sixty. When she hit one Chad had himself under control. He stood up, his breathing still ragged. "Okay, we keep going. I don't know how much I have left, but I swear, I will give every single moment of it to you."

The group walked on, barely more than a crawl. Sometime later the sky ahead of them begin to lighten, just a slight mellowing of the blackness, not really light, but the stars were harder to see on the horizon when they could see the sky at all. Soon after that, the sky began to take on a blush, a dark red stain over the world. There were clouds on the horizon, dark and massive, lending an eerie quality to the light, everything was cast in tones of blood and fire. The clouds were closing.

"Oh, good, another storm. That's exactly what we needed right now," Chad said, a deep sigh in his voice.

"Maybe it is. Remember, the people chasing us have to contend with it too."

Evie tugged on Tamra's sleeve. "Clyde likes the storms. Says they are God punishing the land, and he likes it every time God punishes something. Also, they will have runners to bring them resupply and gear. It's the standard protocol whenever we have someone run. It doesn't happen often, but it happens enough that we have routines and procedures."

"Okay, so, the storm isn't our friend then. Let's get as far as we can before it hits, hopefully, find someplace to set up before the full brunt of it is on us,"

Chad said, "We will shelter as best we can once it hits, and move as soon as we can after."

They kept going through a morning heavy with humidity, through air that was more like soup. All of them were dripping with sweat, near collapse, since they had continued through the dark of the night. When the wind picked up it was almost a blessing, for a moment. Suddenly there was a crack of thunder, and the humidity coalesced into a torrential rain. Chad was soaked through in an instant. That moment it felt wonderful, sluicing the humidity and sweat away from his skin, leaving him feeling refreshed and invigorated. Five minutes later it was dragging the warmth from him, pulling it down to the forest floor, leaving him unable to stop his limbs from quivering. "We have to make it to shelter," he said, his voice rising to a shout to be heard over the rain.

The group started looking around them, unable to see much further than they could when they were walking through the darkness.

Tyson was the one who spotted the cave. Well, a cave was a stretch, but it was an overhang, rock with a shelter below it. Narrow, but maybe wide enough that if they stayed close they could stay warm. They made their way through a curtain of water into the scant shelter. Making a fire was impossible, so instead, they stripped down to underwear and huddled close together, their wet clothing lying on the driest ground they could find other than where they were.

The storm raged, and raged, and raged. They were all shivering, cold skin against cold skin. Slowly they started to warm, the rock face protecting them from the worst of the wind and rain. It wasn't much, barely anything, but it wasn't nothing. Chad just prayed it was enough to keep them alive until the storm ended.

By nightfall nothing had changed, so they tried to find a way to lie down, still cuddled together. Chad found himself almost naked, skin pressed up against Tamra. She was cuddled up in his arms, facing away from him, her bum pushed close into his crotch. He realized that he was starting to get hard, despite everything. "No, damnit, not now. Not now!" he kept thinking to himself, but there was nothing he could do about it. Finally, he fell asleep, praying that Tamra hadn't noticed.

Morning came, with no change in the weather. Chad didn't think they could move yet, it was too much, they were too cold and too low on energy. Michelle was warm, too warm. "Hey, let me see your back."

Michelle turned around to give Chad a clear view. Her wounds were red, inflamed, infected. Her feet too once he checked them. Starting to leak pus. He checked his portable med kit. A couple of antibiotics left, they'd used almost all of their store, including all the powder, on Tyson. "Michelle, here, take this."

"What is it?"

"Antibiotics. Seems like you have a little bit of infection. Nothing we can't deal with, but we have to get on it sooner than later."

"Okay."

An hour later Michelle was complaining of stomach pain. Not a surprise. These were strong, hard on the stomach. They were supposed to be taken with food, but food wasn't something they had. They had finished the dried fish the day before.

They spent a miserable day and night under the rock. Chad made sure Michelle got the last antibiotic that evening. Finally, around midnight, the rain stopped.

Their clothes were still damp. Not soaked, but not dry either. The rainfall had been enough to keep them from ever completely shedding the moisture in them. Chad thought it might be worse for him. The armor, it had kept him alive so many times now that there was no way he would leave it behind, but at the same time the metal transferred heat away from his skin at an amazing pace. Still, he was still better off than Michelle. She was feverish, eyes glassy and empty. He didn't think she had a whole lot longer left. Her back was oozing pus from each whip mark, and her feet were starting to turn dark, he knew that if the smelled them they would smell of rot. There was nothing they could do, no way to even let her rest.

After a few hours of walking, Michelle sat down on the ground. "Leave me here. If I live long enough I'll try to take one of them with me when they get here. If I don't maybe I can take even more."

Chad looked at her, took in her condition. "Okay."

"What? You aren't supposed to say okay just like that, you should be trying to convince me to fight through the pain."

"Michelle, you have hours left. I have no medicine to give you. Even if we got you home in the next hour you would probably have to lose both legs, and there's no way in hell I can amputate without killing you. I hate it, but I've been weighing the options. So long as you could keep walking I was going to keep you going, even if you had to lean on us, even if you slowed us down... but the math doesn't work at this point. I'm so sorry."

"Yeah, I know. I knew it when I signed up. It was always a possibility. Well, looks like it's just you. Funny. The new meat isn't supposed to be the last one standing. One more thing. I want a kiss."

"Didn't think you thought of me like that."

"What? Oh, sorry, not from you. I mean, you're cute and all... but you knew I was a lesbian right?"

Tamra came over and kissed Michelle, deep and long, and then turned away. "All right, let's move."

"Thanks, I always wanted to kiss a TV star."

"My pleasure and thank you. Your sacrifice won't go unnoticed. I'll make sure everyone knows about you guys."

"Hey, what else could a girl ask for?"

They left Michelle behind, sitting on the ground. She had a large stick, they had to keep all the other weapons on hand.

The dawn came, a softer dawn than they had had. The air had the first trace of autumn chill, setting deep into Chad's bones. It seemed that with Michelle's fate he had lost his reason for doing any of it. He could have left with Tyson and Tamra days ago, nothing would be different except that they wouldn't be fleeing pursuit like they were. "I don't suppose this Clyde guy will give up, will he?" Chad asked Evie.

"No, he doesn't give up. Not ever. If he decides you need to be punished he will keep going no matter what the cost."

"Way to make me feel better."

Still, they had to keep going, no matter what.

Days went by, until one day they discovered they were looking at the ocean. The autumn sun glinted off blue waves, crashing surf pounded, distant and far, far below them. They had made it to the eastern shore of that little section of Cape Breton. An almost trivial distance. It had only cost them two lives so far.

Playing Catchup

Junie saw that the camp was still running, the strangers still had power, people, fences, and one of his men. He had a couple of others with him, just a small group, loyal and long-term guys, but also guys who wouldn't be missed too much at home. With everything going on Dad hadn't wanted Junie to compromise the work force too much. Figured his son could handle things mostly on his own, the guys he did have were old, had been with his dad since the early days. Not necessarily the strongest, or the fastest, but all of them were smart enough, and hard workers to the limit of their ability. Junie went and found Earl, his second in command. "Bastards captured Earl, they have him inside now."

"How'd they manage that then?"

"Bunch were outside, just dumb luck. They happened on him as he was crossing to another location."

"Shit luck. Well, guess that's that then."

"Yeah, he'll give them an accounting, I bet."

"Don't know. Earl's in pretty bad shape. Shakes started a while back. Figure he'll go Wendigo on them soon enough. Bet they don't see that coming."

"Yeah, that's true. Bet they don't have Wendigo where they from."

The two of them gathered up the rest and headed back to where they were making camp, an old warehouse that had an elevated interior office that was still intact. They had packed two or three hundred zombies into the ground floor leaving the catwalk the only way to reach their sleeping quarters. It was as secure as they could get and reasonably warm. It was also dry, something Junie had come to truly appreciate in hundreds of hunting trips with his father.

If you knew the routes it was about a week's walk home, but you had to know the way to go. if you lost the old roads it could take a really long time. Junie was pretty set up, a change of clothes, enough food, especially pemmican, they had a water jug set up, comfortable bedrolls. It was almost as good as home. Junie wanted to be back there some bad though. Evie was waiting on him. Evie and his wedding night. He'd finally get to stick it in her, he knew she was a virgin, he'd be the first one to plow that field.

He lay back, drinking some of the shine they'd brought down with them. Sure, the camp hadn't been wiped out, but they'd been hurt, pushed to the brink. Every day they were pushed like that was another day they couldn't get established, and that meant it was a success for him.

He enjoyed the simple comfort. He blankets made the hard floor seem less hard, they were piled three thick, made of sheep skin, much of the wool still attached. The shine caught his throat, rough and harsh, but it left a warm glow in his chest, and then in his head. This was good, doing God's work and getting to lay back at the end of the day. The bunch of them lit a couple of candles and Earl got out his mandolin. Junie didn't have much musical talent, but he could play the spoons, so he did, as Rich started singing, his deep voice melodic in the night. They weren't worried about anyone hearing them, the only ears in listening range belonged to the dead down below.

After a few drinks and some companionable conversation, they drifted off to sleep, content with their place in the world.

The next morning Junie had a slight headache, nothing serious, just a bit of pain around his eyes and the back of his head. He drank as much water as he could stomach and then grabbed some jerky. The jerky was fatty and salty, delicious.

They took the catwalk to the exterior staircase. It was rickety and old, creaked and groaned worse than a woman, but it had held so far, and if it didn't, well, that's what God willed.

Today Junie had a special mission. The interlopers had captured one of his, he intended to return the favor. He wandered the town, near the base. These days there were so many tracks it was hard to tell where the strangers might be, but eventually, he found a track. It was five of them. Too many to take at once, but if he could separate one out. He gestured to Rich to take the left and Earl to take the right. Too bad about Norm, the old timer was a wizard at tracking.

They followed the tracks until they found the patrol, the small group ensconced in an old corner store, long since looted. They were deep in conversation, ignoring the world around them, a fatal mistake in an environment like this Junie thought. He decided that he had a better way to deal with them than his original plan. He said, "Earl, wait there, Rich, over there. I'm setting the store on fire." using hand talk.

Creeping near the store Junie took out a small strip of magnesium, he'd snagged it from a wilderness outfitter a while back and put it against some dry boards. A quick flick of a lighter and the place started to burn.

It took a minute, but it caught. The soldiers, for it was clear that was what they were, kept talking inside. They were lost to the threat around them, focusing on their pointless words. When they did notice the flames were high and partially blocking the exit. Junie heard on of them say, "Oh fuck, fire!" and then they bolted for the flames.

As the four of them leapt through the flames Junie grabbed the one closest to him, getting a small burn in the process, his skin sizzled and blistered, but only on his forearm. It was mostly scar tissue there anyway. His men grabbed the interloper with him and dragged the man into the next building. It was going to burn, no question. This kind of fire tended to get out of control in places like this, but by the time it caught they would be out.

Junie grabbed the strap on the man's helmet, releasing it, and pulled the helmet completely off, revealing a very young, very scared looking man.

"Make a noise, I cut out your tongue what."

They dragged him back deep into the building. It appeared to be an old pizza parlor. Once they were at the back door, Junie grabbed an old piece of cloth he had in his pocket and stuffed it into the man's mouth. The man resisted so Junie punched him in the stomach and then pushed the ratty old cloth into his mouth. They tied another piece of cloth around his head, keeping the gag in place, and then went out the back way, into the cool, bright day. Smoke was starting to cloud the sky, which meant that in no time there would be a lot more soldiers on site. Junie and his men hightailed it out of there, hold a knife under the soldier's chin to ensure he would cooperate.

Once they reached the warehouse Junie took the man's gag off. The man said, "Fuck you. Let me go."

Junie casually kicked him in the stomach, driving him to his knees. Then Junie grabbed the back of his head and kneed him in the nose.

"You will answer my fucking questions, and you will keep a civil fucking tongue in your head when I talk to you. Got it, boy?"

The man nodded.

"Okay, now, what's your name?"

"Bob. I'm Bob."

"Okay, then Bob. I'm Junie. From now on I am your mother, your father, your God. you will say exactly what the fuck I want you to say, got it."

"Sure man, sure, just don't hurt me. Please."

The man was begging, pleading. It made Junie sick. A real man should have more strength than that, more heart. Junie kicked him in the ribs once, just for the hell of it.

"Okay Bob, you hear that sound?"

The noise from below was clear as day, a few hundred zombies, growling and shuffling, reaching up to try and get to the office suspended far above.

"Yeah, I know what it is."

"You piss me off, you don't answer my questions, I dump you over the edge."

"Okay, you won't have a problem with me," Bob was blubbering, sobbing.

"You make me sick, pathetic waste of flesh. Might be all you're good for is feeding the blessed. Now, how many are in your camp?"

"Fifteen hundred and six, last count. Just a small force, to feel the place out."

Junie thought about that number for a moment. Last count his town had just under six hundred, counting everyone, even the newborns and the very old.

"Where are you from?"

"New York. We're from New York."

"How many people in New York?"

"Not sure, somewhere around six million I think. Most of the city died, we only managed to save a few, but we've grown since then."

"Six million?"

"Yeah, around. Nobody has a completely accurate count. We are expanding up and down the coast right now."

Junie kicked him again. Bob coughed, choking and gagging as he did. "Fuck was that for?"

"Six million people. That's bullshit. No place has six million."

"How old are you?"

"Old enough to know bullshit when I hear it."

"New York had more than twenty million when the zombies hit. Like every place else we lost like ninety percent, brought us down to like two million. We kept going, kept fighting. A little while later we had more, we're back up to six, with people coming in from outside, kids being born. There's a ton of room, a ton of food. It's awesome, the best place around. Rebuild from the ashes. You should visit."

Bob started singing "Start spreading the news, I'm leaving today, I want to be a part of it, New York, New York." He was cut off with another kick. "Fuck you, I can drop you."

"So do it. Show me how big a man you are, tough guy. Drop me in the zombies."

"No, I think I make you hurt a lot, then I drop you in the zombies."

"What, no more question... agggh"

Junie stomped on Bob's hand, driving his heel in the bones, hearing it crack.

"No, I don't think you're going to tell me anything useful. Instead, I'm going to beat you until my desire to beat someone passes."

He broke Bob's arm, started punching him in the face, kept punching until the soldier's face was a bloody mass, eyes swollen too shut to see. Every hit made a meaty thud, then a squishy thud. Junie looked at his knuckles. He might have broken the largest one on his left hand. Oh well, not the first time, not going to be the last. He started kicking Bob in the ribs until he coughed blood. He looked down at the bloody mess and said, "Alright, I think I'm in the mood for questions and answers now. So, where the fuck are you from boy?"

Bob looked up at him and said, "Okay, I admit it. I lied."

"Really?"

"Yeah, I'm from Long Island. Guess I just couldn't face the shame."

Junie kicked him again, hard enough to drive him into the wall behind him. Bob slowly crawled up the wall. Junie let him stand, letting him get to his feet so he could take him down, take away his hope, his belief in himself. Bob got all the way standing, still hunched over with the pain in his ribs.

Junie slowly walked forward when Bob turned and ran, straight for Rich. Junie tried to grab him, but Bob had developed some last reserve. He grabbed Rich by the collar and dove through the window to the zombies waiting below, taking Rich with him as he fell. His last words as he jumped were "My names not Bob mother fucker."

A Jaunt Along the Shore

C had looked good in his role. Tamra was impressed with how much he'd grown. Some men collapsed when things got too tough, but not Chad. He grew into the role, became who he needed to be to save them all. Okay, it hadn't worked, but still, despite being ten years her junior she had decided that he was what she wanted in a man. Hell, he'd even developed some courage when it came to interacting with her.

They were trekking along the coast now, making much better time. There was a road for them to follow, not much of one, but so much better than the deep forest.

They were making the kind of time that was possible in the old days. Remote as this area was there was no issue with zombies, it was just a straight shot to Sydney. Well, not straight, kind of twisted and crazy, but Tamra thought they might be making eight to ten kilometers an hour. A respectable pace to maintain, and it wasn't killing them. Water and food were a problem, of course, but that was hardly new.

After a full day of walking with relative ease, they found a small community. It wasn't much, a few houses that hadn't been occupied in twenty years or so, most in an advanced stage of rot, but it was something, anyone who was still alive in this world had scavenged in worse. "Hey, how about this one?" Chad asked.

"Sure, looks good." There it was again, he had picked one, led. Sure, he phrased it as a question, but that was good leadership, making the group feel involved, but not burdening them with the weight of the decisions at the same time. The four of them waked up to the house, it was weathered and ancient, but it also looked like a certain type of place, the kind of place a poor family would have lived in back in the old days. Not trailer trash, not like her family, but still... poor. Working class. Families like that didn't tend to have high-end food, fresh food, all of that. They had bulk food that lasted.

Especially in a place like this, where winter might mean you couldn't make it to a larger center for months on end.

Tyson smashed the door in, not bothering to preserve it. A zombie came rushing at them, but Chad slammed his machete into its head before it could even reach the door. It was an overweight woman, the tattered remnants of a floral print dress draped over her grey, decaying flesh. They stepped into the gloom. There were two more zombies, children. Chad decapitated the first with a savage blow and Tamra took the second, driving a knife into its temple. Tyson and Evie followed along.

The place was awful. Tacky in a way that defied the mind. Every square inch of wall was covered in commemorative plates or spoons. The center of the room was an overstuffed couch and chair set, corduroy covering all of it. There was no way to know where to look, every surface had something on it. There was a large picture of a blonde woman with the words "A Candle in The Wind" written beneath it. Tamra started to feel claustrophobic just standing there.

They looked through an open door into a small kitchen. The fridge was sealed shut, but rust had taken its toll, leaving gaps in the door. The food inside was decades past rot and had lost all odor. It was inert. They checked through the cupboards. This place had never been looted, twenty years and it was untouched. The bottles of water, lined up in plastic, were still clear, no trace of contamination. It was better than they could have hoped for. Chad cracked one open and passed it to Tyson. Tamra realized that in that moment she might actually be in love with him. The second bottle went to Evie, third to Tamra, and finally, he took one for himself. "Bottoms up. Let's see if there's any food."

They ransacked the place and found some. The basement contained shelves of preserves and a good collection of rum. Tamra said, "So, guess we get to go home rich huh?"

"What do you mean?" Chad asked.

"You have any idea what pre-apocalypse rum is worth? And most of this stuff was worth a lot before the world went to hell. You are looking at being able to retire if you play your cards right with this stuff."

"Had no idea. Wait, how the hell does a TV star know the price of things on the black market?"

"Girls gotta have her secrets."

They took one of the bottles and cracked it open. Tamra insisted. "We aren't going to finish it, but you should at least try it, find out what it's like to live the high life."

They all took a swig, even Evie, who said, "I'm an adult now, at least in my home. I've had a drink before."

The rum was smooth and sweet, leaving a pleasant burn in their chests. Evie said, "That's nothing like what I've had before."

"Moonshine, right?"

"What's moonshine?"

"You guys made it yourself."

"Oh, yeah, Clyde lets a little of it be brewed for festivals. Not too much, he believes strong drink is a tool of the devil, but on festivals it's all right."

"Yeah, shine was basically free in the old word. Some of this stuff was north of a hundred and fifty a bottle."

They stopped after a couple of drinks, Tamra had a nice soft glow on, feeling happy and soft. She had found something else. An amazing find. These were the type of people to prepare for an emergency. There were tubes of toothpaste and unopened toothbrushes, many of them. She handed Chad a tube of toothpaste and one of the toothbrushes, then started brushing her own teeth. He took the hint and did the same. Tyson grabbed a set himself and went to brush his teeth. Evie looked at them in puzzlement. "What are you doing?"

"Cleaning our teeth. Don't your people do that."

"No, not ever."

"Okay sweetie, just watch what we do. It makes your teeth last a lot longer."

The girls copied them as well. Once Tamra was sure her mouth felt like it belonged to a human being again she walked into the other room, beckoning Chad to follow her. "So, now that I have reasonable breath I think it's time we did a lot of kissing."

He walked straight to her, took her in his arms and started kissing her, a deep passionate kiss.

It was an amazing moment, an amazing kiss. It was everything Tamra hoped it would be. Chad held her body tight, close to his. He was slender but surprisingly strong. They kissed for a long time until Evie cleared her throat behind them. "Um, guys, we might want to keep going. Clyde is still looking for us."

"Yeah, sorry kid. Tamra, that was amazing! A lot more of that once we aren't being hunted by a tribe of cannibal religious fanatics."

"Agreed. Let's go."

They took as many of the preserves with them as they could, only ones that appeared to still be good, and they went looking for another house. No point in staying inside a place after breaking the door, that just announced their presence.

There was a place a bit set back from the road. The door was open already, no need to break in. They made their way inside; the place was little more than a mobile home and was in terrible shape. It was warm enough that it didn't matter too much, and they just needed shelter for the rapidly approaching night. They huddled under blankets they had raided from the first house, moth eaten and threadbare, but there were enough of them that they kept them warm. It was the first night they had been truly comfortable since they escaped from Meat Cove.

The next morning was rainy again, a slow, insidious rain. The kind that seeps color, warmth, hope from the world. However, they were able to raid several rain coats from the houses. The coats had mold on them and weren't nearly as waterproof as they had been twenty years ago but were better than nothing. Tyson finally had proper clothing as well, it was decayed, falling apart around him, but again, better than nothing. They started down the coast in the grey drizzle.

Later that day they reached the ferry. It was a narrow channel, leading from the part of the island they were on to the part of the island they needed to reach. The ferry was there, three-quarters submerged rotten decks sticking up above the waterline. The boat felt like the death of hope. If there was a ferry that meant it was probably a long way around, and there was no way they could swim that. It wasn't far, but they were too cold. Maybe if it was still the height of summer, but it was a cold autumn day. They would go into the water and not come out.

"We need to find a boat. Might be one of the houses has one, or at least something we can use as one. Let's start searching, remember, any house with a closed door absolutely without question has zombies in it," Chad said.

They split up, traveling through the small town that used to service the ferry. It was slow going, each house had to be cleared of zombies before they could go in, and then once the house was deemed safe they had to search it. Tamra hadn't hit a single zombie so far, which made her decided she needed to be extra cautious.

She heard a sound behind her, coming from outside the small house she was searching. A giant man with a long beard was behind her. He swung his fist catching her in the side of the face, knocking her to the ground. As she fell she realized that he was living. She tried to turn over and crawl away, but he took a giant gaff hook and drove it through her shoulder.

Tamra had always thought that enough pain would make you pass out, but apparently, that wasn't true. There was no relief for it, the giant hook ground inside her flesh, pulling and tearing, but so deep in the meat of her shoulder that it couldn't pull out. She tried and tried to stop, to brace herself, but the giant man holding the other end of the hook didn't even seem to notice. Her hands ripped off of anything she held on to, leaving her palms bloodied and bruised, flesh torn to ribbons. He dragged her through the street, yelling as he went, "You want to see your pretty blonde friend again, come find me."

A Scream in the Daylight

C had heard Tamra's scream. He ran out of the ruined house he was exploring, vaulting over the front railing and running as fast as his legs would carry him. He heard the deep voice telling him to follow. He knew it was a trap, but he didn't care. He ran towards the voice anyway. As he rounded a corner he saw the man Evie had called Clyde walking down the street, dragging Tamra along behind him. The cruel hook in her shoulder shedding her blood into the wet street. Chad ran towards the man until suddenly he stopped short, fell backward onto the street. Tyson was standing above him. "That's just suicide. You want to save her you have to do it differently."

"Fuck."

Chad lay on the ground, back aching. There were a dozen or so villagers around the big man. How they had missed seeing his mad dash he didn't know, but they hadn't.

Clyde had Tamra. Also, Chad loved Tamra. Completely and unreservedly. It had taken him a while to separate that from what he'd felt for women before, the kiss had clarified it, let his head know what his heart was already certain of. He needed to save her, to reach her, but Tyson was right. If he could trade his life for hers, he wouldn't hesitate, but his mad rush would have only served to see them die together. It needed to be smarter than that.

Chad gathered his wits, pulled himself together. He got up off the ground and walked to a nearby porch. He sat down on the step and took a deep breath. "I think I fucked this up."

"Yeah, just a little. We all did. So, how do we save her?"

"Give me five minutes to think and I'll figure it out."

Evie caught up to them a second later. "Told you he didn't give up."

"Yeah, you were right. Now we have to get her back."

"I know. I'm not sure I should stay with you though. I don't want to go back. Not ever."

"What else would you do?"

"I'm away now, I can make it to wherever I want. I can find your people, get them to take me in."

"Okay. Look, it's not like I'm somebody there, okay. I'm just a soldier, but there's enough people who know me. Tell them you know Chad Lee, tell them everything. Hell, get them to send in the cavalry."

"What does that mean?"

"You know, I don't have a clue. It's just something I hear the old folks say from time to time."

"Okay. Thanks for all the help you've given me. I don't think I would have had the courage to leave on my own."

Evie left, walking through along the shore. She vanished from sight. Chad had no idea how she planned to make it to Sydney, but he believed she would accomplish it. In the short time since he'd met the girl, he'd seen her manage amazing things. He was almost jealous of her, provided he didn't remember that she had been raised by a crazed cannibal cult who wanted to marry her to a junior psychopath.

After Evie left Tyson and Chad had to go. If they took too long they could lose Clyde's trail or be too late to save Tamra. The woods were dark ahead of them, they couldn't see Clyde and his men anymore, even though it had only been a few minutes. They started to walk towards the woods, following the path. Chad was on high alert, convinced that at any moment he would find himself face to face with Clyde, unprepared for what was happening. Of course, the whole thing was a trap. Clyde had almost put up a sign saying "Trap". Didn't matter though, it wasn't like he had another choice.

Clyde wasn't far up the path. Chad spotted him before he got too far in. He took his bow off his shoulder and knocked an arrow, sighting on the large man. He was moving too much, Chad couldn't get a shot off on target. He had to get closer, and if he did was probably going to be seen. Tamra was lying on the forest floor, writhing in agony. Her small form looked tiny next to the giant cult leader. Then again, Clyde was almost a head taller than the next tallest man with him. He had a long beard, salt and pepper, full, bushy. His hair was down past his shoulder, somewhere between dreads and mats, there was a lot of it. His body was covered in an ankle length oil coat, layers and layers of rags underneath it. He was a messianic figure, and he had Tamra on the end of a hook. The dozen men around him were armed with similar things, improvised weapons, farm and fishing implements. Chad knew his only advantage was range, and that was negated by Tamra's presence. If he fired an arrow one of them might decide to kill her.

He watched, and then Clyde spoke up. "I know you're there. Come out, face me like a man."

"Why the hell would I do that?" Tyson replied, from off to Chad's left.

"I don't mean you. I know about you red man. I mean the other one, the soldier. I want him to see what his interference in God's plan has cost."

Chad said, "Okay, sure. I'll come out, then you'll kill her, then you'll kill me."

"No, you come out you get to come back to the village, both of you. What happens from there depends on you. If you can find God you are welcome to stay, to join us. If you are found wanting, well, you join the blessed."

"You know, that sounds like a shitty deal."

Clyde twisted the hook. Tamra screamed. Chad stepped out, "Okay, you got me. I'll come quietly."

"Drop the bow, the machete, any knives you have. We're going to search you. If you have any weapons on you, we'll hurt you a lot more."

Chad dropped his gear. All of it. After he dropped all of his weapons he stepped forward. He did as Clyde demanded, dropped everything. The big man gestured to two of his men who started to search Chad. They gave him a very, very thorough pat down, basically prison level. Chad couldn't remember the last time he had felt so violated. He didn't fight back. Afterwards, Clyde came over to him. "Good, you did as you were told. Now, where's my daughter in law."

"You mean the little girl? She jumped in the ocean when she realized you were near."

Clyde slammed his huge fist into Chad's face. The pain bloomed, filling the entire world. Chad fell to the ground, boneless. It took a few minutes for him to be aware of his surroundings again. Once he rejoined the world he realized that he was stripped naked, tied hand and foot. Clyde stood over him, bloody hook in hand. "Let's try that again. Where's Evie?"

"Seriously man, I have no... aggh!"

The hook bit deep into Chad's bicep, separating muscle from bone. Pain, his whole being was consumed with pain. He burned, deep in his soul, the fire tore him to pieces. Then Clyde twisted the hook, pulling tendons and flesh away, the pain was more, greater. He didn't think was possible, but it was. He screamed and screamed. Clyde looked down at him, a slight twist of a smile visible on his lips. The smile reached his eyes, a dark humor twinkled forth, making it clear he found Chad's pain a source of amusement.

He ground a heel into Chad's thigh, pulling up with the hook at the same time. Chad began to retch, the pain in complete control of him. He knew in that moment that he would do anything, anything at all, to make that feeling stop. "Okay, one more time, where the fuck is Evie?"

"I don't know. I don't. I wish I did, but she left when she knew you were coming."

"Okay, I think I believe you. Still, just in case," he twisted the hook again.

Chad screamed more, he screamed until his voice died. After that, he sobbed. The blood leaked from his arm onto the ground mixing with Tamra's. She was lying, eyes closed, just next to him. She was pale, more pale than usual. Despite the pain, he was happy to be lying near her, to have the ability to reach out and touch her, even if his arm couldn't reach her right at that moment.

His world went black.

When Chad opened his eyes, he was lying on a threadbare carpet, it was cold and smelled like mildew. Decaying furniture surrounded him. He started shaking, his arms and legs still bound. He needed to move, to bring his shoulders forward, to get his arms out of that position. The pain in his left bicep was all encompassing. It had no respite, no break. He was desperate to move.

Clyde walked into view. His leather boots scuffed and filthy. "Okay Chinaman, you gonna find God soon. I promise you that. One way or another."

"Please, please, just let my arms go. I need my arms free."

"Sure, I'm pretty certain that you can't even swing a punch. I could let you go, but you know what, I don't feel like it."

Chad strained at his bonds, his left arm was far, far too weak. He didn't know if he was ever going to be able to use that arm again. Tyson was there too, in his view plane, lying on the ground, beaten and bloody. That meant all three of them. All that work was for nothing. They hadn't made it anywhere. He hoped Evie was on her way to Sydney. At least that way there would be one positive thing to come out of all of it.

"On the other hand, I might just let your pretty friend here out of her bonds. She could use a real man in her life, I'm pretty sure.

"You touch her, and I will kill you."

"I thought there might be some life left in you. It's a shame really, you seem like a decent man, at least from the little I've seen. Too bad you had to go and take Evie. I could have just killed you easy and painless if you hadn't done that."

"I told you, she ran off as soon as she knew you were near."

"Yes, I know. I believe you completely, but you put her in a position to do that. I can't have that. My flock has to be loyal, or else their souls will be at risk."

"Wow, I get why Evie ran away."

Clyde kicked him in the stomach, a short kick, not too much power in it. Chad was pretty sure one of his ribs cracked. The sharp pain in his stomach from the rock was still there too. He was a mass of pain, wounds upon wounds, scars upon scars.

Chad threw up, his ribs ached so much he couldn't comprehend it. His arm was destroyed. As he vomited Clyde kicked him again, in the head this time. He saw stars.

"Alright, so Evie took off to visit your buddies in Sydney then. I guess we follow her. Little bitch can't be allowed to think she can just go do whatever she wants, she's going to have to come in line. Sets a bad precedent."

One of the men untied Chad's ankles. A woman, older, but still showing evidence that she had been pretty in her younger days, walked over to Chad and spat on him. "She was my daughter you monster. She was my daughter and you killed her."

Right, the little girl. That might have been his biggest regret in this whole thing, but he was pretty sure he would have done the same thing if it came up again. He didn't have a choice, and despite how she haunted him he still had to put his own people first. Not that it mattered. All that pain, all that torment, and he shackled and in the grips of these madmen, along with the few survivors among the people he had set out to save.

"You get to walk with us. Doesn't sound pleasant? Well, it's walk, or I drag you."

Chad struggled to stand, despite having his arms bound behind his back. The men laughed as he struggled. He coughed, his mouth filled with liquid. He spat it out, staining the floor crimson. Tried to stand again, unable to care that he was naked, the pain stripped even that away from him.

Eventually, after he fell several times, Clyde pulled him up by his injured arm, causing him to scream again. The pain caught his ribs as he did, and he almost fell again, but Clyde kept him standing. "You go down again I don't pick you up. I just pick a meaty bit and haul you along with my hook."

Chad did everything he could to stay on his feet, his vision swam, the world going wavy and dark around the edges. He swallowed, again, again, and got the nausea under control. The darkness brightened, his vision clearing, and he stayed on his feet. Tyson came next. Tyson was beaten and bloody, but it didn't look like they'd done as much to him this time around. Chad wasn't fooled that Tyson had gotten off easy though, when they had first found him he was in at least as bad shape as Chad was now. He was also naked, blood providing his only covering.

Finally, they hauled Tamra out. She had been in a separate room. She was in the same shape as Chad, her shoulder still dripping blood from the hook. She looked at Chad, saw the shape he was in and started to sob. "Shut up bitch," the man holding her said.

"Fuck you. You don't wanna hear people cry, don't fucking torture them. What is wrong with you?"

"God has ordained that we and only we are his chosen. You are nothing, grist for the mill, no more," Clyde said.

"You know, when I was little I read the bible. I don't remember anything about psycho cannibals being the chosen," Tamra said, "In fact, I'm pretty sure that there was a whole said about this kind of shit being bad."

Clyde backhanded her, sending her naked body tumbling into the wall. It was clear he hadn't put much effort into the blow. Chad was sure it would have knocked him down just as easily. Clyde was a monster, a giant. How the hell was he supposed to fight that?

"You will shut your mouth whore. Treat me with the respect I deserve, or I will thrash you to the edge of death, and then let the men fuck your whorish parts until you die."

"Right, it's always rape with you types. Well, if that's what you need to do to get your little pecker hard, that's what you gotta do. I notice you didn't threaten to rape me personally. Bet you can't even get it up for a woman huh? So, is it little boys or little girls? Bet it doesn't matter to you."

"Gag the slut."

One of the men stuffed a filthy rag into Tamra's mouth, tying it tight around her head. Clyde lifted her off the ground and set her down on her feet. "You will walk, and you will do so in silence."

The group started traveling, looking for tracks. They picked up Evie's small feet after a few minutes. Just a single print. A bit further there was a broken stalk of grass that was recent and out of place. It was slow going, and the day was cold. It wasn't long before the pain was only Chad's second highest priority. "Look, if you wanna kill us, just kill us. Otherwise you have to put something on us, because too much more of this and we die of hypothermia."

"You outsiders are weak. Pathetic."

"Well, let's trade. You give me the coat and layers of warm clothes, you march down the road naked, we'll see how you stack up," Chad said, teeth chattering.

To his surprise, Clyde laughed. He took off his coat, then started stripping down until he was naked. "Give them covering, just blankets. Enough to keep them alive. Shoes too. Also, someone carry my things."

Clyde was huge, muscles on muscles, greying hair covered his body, almost like a pelt. It was more like a bear than a man. Clyde started walking, comfortable and relaxed. Chad regretted his choice to speak to a degree, but the warmth of the blanket on his shoulders made up for a lot.

They marched on, through the cold. Every time Chad faltered one of the men poked him. Clyde didn't put anything else on, apparently completely unaffected by the weather. After several hours when they finally stopped Clyde said, "Satisfied? God provides all the warmth I need, and no soft mainlander is going to make me believe otherwise.

Chad took more from that statement than was probably intended. He realized that Clyde didn't know where they were from, that meant there were gaps in his knowledge. Maybe not something he could exploit, but maybe he could as well.

When they finally settled for the night Chad was placed on the ground between Tyson and Tamra. He looked at the blonde woman and said, "Hey, how are you holding up?"

They had removed her gag when they set her down, she replied, "Well, that gag tasted like sweat and mold. I think they grabbed it from the dirty laundry basket in the house. I mean, twenty-year-old dirty laundry... I'm probably going to die of some sort of rare disease, if the blood loss and infection don't get me first. Other than that, peachy. How are you?"

"About the same. At least I didn't have the rag in my mouth. That seems like it might be a fate worse than death."

"Oh yeah, well it's your fault I had to watch Clyde's hairy ass crack all day. That might be a fate worse than death."

"Good thing we probably won't live very much longer then."

Tyson sighed and then said, "Could you two stop being so fucking cute? I mean, I don't mind dying too much at this point, but to have to listen to adorable couple shit? That's too much to ask." Despite the circumstances, his voice had a touch of laughter in it.

"Okay, so, we're about to be killed by psychotic cannibals in terrible ways. The hell are we all laughing at?" Chad said.

"Well, not like we can do shit about it, might as well laugh while we still have breath right? I mean, if I die at least I can die smiling. It's the only thing I can do to defy that bible thumping sexist mother fucker." Tamra shuffled closer to Chad, her shoulder rubbing against his."

"I think you forgot racist. Seems like his followers all share a skin color with you."

"He might be, but he did try to convert me, and I ain't exactly white either. Thought that shit died with most of humanity."

"Yeah, back home I'm not Asian, I'm just breathing, seems like they didn't get the message that it's just dead or living here in Meat Cove."

"Yeah. It's weird, I hear old people talk about it all the time, how there used to be different races, how unfair the world was. Until this group I hadn't seen it though, just us and the dead."

Tamra said, "I was ten when it hit. I saw a bit of racism before. Hell, my own family were pretty terrible. Thing is, once everyone died there was no point in it. We couldn't be so damned stupid anymore, the few of us still alive had to pull together, didn't matter race. Dad went and married a native woman after mom turned. Took a while, but hey."

"This shit is so stupid. There's what, a few hundred million of us worldwide, at the most, and we're fighting over scraps of land. There's enough space for everyone. Hell, it takes a week to get from Meat Cove to Sydney. Not like we wouldn't share." Chad said this last loud enough to make sure that everyone could hear him.

"So, the Chinaman wants to share our land, does he? Well, it's our land and the Godless don't get to share."

Tyson said, "It was my people's land before it was yours, so why don't you just give it back? I mean, not like you are making use of most of it anyway."

"How did I get saddled with fools like you? Don't you understand that you are my prisoners, that if you provoke me I might just torture you to death?"

"Yeah, we get it. Thing is, we don't really give a shit. With what you've done to us you might as well. It's not like we have any reason to hope for nice treatment."

"Oh, you still have something. You don't know how much pain a man can endure. I may teach you if you insist on this insolence though."

Chad decided not to provoke the big man anymore, so he shut his mouth and sat, observing. It was the same strategy he had employed at the village, provoke, create chaos, hope that led to mistakes, slip ups. Chaos in your enemy was opportunity for you.

Sometime after he had fallen asleep he woke to feel a tugging at his wrist, then a sharp dig. He suppressed the outcry that was on the tip of his tongue as he heard a young voice say "Shh".

In a moment his wrists were free, a shape flitted to Tamra and started working on her wrists. Evie said, "Go, get Tyson free. If we move fast they might not wake up." Her voice was quiet, soft, the kind of voice that didn't carry in the night.

Chad started working to free Tyson's wrists, pulling apart the knots. In a minute he had him untied and ready to move.

Evie led them into the trees, they followed her as quietly as possible.

She led them to an old cabin, about an hour away. It was a simple log building, no lock on the door. Evie took them inside.

Once they closed the door behind them she said, "I got a little ways then I realized I didn't want to leave you. You risked a lot to let me come with you. It would make me like him, a monster. So, I came back. I've been following you all day. I never heard anyone talk to him like you guys did. I'm surprised he didn't just kill you."

"Nah, he needed to break us in front of his men. Killing us wouldn't do it. I've met lots of men like him. They don't think, not really."

"Wait," said Tamra, "You were goading him on purpose?"

"Yeah, I figured he would hurt me for it, but he would make sure to keep us alive. He couldn't kill us while we were still defying him. I thought you were doing the same."

"No, he just pissed me off."

The cabin had been occupied somewhat recently, and the original occupant was still there, a skeleton lying on a lone bunk bed, the flesh rotted almost totally off its bones. There was a clean hole in the center of the skull. Whoever it was had made sure they wouldn't be coming back.

The cabin was rough, clearly made by hand. It contained a few meager supplies, mostly in the form of old cans. Nothing that seemed appetizing right away, but it was something and at this point calories were calories. They opened one of the tins and discovered a thick, grey mush. Chad didn't recognize it, but he took a tiny bit on his finger and tasted it. It was salty and rich, thick. It tasted vaguely like mushrooms. He decided it was good and they shared it between the four of them, not talking as they ate.

The food left them thirsty, so Chad took a pair of threadbare overalls from the cabin, threw them on, and took a pot to see if he could find water. He also took a small hatchet that was there. It was the kind of tool that would be used for splitting small logs. Still, at least he had some sort of weapon.

RESOURCE ECONOMIES: RECLAIMING THE ZOMBIE APOCALYPSE

The night was dark, heavy clouds obscured the stars. There was a chill in the air, it was too cold for his overalls, but they were still better than nothing.

He wandered through the woods, carefully. With the lack of light, it was a terrible risk. He knew thought that all of them were too beat up, that they needed to take care of their bodies for the next little while, they were near the point where their bodies wouldn't keep them alive much longer if they didn't do something to change the dynamic.

After an hour or so he found a stream by stepping in it. He scooped the pot full of water and headed back to the cabin. He was able to find it quickly, he'd been careless, but lucky. It could have ended with him wandering the entire night, lost to the world. When he got inside Tamra and Tyson were asleep on the floor, while Evie was curled up where the skeleton had been. Apparently, they'd moved it while he was away.

He lay down, just for a minute, just to get a tiny bit of rest. When he woke up sunlight was streaming through chinks in the log walls. Everyone was up.

"Hey, turns out there's a stove in here. We boiled up the water, it's ready to go." Tyson was standing over the stove, heating something in a pot.

"Huh... oh, yeah, cool. Boiling it, good idea."

"Yeah, also there's a few more cans here. The grey stuff if cream of mushroom soup. It's pretty tasty, especially when you cook it right."

"What should we have done?"

"Well, you're supposed to add water and heat it up. That's it. Here, have a bowl."

They set some food on the rickety table, a few sticks underneath a board. Chad ate it, and it was ambrosia, the greatest thing he had ever eaten in his life.

"How old are these cans?"

"The expiry date is almost twenty years ago. We're lucky opening it didn't kill us all. Still, they knew how to make soup back before the world died."

"Apparently. The amount of salt in this, I don't think there's a bacterium in the world that could survive it."

"Yeah, guess that's why we got to eat this sumptuous repast."

They ate and searched the cabin. It was a single room, a latrine pit dug out back was long since gone to soil, but they could tell what it had been once upon a time.

There was the pair of overalls, a long shirt, a jacket, and a pair of long johns. Tyson took the long johns and the jacket, Tamra the shirt, since it was long enough to be a dress on her. Chad kept his overalls. There was also a pair of socks and pair of boots, but they were too small for Chad and Tyson and far too large for Tamra. The socks were worse than nothing when trekking through the woods if they weren't accompanied by boots.

The four of them started into the forest, Evie was the only reason they weren't completely lost. She'd scouted the general area the night before. She led them to the shore in minutes. The ferry was there, a little way up the bay, grounded as they had noticed before. It was a long, narrow bay. They were near the head of it, just a short jaunt until they had a possibility of crossing, a ruined stretch of road that had clearly flooded many times but was above the waterline at this point.

They crossed the bay by the road, trying to stay out of sight. Last time they had screwed up by going into a town, by being visible. This time Chad was determined to do it right, to stay out of sight. That is until he saw the lodge.

It was remote, isolated, made of logs, but carefully constructed, clearly weatherproof. The roof was made of some sort of black, shiny material, and despite the dirt on it, it appeared to be perfectly intact. They walked up to the front step, log, but intact and secure. The door proved to be unlocked but latched. They walked in, carefully.

Inside there were three residents. Old zombies, possibly even first night zombies from the condition of them. All three turned to the open door, making their way slowly towards the group. Three men, tall and fit from the look of it, at least once upon a time. Now they were emaciated, well-dressed corpses.

Chad moved into the closest one, bring his hatchet into its knee, using the blunt end. The knee shattered, a sickening pop momentarily overwhelming the moaning of the creatures. The zombie fell to one side, still reaching for Chad.

RESOURCE ECONOMIES: RECLAIMING THE ZOMBIE APOCALYPSE

Tamra took the second one, grabbing its outstretched arms and spun it, moving it out of the door. She shut the door behind it. Evie and Tyson worked on the third. Evie baited it, staying just out of its reach. Tyson grabbed the nearest heavy object he could find, a silver tipped cane, and smashed the creature as hard as he could in the temple. It fell to the ground, grey matter leaking across the wooden floor.

Chad took the opportunity to hit his zombie with the sharp edge of the hatchet, cleaving deep into its skull, another corpse dealt with.

Finally, they opened the door and Tyson brought the cane down on the third, no point leaving a sign post to where they were.

The inside of the lodge was luxurious. Somehow the windows were intact, although almost impossible to see through, scratched and pitted. The material wasn't glass, it was something else. There were large chairs facing a fireplace, a set of stairs leading up to a second story, and a door leading deeper into the building. Every wall had an animals head on it.

There was a safe on one wall, underneath the head of a massive buck. It contained rifles and shotguns, a dozen of them. They didn't see any ammo, but that didn't mean it wasn't there.

Chad said, "Let's search this place, as fast as we can. If we can get ammo, good. If we can't, let's find whatever weapons we can use. We need to be out of here fast though if we can't get the guns. If we have them, we hang out and wait for a bit, hope Clyde catches up with us. This place with guns on our side, we win."

They started the search. In the end, there was half a box of ammo, nothing more. The gun safe was locked up tight. They could see the weapons, even touch them, but not get them out. There was nothing edible, not that had survived the twenty years. It was a bust. The only clothing was what was on the zombies. They did manage to gather up a few hunting knives, one bow with ten arrows, and an axe. Tyson took that, it was full size.

"We're a bit better armed than before, and a bit warmer. Let's keep going, get as far as we can by daylight. We still have days and days of walking in front of us before we reach safety."

Make Them Pay

Junie was pissed. He only had Earl left with him, and the prisoner was dead. Time to unleash the last horde. Maybe that and some explosives would convince the camp to leave or at least kill them all. He was getting ready to go when he heard a sound from outside.

The soldiers were on the stairs! A whole lot of them. Well, he had a plan for that. He pulled a rope and there was an explosion. The stairs fell away from the side of the building, leaving only the small platform at the top. Junie walked out on it, looked down, and laughed. A dozen of the black clad men were lying on the ground, in a heap.

"You should have stayed away. This place is ours."

"Why don't you come down and we can talk about it?", a tall man with black hair said.

"Naw, why don't you fuck off back to New York. I killed your boy, he's lying on the ground floor inside. You should go get his body."

"You think we're deaf? We know what's in there."

Junie spat at the tall man, hitting him in the shoulder.

"Alright, that's the way you wanna play it. Keep in mind, we have guns."

"Yeah, I know what you all got. So, here's what I got." Junie pulled another chord and the warehouse doors blew, falling open. The zombies started to stream out, hundreds of them, all reaching for the men in front of them. The men Junie wanted to see dead.

He knew he didn't have a chance, but at least he could take out as many of the Godless as possible.

The blessed started grabbing hold of the black clad men, biting at them, trying to bear them to the ground. The soldiers fought back. Junie laughed and grabbed his bow. It was an old-fashioned longbow, the kind that had been used for hundreds and hundreds of years.

He fired an arrow, aimed at the tall man's leg. The man went down, the bolt through his thigh. He found another target and fired, this time through an arm. He was drawing a third shaft back when a crack broke the air. It didn't even hurt much, but suddenly he had no strength. The arrow fell, useless and broken. Then Junie joined it descending to the ground, a swan dive into the waiting horde.

I Fall Down

Bennett felt a momentary tug at his right leg. Nothing much, for a moment, then the pain hit. His leg went out from underneath him and he fell, the zombies piling on top of him. This was the second time in a couple of days he'd been in this position. At least he had his blade on him. He stabbed one zombie in the temple, then another, then another. His arm was lead, no strength left. The zombies were chewing on his armor. It was strong. He could take this for a while, but eventually, the links would give if he didn't get clear.

Each zombie he dropped was replaced, after a while it took a little longer for the next one though. There were brief moments of respite, brief moments where he thought he might be able to get through them before they got through his armor. If any of them hit his injured leg that would be a different story, the links were already weak, and the odds of them breaking were much, much higher than the rest of the armor.

He fought on, long past the end of his strength. His arm shook, shook worse, he felt bile rise in his throat, his breath caught in his chest. He kept stabbing, brains and ichor flowed over his helmet, covering his visor, until finally, he couldn't see. He kept stabbing, by feel alone. The corpses weight bearing down on him. At some point, he realized there was nothing left to stab. He pushed, found himself unable to move the corpse on top of him. There was nothing left in his arms, at least not enough to push himself free. The dull red in his visor faded to pure black. He woke some time later, hands pulling him up.

"Hey boss, good to see you."

Bennett pulled off his helmet, allowing light to reach his eyes.

"Hey. Did we win?"

"Yeah, nobody without a pulse still moving here. We did it."

"Thank god. The villagers?"

"Two fresh, the guy who fell and another one. He put up a bit of a fight, but we took him out. There was another one, he had Coschek with him, on the floor where the zombies were. Neither one turned, heads destroyed in the fall."

"Okay, well, that was a fucked up situation. You all did amazing. Now, we have more work to do. These bastards need to be put down."

Naomi came up to him, her armor covered in gore and dirt. "So, we lived through another one. Time to bring this shit to them."

"That an order boss?"

"Yep. Damn, right it is. Motherfuckers need to pay. I was on board with killing them before, now I want them exterminated. Sooner than later."

"Okay, we leave a skeleton crew behind, make our way up to Meat Cove. Take them all down."

"You know how bad this is going to be right?"

"Yeah, I do. I know we can't leave any of them."

"Kuru can show up decades later. They've been eating people, none of them can join us, they pose too high a risk. That means kids, old folks, women, whoever."

"Yeah, I know. We've talked about this in council meetings."

"You ready to shoot a kid?"

"Yeah, if I have to."

"Well, we have to. No question at all."

They gathered the soldiers together back in camp and started to develop the best plan of attack they could. The next phase was to call the council and brief them. As they were waiting for the radio Naomi said, "I'm pretty sure I'd rather be covered in honey and left out for fire ants than make this call, how much you want to bet Barbara tries to veto?"

"She won't, she can't. It's policy, and policy she drafted. We don't let cannibals survive. Too many dangers to us. They can't be reintegrated, they can't be reasoned with. It's not a workable solution. We have to fight them, and we have to kill them."

The voice on the other end came over, static filled and distant, but clear enough. "Go ahead. Over."

"We have identified the source of our issues. We have a community of cannibals in the area. Over."

"Okay, I'll bring the council in. Over."

The first voice they heard was clearly Barbara. Her tone was flint, mixed with Iron. "Cannibals. Of course. It had to be cannibals, didn't it? Well, that changes things. Over."

Taylor spoke next. "No, it doesn't. It delays things by a bit, but it doesn't change things. There's enough material in salvage to justify this expedition, already waiting at the dockyards here. I've run the numbers and even with everything we are up by a huge amount. You are trying to sabotage this, again. I've had enough of it. Stop trying to tear things apart, we need someone who's willing to build, not destroy."

They could almost hear the silence on the other end of the radio. Nobody talked to Barbara like that, and it was likely that nobody other than Taylor could get away with it. Everyone was full of tension, on edge with the rift. Finally, Barbara spoke. "It was never my intention to jeopardize the mission. As you know I had concerns about resource usage. Once the materials started flowing in I made peace with it and gave my blessing. Now, with these cannibals, I have to wonder if we wouldn't have been better not starting, following my original thoughts, but that ship has sailed, and now we have to hope that even with the added complication we are able to make it all work. Over."

Bennett said, "So, as per policy we are going to root out the nest. These people can't be allowed to stay in place. Over."

"Of course not. I proposed that policy myself. Once we know of a cannibal group we have to exterminate them. Do we know numbers? Over."

"Not exactly. Less than a thousand, more than five hundred. They are in a place called Meat Cove, of all things. Over."

"They are proud of their cannibalism? Over."

"No, it's a pre-apocalypse name. The place has high cliffs and the natives used to drive herds of animals over them, harvesting the meat from the rocks below. It's a very, very old name. They have incidences of Kuru showing up frequently. They call it going Wendigo and seem to have adopted a variant Christian cult status. Messianic leader, all that nonsense. Nothing we haven't seen a few times before. Their numbers are high though, it's going to be a bitch. We could use more men. Over"

"Not a chance in hell. You have to do it with the team you have. Over."

"I figured. Well, nothing for it but to get started. Once we have this in hand we will get back on schedule with shipping resources back. Over."

Barbara said, "Good luck. Come back in one piece. Over and out."

The radio clicked off, leaving dead air. Bennett wondered if this was really how people used to use the radio. It was so stilted, so strange. Not something that was ever part of his world.

"So, she didn't get a chance to bitch," Naomi said, "Guess you win that one."

"Yeah, but Taylor is going to face some pretty heavy consequences pretty soon."

"Yeah, nothing we can do to help either. I hate that woman, a lot."

They went to Bennett's tent and laid out the old-world maps, updated as best they could be.

"Looks like Meat Cove is at least a week away on foot. Best to go with as many troops as we think we can spare. Maybe leave a dozen here to cover off, plus support people. Get the troops out there, in some force."

"Yeah, fuck. This is the last thing I wanted this trip to turn into. We are supposed to be bringing hope, not destruction. Now I gotta go kill a bunch of people. Damnit."

They drew up plans, set marching orders in place, and started their people moving through the wilderness, fully equipped. Bennett took the lead. Naomi was against him going, but he couldn't leave something like this to someone else, he needed to look at these people as he gunned them down.

"Look, babe, I don't think I would ever be able to live with myself if I told my soldiers to shoot children and I didn't go to at least face the reality. Would you really be able to look me in the eye again?"

"No, but I don't like it. You're a commander now, not a field soldier. You don't belong out there."

"Field soldier? I think you forget that I'm an accountant. The rest of it is just what happened when everything went to shit."

"Babe, you were an accountant for what, three years? That was twenty years ago. You're a soldier, a survivor, a general. Face it, that idea you have in your head isn't true, not even a little bit. It's old world thinking. In a way I can't wait for the rest of the world to catch up to the reality, none of us are what we were before first night, and who we are is who we've been for twenty years. Hell, do you know what Barbara did before the zombies?"

"You know, I don't. Everyone knows about the farmhouse and how incredible her story is. I think she writes it at the bottom of every memo, but I don't have a clue what she did."

"Nothing. She inherited a tiny bit of money from her mother and she lived off that. Never had a job, never married, no kids, she did literally nothing. She's just what she is now, a former colonel turned politician."

"Well, that's actually kind of interesting. I always thought she was a student or something."

"No, a waste of space really."

"So, kind of like now?"

"I have to be fair to the woman, we needed her in the early days, but we don't need her now, and she's poison. She's too stuck in immediate survival mode to see that there can be a larger vision for the future. That's why I backed this idea, expanding our civilization, building new colonies, new homes."

"Still, she's a bitch. No doubt, no debate."

"Somewhere along the line I think power became its own motivator, now she does what she does to keep it. I don't know, if I ever got to that point, shoot me in the head."

"Nope, I'll shoot you in the stomach and then set you loose in a council meeting. Might be that would be the best thing that could possibly happen."

"Not unless you make sure Taylor is gone. She still trains every day you know?"

"Really? Every day? It's almost like she survived a zombie apocalypse or something."

"I know, but don't let on. People might start expecting council members to be able to do things. I sure as hell don't want to go back to training."

"You sure, I do it. Part of the job. All officers have to keep their field skills up. You never know when something like this might happen."

It took two days to get ready for the mission. They gathered supplies, got restocked with ammunition, got their armour cleaned and repaired, then they started along the road.

RESOURCE ECONOMIES: RECLAIMING THE ZOMBIE APOCALYPSE

They were exhausted from the days of fighting zombies. Bennet decided to move anyway because waiting meant giving the people at Meat Cove more time to prepare, a higher chance of sending another like the ones they had killed. It was amazing, primitive hillbillies had given his forces a serious challenge, despite their tiny numbers. It was a matter of using every weapon at hand, using zombies against humans. Bennett had some serious moral qualms about that, but as he marched through the early autumn sunlight he thought about how much more willing he might be to do that with a group like this.

The days were still mostly warm, but storms were picking up. They'd already had a couple. This day, the one they left on, was beautiful. Warm air with gentle breezes carrying the autumn scents of harvest. There were apples and blackberries everywhere. Many of the trees had gone wild, the apples changing to small, hearty varieties, better at producing seeds than at producing a large amount of fruit. Yellowed grass grew long, through cracked roads and along the side of them. It was peaceful, tranquil even. A tranquility that was broken by hundreds of black clad soldiers in full combat kit.

The lightweight chain mail they wore was ideal for zombies. It wasn't heavy, at least not compared to the armour of old, and it wasn't too hot. It was however much hotter than not wearing armour at all. The troops had to keep their pace slow, walking down roads that hadn't seen repairs in at least twenty years, twenty years of ice, snow, slush, melting, freezing. It was rough going. Not for the first time Bennett wished for the old days of smooth roads, vehicles that could make this drive in a couple of hours, not a week or more.

Night fell, and they made camp, setting a simple, flexible barricade. It wasn't going to work against the thousands of zombies they had faced in Sydney, but it was enough for this, a combat mission with every person both armed and armored. There were a couple of zombies in the night, quickly dispatched at the barricade.

Days blurred until Bennett found himself looking at high cliffs over booming surf, a small village visible in the distance, ramshackle and damaged. They had arrived.

But I Get Up Again

Clyde was pushing his dozen men hard. He almost ran, keeping his speed low only because he needed to be able to search the area surrounding the road. The Damned, the Godless. They needed to be broken, to be made to pay and surrender. His people needed to see that the wages of sin weren't just death, but suffering, pain, damnation. He needed to break them. Needed to.

There were traces. A hunting lodge with recently dispatched zombies, broken stalks of grass that showed footprints. He didn't think they had much going for them. The weather had stayed nice, but it was cold at night. No way the godless were staying indoors, he'd know. Every night he marched as late into the evening as he could. He was confident God would protect his people from the blessed. It had worked so far. Two had wandered into camp, only two. He had dispatched both of them. After all, the blessed needed to be contained, they were empty vessels, souls that had been taken to heaven already, or else damned to hell. His people, the truly righteous, they were being tested, shown the path so they could inherit earth reborn as paradise. It was clear, obvious even. He didn't understand why everyone didn't just see it. God was testing man, and only through faith could they survive.

It was like he was Jobe and the Godless were his trials. He would follow them to the end of the earth, and he would destroy them. He owed God, he owed his people.

He started to see more signs of them, fresher signs.

Clouds move in, dark, terrible, storm clouds. Twice the Unbelievers had used a storm to escape him. Twice. Now it was time to reverse that, to use the storm to catch up. He would march through the storm, march into hell if he needed to. He would, nothing could be allowed to stand against him.

As the wind began to pick and the sunlight got lost under darkness one of the men yelled, "We need to get to shelter."

"No. The Godless have used Gods storm to their advantage because we didn't have the courage of our convictions. Now it's our turn, now we use the storm to corner them. We will run them to the ground and we will destroy them."

Clyde started moving forward, his coat flapping in the wind like a pair of wings. The image of it appealed to him - like he was an avenging angel. He needed a flaming sword to brandish, to show them the truth of what he was. He grabbed a branch from a nearby tree and held it aloft, somehow it didn't seem as childish in his giant hands as he had feared it would.

He walked forward, bent against the wind. Branches flew, trees fell, still, he walked on. Nothing touched him. It was true, another sign, he was Gods messenger. Now, he needed to find where the unbelievers were hiding. Lightning crashed, highlighting a derelict shack, tar paper shingles mostly missing. It was odd. The shack, the door was closed. That door should have been flapping in the wind, open to the night. He knew, just knew, that they were inside.

"There."

They walked forward, a dozen of them. Twelve men and one woman. It was like they were the people at the last supper, they were the new apostles. He reached the door and tore it off its hinges. Inside, exactly as he had predicted, the Unbelievers were huddled. Evie was with them, the little whore. Well, if her maidenhead was still intact she could maybe marry Junie, but he didn't buy it for an instant. Girl that age probably spread her legs first chance she got.

The Chinaman was yelling, his words carried away by the wind. He rushed Clyde, a hatchet held high. The redskin was closing in as well. You'd think they'd know better by now. He casually backhanded the Chinaman, smashing him into the far wall. The redskin fell to a kick to the stomach. That left the women. Evie was huddling behind the blonde-haired harlot because of course, she would be. Maybe she hadn't spread her legs for the men. Maybe she'd discovered the unnatural ways. That was one of the greatest things about the apocalypse. Those with unnatural passions had died, no more of this bull about men marrying men and women marrying women. It was back to what it should always have been. Women submitted meekly to their husbands, their husbands took them in hand, caring for them, and exhibiting mastery over them.

Clyde walked forward, his men behind him. He grabbed the girl's blonde hair, pulling her up by it. "Did you think you could escape God's judgment whore? It was always going to come to this. If you had submitted when you were given a chance you could have been one of us, but no, the devil is too strong in you."

The girl said, "Yes, I see, I should have submitted. I should have let you put your filthy diseased cock in my mouth and bit it off!" and then she spat in his face.

He lifted her off the ground, ready to throw her when he felt a pinch. Evie was crouched between his legs. In one hand she held a knife, the silver blade stained red. His thigh was covered in blood, spurting, pouring onto the ground. He mustered one last moment of strength and threw the whore, punching down at Evie. His heavy fist caught her head, then he collapsed to one knee. His men rushed in, protecting him, surrounding him. He went dark

You're Never Gonna Keep Me Down

Chad stood, legs shaking. His head rang, everything was distant, through a layer of cotton. Once his vision unblurred enough for him to see he could tell that Tyson, Tamra, and Evie were all down, but the villagers seemed to be completely focused on Clyde, applying a tourniquet to his leg. Chad grabbed his hatchet from the ground and grabbed Tyson. Time to get the hell out while they still could.

Tyson came to his feet suddenly, springing up. His eyes were wide, wild. He still had his walking stick in his hand. Chad grabbed him, put his hand over his mouth. The villagers were so occupied with Clyde they didn't even seem to notice. Tamra was slowly coming too, pressed against the wall. The only one who was in the middle of the villagers was Evie, her nose dripping blood. She spotted them and started sneaking, moving slowly. She was almost out when one of the men noticed her, reached down to grab her. Tyson jumped, swinging his stick. It caught the villager in the temple, dropping him like a stone. There was a dull, sickening thud, a wet sound. The man was down, showing no signs of getting up. Tyson grabbed Evie and ran for the door, a mad sprint. Chad and Tamra were a pace behind. The four of them fled into the storm, the wind hitting them like a wall, they were drenched instantly.

They ran, ignoring the storm. If Clyde survived his wounds he might just decide to kill them all, and if he didn't his men probably would. It was time to make some distance, despite the weather. Tyson put Evie down so she could run on her own and they fled, Chad in the lead.

Chad ran as far as he could, as fast as he could. He ran without thinking about where he was going, he ran without stopping. He felt strong hands grab his arm, he spun, facing his attacker. It was a long dead man, grey hair cut short, his face was nothing but a bloody mess. There were a few more behind him, not a large group. The kind of group that normally wouldn't have given him pause. As it was, weakened as he was, as his group was, this was far from a small threat. Chad dropped his weight down, pulling his arm free. The zombie followed him down, getting another grip almost right away. The thing had rotten teeth, jagged and black, full of blood. Its foul breath wafted over his face as he went all the way to the ground, the zombie on top of him.

It was easy, when you were fresh, when you had your strength, to dismiss the risks zombies posed. They were slow, weak, uncoordinated. A zombie wasn't a match for a trained human operating at peak condition. Chad was exhausted, so weak he could barely lift his arms. The zombie wasn't just a match for him, it was stronger. He'd forgotten that for a moment, forgotten that they could be a threat. He pushed as hard as he could, trying to lift the creature off him, but it bore down, teeth gnashing, inches from his face. Ichor dripped from its open mouth, landing on his cheek, a dark, thick substance. It was so close he could make out the decay on its cheek, the flap of skin that wasn't attached anymore, giving a clear view of the smooth cheek bone below. The things eyes were milk, tainted slightly blue. Chad knew he had one chance, if he couldn't get free with this burst of strength there wasn't another one left in his body. He jerked his head to one side and pulled the creature down, smashing its forehead onto the ground below. As he did this he shifted his hips, pushing his weight sideways and up. He managed to get free, his arm following his body faster than the zombie could move. He was standing, and it was still on the ground.

His hatchet was missing, he scanned the ground quickly, spotting a rock. He grabbed it and brought it down on the zombies' skull. There was a sharp cracking noise and the creature went still, lying at his feet.

He looked around to see how the rest were doing. Tamra was backed against a tree, two zombies approaching from the front. It was a wide tree, covering her from the back. Tyson was wrestling with his own zombie, he seemed to be winning. He was a large man, and physically powerful, maybe even with his injuries he was able to handle one of them. Evie was up in a tree, yelling at the zombies, nonsense words. She had four around her, they were staring up, snarling and grabbing, but she was at least a foot beyond the reach of the tallest one.

Chad didn't see the hatchet, the storm was still raging, it was hard to see anything. Instead, he grabbed a log and walked over to where Tamra was.

He swung the log down on the head of one of the zombies, a small woman dressed in the tattered remnants of a bikini. Her head became flat and her lifeless body dropped to the ground. In the same instant, Tamra struck with her knife, jabbing it into the remaining creatures eye. It dropped like a stone.

Okay, so far so good. Three down. Tyson was finishing off his, bashing it with his walking stick until its head was a fine pulp. There was very, very little left once the rain hit is, washing grey matter and ichor into the ground.

Four left, time to get to work. The three of them closed, it was so much, so much more than Chad had anticipated. Lifting his log took all of his strength. The first time he brought it down on one of the zombies he missed, catching it with a glancing blow to the arm. The zombie turned to him and Chad started to lift the log again, pulling it above his waist. The creature shuffled forward, grabbing for him. Chad noticed that it was missing an arm just below the shoulder. He put the log in front of him, pointing it into the zombie, and he pushed, using his weight to drive the zombie back.

The log was thick, six inches in diameter. He pushed forward until the zombie was pressed into the tree and kept pushing, trying to make sure the zombie couldn't reach him while he caught his breath. He kept his weight forward. There was a wet cracking sound, rotten ribs breaking under the pressure, and then his log was pressing into wood, not zombie. The creature started to pull itself along the shaft of the log, a single grasping hand, claw like, almost skeletal, dragging it forward. It had seemed like a good plan.

Chad let it get closer, then he let go of the log and pushed it aside, spinning the zombie so it was no longer facing him. He grabbed the back end of the log and pushed it up, putting his body underneath it, forcing the zombie to lean forward. Then he pushed, dropping the zombie face down on the ground. He kept hold of the stick and walk around, keeping his legs clear of teeth that were still gnashing for him.

He couldn't figure out how to destroy the things head without letting go, so he pushed the log down into sodden ground, staking the zombie down. It tried to push up, leveraging itself up with its single weak arm but it was in a position where there was very little it could do. Chad left it after making sure it was properly stuck and moved on to the next zombie. The remaining three were giving Tamra and Tyson a hard time. They were having trouble getting in a good angle. Chad picked up a rock and smashed one in the skull. Apparently, the rock wasn't heavy enough and his arms didn't have the strength left to do more than a glancing blow. The zombie turned to him, reaching out. Matted hair hung down over its face, one malevolent eye peeking through the sodden locks. He backed up, turned, and led the zombie away. He needed to find some kind of advantage, despite barely being able to see. Periodically lightning would flash, sending the landscape into sharp relief, stark shadows, and bright light.

The pursuing zombie was slow, but not much slower than Chad was. He was barely able to keep ahead of it, hobbling on feet that were near their breaking point. There was no adrenaline rush, he'd exhausted all his adrenaline reserves. He wasn't even afraid, he'd burned out his ability to feel fear, at least the immediate kind of fear. It was down to sheer will to survive, nothing else left.

He saw something that might work for him. A small cliff, not very high, a few rocks in a hill. He went to the edge, standing almost off it. The zombie closed, reaching. Chad dropped and rolled just as it reached him. Not the well-executed roll he'd learned in training, more like a log, rolling on his side down the rocky face. He caught the zombie's feet as it reached down, knocking it over. It fell, ungracefully, most of its body going over the edge, and then it went over completely. Chad looked down, seeing it smashed on rocks below. It was still reaching for him, but both legs and one arm were broken, unable to move. That counted, as good as a kill, it couldn't reach him any longer.

He stumbled back through the storm, moving towards his friends. By the time he arrived the last two zombies were down.

"We need to get out of the storm," He yelled.

"What?"

"We need to... fuck it. FOLLOW ME!"

Chad made his way back to where he saw the cliff. There was a semi-sheltered nook close by. Not a real shelter, but the best they were going to get. As he walked he stubbed his toe on something sharp. It was his hatchet, now covered in some of his blood. He picked it up and kept limping.

The shelter was a spot next to a large rock that sort of overhung a tiny bit. They were still getting pelted with rain, but a small amount of the wind was cut.

Chad took his hatchet and lopped a few limbs off a pine tree. The soft wood cut easily, but it was still almost more than he could manage. He took the pine boughs and laid them at an angle across them. The rain still dripped through, but slightly less. The four of them curled into a ball and tried to sleep.

Morning came far sooner than they would have liked. The storm was still blowing but it seemed to have lost its teeth. It was a grey, cold day.

They started walking again. They kept walking until Evie dropped. Chad had never seen anything like it. The girl was walking along just like the rest of them, then her legs went out from under her and she collapsed in a heap. It was impossible to tell how late in the day it was, the sky was a uniform grey, the location of the sun impossible to estimate. They rushed to Evie. Her pulse was steady but weak. Chad took hold of her hands and discovered that they were freezing. All of her felt cold. Her lips were slightly blue. "She has hypothermia. We need to warm her up."

Somehow the girl, the stranger, had become as much a part of them as they were. Chad picked her up, his legs going wobbly with the extra weight. She was tiny, almost birdlike. Didn't matter. He was weak, so very weak. He staggered along, carrying her as far as he could. Finally, his legs gave out and he fell to his knees. Tyson took over and Tamra helped him back up to his feet.

"We need to get inside, I know we don't want to risk it because of Clyde, but we won't live much longer if we don't. We need to get out of the wet, out of the wind," Tamra said.

"Okay, yeah... maybe Evie killed him."

"I wouldn't count on it, but we can always hope."

They were on an empty stretch of road, nothing but forest around them. There were no houses anywhere in sight. High cliffs on one side, thick woods on the other. As they staggered along Chad felt his body start to shake out of his control. That was okay, meant he was still generating warmth. If it stopped he was pretty sure that meant he was dead. The cold left his hands numb, unable to close properly. His feet were in similar shape. He knew they were cut in dozens of places, he could see the blood on the ground as he stepped, but the feeling was distant, muted. He walked on, slipping into a daze. Everything was the same. It was some time after Tamra started tugging on him that he registered it. "Huh?"

"House, there. Not much left of it."

It was an old farm house, missing most of its roof, but it was a two story, and despite massive holes in the walls there was a chance they could find shelter.

Inside it was bad, decayed, ruined. The furniture was covered in mildew, and some parts were thick with green mold. There were massive holes all over the place. The kitchen itself was the most intact room, cheap linoleum peeling off the plain wood of the floor, the wood itself soft and spongy. It felt like it might give way at any moment, sending them into the basement. There were a few spots where the floor had fallen in, showing them a lake in the basement. It was the best shelter they had found, and the only option they had.

The three of them put Evie in their middle, huddled around her, in a corner between kitchen cupboards. Impossible to know if the girl would survive, but she was still breathing, still had a pulse, they had to try. Chad wasn't sure he had much longer anyway, so might as well try.

They slept in the farmhouse, huddling together, and shaking. None of them had any tears left, any strength.

The Shining City on a Hill

The storm rolled over them like an avalanche. His troops were prepared for it, disciplined and well equipped. Each man had a mini shelter in his pack, quickly erected and secure. They hunkered down and waited out the worst of it. It was a far cry from the command tent, but Bennett was happier here than he had been there. Most of his adult life had been spent engaged in operations, mopping up zombies, making sure the marauders were driven away from New Hope and the surrounding area. Before New Hope became what it was, there had been years where he spent months in the field with Naomi and Jasper, securing a future for humanity among the dead. Now, they had an island, an entire island without zombies. Now he was supposed to be the general, the man in charge. He didn't really want it, didn't know if he could do it, but there wasn't anyone else, so he did it.

Still, huddling in this small tent near the top of a rocky outcrop he felt more at home, more like himself. The men waited, and by morning the storm was mostly gone.

The village below was pretty, prettier than Bennett had expected. It was ramshackle of course, built on the bones of an older village. Much of what made it so pretty was the children. Children were rare in New Hope, but in this place, they seemed to outnumber adults by a large margin. There were fishing boats out on the water, men hauling lobster traps on board, fish drying in racks. It was amazing in so many ways, but horrible in others. There was a large shack in the middle of the town that had boards holding it together. It had a basic gate, held in place with a large board. Arms reached out from time to time. It was clear that the arms belonged to the undead. There were other ways it was obviously wrong, that first impressions had very little to do with the reality of the town. There was the number of residents who walked oddly, almost a shuffling, lopsided gait. They had more in common with the zombies than with normal humans. There was also the redness around the eyes. All the classic signs of widespread Kuru. For it to be this common they had to have been eating humans since the very beginning.

It was time to make an impression. Bennett got his people together and marched forward, a line of soldiers with automatic weapons, clad in black armor, faceless beneath their helmets. Bennett had a moment of reflection. If this was a movie his people were the villains. Faceless soldiers about to exterminate a village full of women and children. Still, it had to be done. The risks were far, far too high.

Bennett gave the order and they moved forward in a line, firing as soon as they were close enough to be spotted. Automatic weapons fire barked out, the smell of cordite filling the air. It was instant, bodies started to fall. His soldiers were indiscriminate, killing everyone in front of them. It left him sickened, but he did it anyway. He spotted a small boy, running away from the noise, crying. He fired, dropping the small body with a single round to the head. The boy might or might not have been infected, and it could easily take thirty years before there would be symptoms. It was worse than a zombie in many ways because someone with Kuru might be a normal person and suddenly go into a murderous rage, but they would still be a rational, thinking person, driven to kill as many as they could. Each of the people they killed would probably become a zombie. One case of Kuru had almost ended New Hope fifteen years before. Bennett hadn't been there, but he'd seen the aftermath, the burned areas of the city, the mass graves. It was heartbreaking, but it was better this way.

For a minute it seemed like Bennett and his people would walk straight through the town, no opposition at all, but then arrows started flying at them. Their armor wasn't built for arrows, and a couple of his men went down. They concentrated their fire on the source of the arrows and after a minute there were no more arrows.

The houses that had seemed pretty from afar were obviously hastily and poorly built once Bennett saw them up close. There were probably people hiding in most of them. Well, they had a protocol for that. Bennett took a torch and started setting them alight, as did his men.

The village only contained about a hundred structures, including the church. In a few minutes, they had half of them on fire. The ships out on the water were all heading back, but far, far too late. By the time the fishermen reached shore the village would be ash. The landscape heavily favored the soldiers. The one building that looked like a potential challenge was the town church. If they held out in there it might take some real work to root them out.

A child ran out, flames streaming off its small body. Bennett couldn't tell if it was a boy or girl. He took aim and fired, crying as he did it. This was the worst part of what he did.

A single rifle shot fired from the church steeple. One of the black clad figures near Bennett fell, blood splashing over the landscape. Bennett had been instrumental in the design of the armor and he had a sneaky reason for one of the features. The man rose and tried to bite the soldier nearest to him. Of course, the face shield made that impossible, no reclamation soldier would be able to bite his squad mates after rising. The men hated the face shields.

There was no way to get a good bead on the church steeple, the cover was too good. Bennett walked to the church door, leading a squad of soldiers. It was sealed up tight, the large main doors were locked when Bennett tried them. "Take the door."

The soldiers with him started firing at the door. It was a waste of ammo but under the circumstances, time was their most important asset. They had to be on top of the cliffs before the fishing boats made it back home. If they were it would be a simple slaughter, otherwise, they took risks. Bennett hated taking risks.

Enough bullets hit the door, splintering it. Each round did almost no damage, cumulatively they broke the wood around the locks into a million pieces. When Bennett tried the door again he found that there was a heavy board across it, but almost nothing left of it. He slammed the door with his shoulder. It gave, at least a little. He did it again, motioning the other soldiers to join him. In a minute the wood splintered apart, and they were inside the old building.

Rows of pews lined the room. A traditional church in most respects. The one things that stood out was the crucified body. They had a figure splayed open, hands and feet bleeding, blood dripping down the walls. It was dead, although it was clear that it had once been a young woman. There was no damage to the head. The body was trying to pull free from the cross it was attached to, slowly working the wide nails out. Bennett took aim and fired a single shot into the creature's head. Her long hair dropped across her now still body.

There was nobody else here, not on the main floor. A quick search showed that there were stairs going up and down in the back of the building. Bennett motioned two soldiers to accompany him, the rest to go downstairs and make sure it was clear.

The stairs led up, poorly lit, but not dark enough for the NVG's.

Bennett was on edge, waiting for a shot, but it was still a surprise when it came. He felt a burn in his shoulder, and his right arm went limp, useless. He dropped his gun and fell back. The soldier behind him fired a quick burst up the stairs and moved in. The two soldiers he had with him leapfrogged out of sight, taking turns firing. When they came back down Bennett was lying against the wall, bleeding and suffering.

"We got him, sir. One guy with an antique deer rifle. I'm surprised that thing worked at all."

"Antique or not, damn thing still got me. Teach me to stay in front."

"Yes sir, officers should be home staying out of the way, not acting as bullet stops. Next time try to remember that."

There were a few sporadic bursts of fire from downstairs, and then it went silent. The gunfire outside had also stopped. It was over - at least the first part. They still had to deal with the fishermen, a small issue, one easily surmounted. Bennett knew that his mission was done though. He could still give orders, but he wasn't going to be able to take part in the shooting. He was glad for that, one small mercy in this world.

He walked outside, helped by one of the soldiers who'd taken the tower. It was still a beautiful day, clear and sunny. The storm had washed away the mugginess in the air, leaving a perfect fall day. So long as he looked up, so long as he ignored the ground, he could pretend the world was okay.

He made himself look down. The ground was littered with bodies. Almost all were women or children, only a few old men mixed into the group. The men would be out fishing, or farming, or whatever else it was these people did to eat. There was a cluster of small corpses just to his left, it looked like a daycare had been mowed down, and in fact, that might have been what happened. Each body had a single bullet wound to the head, along with whatever other wounds had been inflicted. His men were efficient.

This. He didn't know if he could justify this. Every time they'd cleared a group of cannibals it had been a few, once a dozen. This was hundreds, a town full of people. All of them dead, slaughtered without a chance. The zombie paddock hadn't

The zombie paddock hadn't been dealt with. Bennett figured it would wait until they had a chance to deal with the men.

He got his aide to bring him to the cliff face. The men were pulling ashore, heading for narrow stairways that had been erected against the naked rock. Ragged men, weathered and hard. They were rushing up, every one of them trying to reach their homes. Once again Bennett felt like he was a monster, like everyone with him was a monster. He gave the order and fire rained down on the villagers, killing them by the dozens. A few soldiers focused on boats that were still in the water, punching holes in them by the hundreds. In minutes every single boat that wasn't docked was sinking, every man was felled. Not all of them were head shot yet, but that was mop up, not the main operation. The town was dead.

Bennett directed his squad back to the zombie paddock and they took out all the zombies inside, a few dozen. None of them appeared to be his people, nobody from New Hope. They searched the village and did find a few, less than he had feared.

Burning the village took very little time. They took all the boats that could still float and put enough crew on them to get them to Sydney. It was over, and it was time to go back to base camp.

Bennett knew he'd see the face of that first little boy every time he closed his eyes for the rest of his life.

Clyde Catches Up

Tyson was the first one to notice their pursuers were catching up again. He heard them while he was trying to find something to put on his feet. It was getting desperate, reaching a point where he thought he might lose his feet if he didn't do something, so he said to Chad, "Hey man, catch some alone time with your girl. I'm gonna see if I can find something in a size thirteen."

"Sure, be quick though."

"Yeah, will do. You think we're close?"

"Pretty close. Evie doesn't really know, I asked her. She's never been to Sydney, although it is somewhere her people use a lot."

"Yeah, cool, look, I gotta find shoes man. If I walk much further barefoot I might not be able to walk again."

"Go."

Tyson went. He found a few houses and started looking through them. Most of the shoes had given way to mold years earlier and now they were unusable. Time to get creative. He found an old wooden table and smashed it to pieces. A few of the pieces were larger than his feet. He'd just started carving a couple of them into shape when movement caught his eye.

It was through the missing glass in the living room window. He could see a fair distance. The giant shape of Clyde was plainly visible in the clear day. Just for a moment, but Tyson thought they were about fifteen minutes away from being able to see him.

Ignoring the pain in his feet he ran, each step agony. He reached the others quickly. "Clyde, closing fast."

"Fuck." Chad stood up and they started moving, as fast as they could. How Clyde was able to walk so soon was a mystery to Tyson. Time to run again. They ran, fast as they could. The beautiful day had a bite to it, a bit cold to get their blood going. They pounded down ruined road, using every single ounce of strength left in their bodies. Tyson had gone far beyond the wall, beyond the point where his body felt like it was going to die. He started to feel a euphoria, still, he ran. His feet started to recede, the pain no longer registering for him, and he kept running anyway. There was a loose feeling in his entire brain, it felt like he could run forever. Then he couldn't. His legs gave way under him, pitching him on his face. He turned, looked back to see what he had tripped on. There was nothing. He tried to stand. His legs didn't work. There was nothing left in his body, everything around him was distant, meaningless. He saw Chad walking over to him, heard him saying something, but he couldn't make sense of the words. Chad grabbed his arms, seemed to be trying to help him stand. He tried to say that it wouldn't work because he didn't have legs anymore, but he couldn't make words.

Chad started dragging him off the road. That seemed like a good idea. For some reason being in the road was a bad thing. He wasn't really sure why, but he'd been running from something right? It was all blurry. When he woke up he was in the bushes, lying there with the others. They were huddled together when a noise came.

Clyde was there, almost right on top of them, bellowing "God will judge you through me. you whores, you sons of whores. You wear your sin on your face, it's clear as day. I will cleanse you, I will send your souls to the next world and I will WEAR YOUR FUCKING SKIN."

He wasn't making any sense at all, just screaming. Tyson tried to point this out, but Chad put a hand over his mouth, so he stayed quiet.

Clyde walked over to the bushes, his long coat sweeping the road. He looked right at them. "I found you. Time to come out and play."

Chad did. Chad stood up and ran at Clyde, hitting him in the chest with his shoulder. Clyde didn't seem to notice. He picked up the much smaller soldier and threw him into the wall.

Evie came, sneaking, sliding, she was half hidden by the bushes but there was too much distance between the edge of the bushes and where Clyde was still standing. Only a foot or two, far too much. Evie sprinted the last foot, blade outstretched. Clyde grabbed her hand. "Whore. I was going to marry you to my son, I was going to make you part of my family, part of the chosen. This is how you repay my kindness?"

He threw her against a tree. There was a cracking sound and the girl cried out, the first time she'd reacted to pain in the brief time Tyson had known her.

Tamra was right behind her. Tamra stood in front of Clyde. "You call me a whore? You're a cannibal, you'd be a rapist if your cock worked. I don't even hate you, I just pity you."

Her hands were behind her back.

Clyde swung at her, moving a little slower than he had in the past. Tyson was slowly coming to, slowly understanding what he was seeing in front of him. Tamra had a long blade in one hand, Tyson's walking stick in the other. She slipped under Clyde's arm, slicing into him with the blade. Blood flowed from his wrist. He bellowed and charged but the slender girl was faster. She stepped aside, and the blade flicked out again. It drew a cut on his side.

The rest of his men closed on her, she turned and slashed at the nearest one, drawing a line of blood across his face. The blade kept flashing, moving fast. Each time someone was cut. For a moment it even looked like it might work, but there were twelve of them plus Clyde and only one of her. Finally, they bore her down to the ground, piling on her.

Tyson managed to stand, legs shaky. Time to run again. He ran, straight for the villagers. The first one he hit flew, Tyson was a very large man himself, if not nearly as large as Clyde, and his weight, even with his strength diminished like this, was still enough to knock the men senseless. Tyson started kicking, stomping on anyone he could get near.

A hand closed on the top of his head, enveloping his skull. Right. Clyde was still there. Tyson felt himself lifted from the ground, then he flew until he landed on the ground in a heap. When he managed to look up he realized that two of the villagers were lying away from the group, dead. A third was looking like he didn't have long to go. Chad was up again, smashing his way through the villagers with a long stick. His compact frame nearly obscured by the villagers. His staff whipped out, knocking wrists, hands, knees. One of the villagers cried out, his knee bent at an impossible angle. Now there were only nine of them. The woman was trying to hold Tamra down.

There, in the middle of the road, they were fighting to the death. Clyde tried to close on Chad, but Chad moved around, keeping the villagers between him and the giant. He was whirling the staff in intricate patterns, each time it whipped out someone cried out in pain.

Tyson stood, even shakier. With everyone except the woman focused on Chad he had an opportunity. The woman who was holding Tamra down was young, probably had been pretty before life beat her down. Oh well. Tyson had enjoyed playing football when he was a child. He'd been especially good at kicking. He moved in with a loping run, building momentum as he went. Two more steps. One. He kicked, exactly like he would a ball, driving every ounce of his frame into it. That was a three-hundred-yard kick if he ever saw one. He hit the woman in the ribs.

Her ribs cracked as her body lifted off the ground, flipped over, and landed on her back. Tamra was on her instantly, slicing her stomach open with the long knife. Her body spurted blood into the air and she convulsed. Tamra stood, her blonde hair completely covered in blood.

"Fucking bitch."

The woman started to stand, having turned instantly. Tamra and Tyson ran towards the main group, drawing the new zombie with them. Most of the dead villagers were turning.

Tyson ran past the group, leaving the zombies to attack from behind. One of the villagers screamed in pain as the woman, her intestines dragging in the dirt, bit into the top of his spine.

Chad whipped the staff around again, catching a villager in the wrist, breaking it. The man dropped his weapon, a machete. Another villager swung overhand at Chad, well into his guard, but Tamra caught the blade on the walking stick, turning it. The stick broke under the blow, but the machete didn't manage to strike flesh.

It was chaos, the three of them now facing only five. Of course, one of the five was Clyde and Clyde counted for a lot more than a single man. He was a mythic hero in build, in stamina. The only thing that prevented him from being a hero was the evil. Maybe a monster then, something from one of the old myths. A minotaur or a Jason.

Suddenly one of the other men fell, screaming. Then a second one. They were grabbing their ankles. Evie was there, holding a paring knife she'd acquired somewhere. She was about to stab another one in the thigh when Clyde got hold of her. He lifted her with one hand, then grabbed her with the other, twisting as hard as he could. Her neck snapped, and he dropped her lifeless body to the ground.

Tyson screamed with rage. He hadn't known the girl for very long, but he'd grown close to her. He charged at Clyde. The big man grabbed him and threw him again, slamming his nearly decimated body into the ground. Once again everything went black for Tyson.

Running Again

When Tyson came running Chad wasn't prepared for it. He'd barely managed to get his breath from last time, and now they were running again. He felt himself falling behind, unable to keep up with Tyson's long legs, Tamra's endurance, Evie's limitless energy. He ran though, he had to run of course. There was no way around it. The road they ran on was cracked and broken, but relatively clear. It was obvious that it had been a major roadway once upon a time. They were able to move fast, almost completely unobstructed. Then Tyson fell, he tall body dropping like a stone, boneless. He didn't trip on anything, he legs simply stopped working. Chad caught up with him, a clearing in the tree cover lent the area they were in a peaceful feel, lazy insects flew in the cooling air, the tranquil sunshine. It was beautiful, almost perfect. The scents on the air were subtle fall smells, apples, blackberries baking in the sun. Chad said, "Come on man, get up. You can't rest now. Get your ass up."

Tyson didn't respond, so Chad grabbed his arm, tried to pull him up. No luck Tyson was murmuring something, but it didn't seem to contain any actual words. Chad grabbed both his arms and pulled him, trying to get him off the road. Evie and Tamra came over and helped. They managed to get their friend a little way into the bushes when Clyde came striding around a bend in the road. The preacher stood there, long hair hanging down, looking for them. He spotted their trail, still clearly visible, and walked toward them. He started screaming at them. Chad had enough, he didn't have any fear left in him, not even any survival instinct. It was down to anger, and only anger. He ran forward, trying to tackle Clyde. The ground came up hard and fast, knocking the air from his body.

What was this man? He wasn't human, that was clear. Some sort of demon, a monster. Chad stood up, realized he'd been thrown clean through a dead tree. The remains of the tree were there.

In basic, they had drilled with staves. It seemed like a stupid idea at the time. Now though, he thanked his drill sergeant from the bottom of his heart. He took the fight back to the villagers, whirling the staff around his body as he went. It was a blur of motion, patterns drilled into him until they required no more thought than breathing. He started taking them down, the piece of wood an extension of his being, no longer a weapon. He thought about hitting someone and they shrunk back from him, injured, broken. Tamra and Tyson were there suddenly, also doing damage, also breaking people. Then Evie. He watched her tiny body twitch as the life left her. Her eyes went grey, filmed over in death. Clyde threw her aside, not even able to rise. Tyson screamed and was put down in turn. It was time to end it. There were no more villagers between him and Clyde. One was busy with Tamra and the others were either zombies or too occupied with zombies to get involved. Chad closed, maintaining enough distance that he could strike without getting into Clyde's reach. It was hard, even with the staff he was close to Clyde's reach.

Clyde swung a giant fist Chad's way. Chad whipped the staff around, catching Clyde on the back of the hand. There was a crunching sound, but the giant preacher didn't seem to care. He closed again, grabbing. Chad swung again, catching him on the inside of the wrist. No crunch, but Clyde did drop his hand, pulling it away.

Clyde kept closing, stalking forward, a monster, unstoppable. Chad danced backwards, keeping light on his feet. It took everything he had, every ounce of will, not to let his feet fall flat, not to let his body slow down. Clyde swung again, his combat style basically coming down to a punch or a grab unless he had a weapon. Chad smacked his hand again, this time he knew he broke something, he saw one of the big man's fingers shatter, becoming a formless mass of meat. Clyde didn't even flinch. He did seem to remember his hook. He drew it from his belt, holding it in his left hand, the only thing he'd done that let Chad know he'd even noticed what was happening to him.

Chad backed up further and the hook swung just past his face, the wind of its passing blowing against him.

Clyde swung again, going low. Chad brought his staff down, smashing Clyde's left thumb into a bloody pulp. Clyde dropped the hook, sending it clattering to the ground. He bellowed with anger and charged straight at

Chad, his body accelerating much faster than Chad had thought possible. Chad saw this giant closing on him, coming toward him. He tried to backpedal, tried to get out of the way, but Clyde was coming too fast, like a freight train. Chad fell, the giant on top of him. Clyde swung a massive fist at Chad's face, pain blossomed in his nose, there was a crunching sound. Another fist came right behind that one, snapping Chad's head into the dirt behind him. Chad bucked, wild, trying to get his hips out from under the larger man, but he couldn't move him.

Something happened inside Chad, a calm came over him. He breathed, through his mouth since his nose was filled with blood. Time slowed down, details became more precise, clearer. He moved his head to one side as Clyde swung down again. Clyde was full of power, full of fury, but not the most precise person in the world. He missed Chad's head, clipping the ground. Chad wrapped his arms around Clyde's hand, pulling him down. He bit, as hard as he could, into Clyde's cheek. As he pulled a chunk of flesh away with his teeth Clyde recoiled in pain, giving him just a moment. He scooted his hips to one side and out, pressing Clyde in between his legs. He quickly shifted his arms to behind Clyde's neck, keeping him in close.

Clyde tried to lift away, but Chad went with him, his body lifted off the ground. Again, the training was working, he was in the classic guard position, a position excellent for minimizing the damage an opponent could inflict, and one with many options for attack. Clyde shook, jerked down, slamming Chad's back into the ground, but Chad kept his arms locked. Finally, he felt his opportunity. Clyde came up unevenly, his arms too low, one still on the ground. Chad flipped his legs around, locking his entire body around Clyde's left arm. He pushed his hips up, straightening the large man's arm. As it straightened Chad increased the pressure. It wasn't working. Something was wrong. Right, the thumb. He turned Clyde's thumb to the side and bucked again. There was a sickening crack and suddenly the resistance against his hips decreased. Clyde screamed, bellowing like a mad bull and stood up, his left arm flopping, useless.

Clyde swung a kick, but Chad was already rolling backwards over his shoulders. Clyde's leg hit nothing but empty air.

They stood, facing each other. Chad was bleeding from a dozen places and Clyde had broken bones in both of his arms. Other than the natural difference in strength Chad felt he'd done remarkably well for the circumstances, but the fight wasn't over. The big man was still standing, somehow. His left arm was useless, he still had all the cuts Tamra had left on him. There was a red stain on his pants where the blood was soaking through whatever bandaging the villagers had put over his leg. He snarled and launched himself again.

Chad leapt backwards, staying out of range. The big man was slowing down, the myriad of injuries he'd sustained starting to take their toll. Chad wasn't in better condition, but he was a much smaller person. Clyde hit the ground, his knees driving into the hard-packed earth. Chad kicked out, catching Clyde in the head. It was a brutal kick, the preacher's head snapped back, he wobbled, but stood again, using his one working arm to lift himself off the ground.

"What the fuck does it take to stop you?"

"More than you have, boy. More than you'll ever have."

Chad swung a low kick, contacting Clyde just above his knee. Clyde grunted in pain but kept walking forward. Chad kicked again, hitting the same point, and again, and again. Finally, Clyde toppled, his leg no longer supporting his weight. Chad circled around behind him and wrapped his arm under Clyde's chin, locking his other arm around his palm, hand on the back of the preacher's head. He squeezed, putting every ounce of strength into his two arms, he wrapped his legs around Clyde's waist, locking him tight. Clyde dropped back, slamming Chad into the ground. Chad kept hold, even though he had no wind left in his body. He strained, holding the preacher tight. It felt like his right shoulder was going to dislocate, his arms were almost rubber, and then Clyde stopped, his weight went slack, his arms stopped thrashing. His head dropped to the side.

Chad let go and took a rock, bashing the big man in the head over and over again until there was nothing left of his skull, it was deflated and flat. He finally looked around. Tamra and Tyson were standing over him. Tamra was kicking Clyde's corpse, a flurry of kicks, all hitting dead flesh. Tyson was just staring. His face was curled in a snarl of hatred. Nobody was stopping him, nobody wanted to take any chance that Clyde would recover, or even that he would come back. He was so huge that just his weight in a zombie would be almost impossible to deal with.

Monopoly Teaches us Finance

C had started searching Clyde's pockets. He ignored the stench. The man's bowels had let go when he died, but that didn't matter. They needed things to survive the night. They might not be pursued anymore, but they were hardly safe. Battered and out of resources Chad knew they wouldn't survive until morning.

Clyde had a stick of magnesium and a striker in his pocket, along with a wicked hunting knife. That meant fire, fire could mean life.

Setting up their camp was easier, they knew they could take their time now. None of them wanted to talk, Evie was still lying there, Tamra took a moment to push a blade into her skull, preventing her from coming back, but they needed to honor her, to burn her body. It was less important than the warmth a fire would produce, but only barely. They built a pyre, slowly. They set her on the pyre gently, lovingly. Her small body was so light.

As night fell they set her alight. The pyre burned into the evening, sparks floating in the night air. Evie was consumed. They hacked apart the other bodies, beating and smashing them. Let the wild animals take care of the corpses, no reason to waste good firewood on them. They stripped every single thing they could from them. Clyde's greatcoat was large enough that they could use it as a blanket.

That night they slept in a half-ruined shack, getting up with first light and stumbling along. They found themselves walking next to a body of water that looked much calmer, much more restrained than the wild ocean. There were buildings alongside it, small places for the most part, but sheltered and relatively intact. It looked like this area was different from where they had passed before.

That night they spent in comfort, sitting in a home with a wood stove that still worked. It was hard to know exactly how far they would have to walk, but they knew that if they followed remains of the road eventually they would reach Sydney.

They walked day after day, the remnants of the road forming a guide post. Chad and Tamra talked all day, they began a more serious romance, sharing a sleeping bag they found in one of the cabins. It was well preserved, the owners, while living, had clearly set the place up for long absences.

Tyson healed, better than he had hoped. One day, as they walked through the remnants of ruined roadways and buildings, he said to Chad, "You think I could sign up for the Reclamation Force?"

"You sure you want to?"

"Well, yeah. Seems to me that what I was doing before was just as dangerous, but now at least I would have a gun..."

"Sure, of course. I'll put in a good word, not sure if it's worth anything. I'm a rookie, brand new. This was my first deployment."

"Sure, but it's a new force, right?"

"Yeah, but most of the guys were with the guard before. Anyway, training is hard, I'm sure you'll kick ass at it."

Tamra said, "I'm going in too. I can't work as an actress anymore, it's not... well, it's not real. Plus, they want me to be the kind of woman I wouldn't ever want to be."

They saw something in the distance, an overpass, huge chunks missing, the whole thing was lilting down, but it was still there. They could see the harbor in front of them. The base wasn't visible yet, and the city was anything but safe, they still had miles to travel, but they were officially in sight of Sydney. It gave them hope, allowed them to pick up their pace a little.

The harbor was beautiful, long, and narrow. They could see the skeleton of a bridge ahead of them. It was damaged, it leaned dangerously to one side, and there were a dozen zombies along it. Of course, there was another way to go, but it was probably another day at least to walk it, maybe more. Chad said, "What do you think? Do we chance it, or do we try to make our way around?"

"Fuck it. We can handle that many. I say over." Tyson looked stronger than he had since the day Chad met him.

Tamra didn't answer, instead, she started walking forward, readying the long piece of wood she was using as her main weapon right now. She'd been getting Chad to show her staff techniques at every rest stop.

The bridge still had some decking on it. Enough for the three of them to walk. Zombies started following them from the shore, with the dozen or so on the bridge trying to converge.

The trio jogged forward, intercepting the first pair of zombies in a moment. Tyson smashed one over the head with the shaft of the gaffer hook. He'd taken Clyde's weapon as a trophy. Chad and Tamra converged on the second. Chad took its legs out from under it with a low swing, while Tamra hit it in the head, a solid blow. It was only a moment to take the two zombies. The ones behind were cutting off escape, but they had been building for a while now, more and more appearing every moment they spent in the small city.

The next one was alone. They took it out instantly, but then thing started to get more difficult. There was a cluster of six zombies closing. No way around it, they had to take them as a group. Chad jogged left, drawing them towards him, while Tyson and Tamra set up behind them.

As the first zombie reached Chad he swung his staff, low and hard, hitting it in the knee. The zombie stayed up, but it was knocked slightly off course. He used the impact of the hit to redirect the other end of the staff to the nose of the next zombie, knocking it off its feet. He kept the staff bouncing and moving. It didn't stop, a whirling wall of wood. He took out his two zombies and moved for the next one, only to find that the others were gone. Tamra and Tyson had done their job.

There was almost nothing left for them to kill. They ran across the rest of the span, a growing entourage following them.

"We have to keep moving, we stop they catch up"

"No stopping. Got it."

"We should try to lose them before we hit base camp."

The next few hours were spent moving around abandoned buildings, trying to run, trying to move as fast as they could.

No Place Like Home

Bennet returned to the camp, a conquering hero. People cheered, they clapped. He felt sick to his stomach.

Naomi took him aside first chance she got and said, "Hey lover, you know it needed to be done right?"

"Did it? I mean, I know they weren't the good guys, but are we? I shot a little boy, he was running, trying to stay alive, his parents had just died. I shot him, I stared right at him and I pulled the trigger. How am I supposed to live with that?"

"You just live with it. I know, it was hard."

"No, it wasn't. It was easy, no effort at all. It should have been hard, I should have had to work, to strain. It should have had a cost for me. It didn't, I squeezed my finger and his life ended. Nothing to it. Hell, I got shot but I'll be fine in a few weeks, no big deal, not even the biggest injury I've sustained, but his life is just done."

"You know why."

"I don't know, I don't know if it's right. I was sure it was, but now... I mean, we watch everyone anyway. We have precautions in place for people turning. Would Kuru really be any harder than that?"

"I don't know. Here's what I do know, we have a home, a city full of people who rely on us. They are able to rely on us because we do the hard things, make the hard choices. This isn't a world where mistakes are something we can recover from. Think about it, what if we'd let a community like that survive near New Hope? If we had a breach there like we had here we would be dealing with hundreds of thousands of zombies."

Bennett didn't sleep that night. He was driven for the next few days, working harder than he ever had before in his life. He was organizing things, working to make the place perfect. Every time he had a chance he would pitch in physically, hauling boxes, lifting, carrying. He worked until he was exhausted, then he worked some more. He collapsed every night, having worked his body until it couldn't move anymore. He ignored Naomi. She said to him, "Killing yourself isn't going to work, it isn't going to help anything."

"I'm not trying to kill myself."

"Really? Could have fooled me."

"Everything is fine, there's a lot of work to do and I need to make sure that all of it gets done."

"Bullshit. I can't make you behave like a reasonable person, but I'm not going to stand around watching you destroy yourself either. I'm going back to New Hope on the next boat. You come find me as soon as you realize what you are doing to yourself."

The problem was he knew that she was right, but he didn't care. He couldn't look at her without seeing the little boy, without knowing that she was the one that gave the order that ended that little boy's life.

The work progressed, the camp grew, improved. They had most of the waterfront now, and they were building from there. Each boat brought more people, more workers. They were pulling resources from the corpse of Sydney, but even more important, they were taking parts of the city, turning them into places where citizens of New Hope could live, expanding to accommodate their limited space and rapidly growing population.

One day there was a commotion at the gate. He hurried over to see what it was. There was a group of three people, a woman and two men, ragged and filthy, walking up to the gate.

Finale

The walls came into view. They were exhausted. The last few hours had taken away most of the gains of the slower journey. Despite having evaded pursuit, they were still on foot, traveling with almost no equipment, desperate and cold most of the time. Hunger had left them hollow.

The base camp was larger, so much larger than when Chad left. It had grown from a tiny outpost to a walled city, hundreds of people milled around in the central square, all running from activity to activity, filled with purpose. Hard to believe it was only a few short months since he had walked out of there with his team. Tyson followed him closely, bloody, battered, barely walking, but alive. Tamra took up the rear, heavy rifle at the ready. The gate guard got a look at them as they approached, covered in filth, and sounded a call. Chad dropped to his knees in front of the gate, spent. He had nothing left to give, no more reserves. A group came rushing toward him "Who are you, what are you doing here?"

"Chad Lee, reclamation forces. I have Tamra Duchene and Tyson... shit, I don't know his last name"

"Sylliboy."

"Right. Sylliboy. He's the last member of the salvage group. It's been a long, long journey."

"Okay, son. You just relax, you can tell me all about it once you get a bit of rest." Bennett Matheson said, a look of concern on his face.

Chad felt himself getting lifted onto a stretcher. He was carried inside the gate, finally safe.

The End

About the Author

Traverse Davies was raised by a pack of wild hippies, during the seventies and eighties when such creatures roamed the forests unfettered and free. He discovered a love of books at an early age, and that love has only grown over the years. After years of working in IT he decided to branch out in the activities he did while hunched in front of a glowing screen tapping at a keyboard and added writing to his task list.

His skills outside of programming and writing include Taekwondo, Wilderness Survival (sort of), Ninjutsu, Parkour, Drawing, Photography, and crappy Photoshop work. He has lived in various countries, although he currently resides on the east coast of Canada. He is obsessed with post apocalyptic survival and subverting as many genre's as possible.

Come find more of his work at *http://dreamtime.logic11.com*[1]

---

1.   *http://dreamtime.logic11.com/*

Want More?

Join my mailing list at *http://bit.ly/2K99oBP-resource-economies-free-ebook* to get lots and lots of freebies and cool stuff! I run contest from time to time as well as giving away lots of unpublished material.